Tom Blackburn

ASSISTED LIVING

A Novel

By Tom Blackburn:

Fiction:

The Cello Francesca, or, Balderdash

The Hap Maryland series:

Surviving Mozart

Thanks to Mister Merrydown

Roots of Evil

On Honeyman Bald

Dancing With Granny

Assisted Living

Nonfiction:

Equilibrium: A Chemistry of Solutions

Getting Science Grants

Tom Blackburn   ℈   Books

Prologue: What the bones have.

Here are some things the bones have kept, while so much else was subtracted during the days of waiting:

Articulation. For the most part, they remember and cleave to each other still.

Elegance. Like those of any animal, these are sinuous, even graceful, matched to their function, symmetrical to a first approximation.

Orientation. Not yet a clacking bundle of castoffs like the auto bodies at Mercer's Convenient and Parts a few miles south, the bones match to a hair a north-south meridian, the right arm straight as a die beyond the skull, indexing steady Polaris as if earth and the seasons swing them on a tight line. The left arm lies beside the ribs, pelvis and femur, while the slowly disarticulating bones of the feet point like the toes of a diver toward Mercer's. The slackjaw bonehead, looking neither left nor right, watches the leafmeal.

Scars and spurs. These are the bones of one who lived hard, heard them crack in times of crisis, who healed and winced at the stiffening of age.

Here are a few things from the list of what the bones have lost:

Chill, feeling, breeding, tiredness, the whole catalog of what people speak of as the particular business of bones. These bones, though they hardly have stirred in twelve months, are neither lazy nor having their fingers worked.

Cover. The envelope of flesh, that ghostly halo that x-rays show us wrapping the solid core of ourselves, took early and smelly retirement. Its gassy going was not marked by humans; humans almost never come within a mile of this place. Birds and animals, of course, but the bones lie in a thicket of briar, and only very small creatures could help with the disrobing. The hair and clothing faded to rags, to shreds, to beetle dung over the short course of a year. A buckle lies beneath the pelvis, and some coins.

Momentum. Still moving, but at speeds a great deal less than once. Now it is a matter of adjustments, small settlings. Once in a while, when rains bring the water back to them, the nudge of a hungry crayfish. Still, the compass points for the pole, and the crumbling feet show this world a clean pair of heels.

1.

Lee Morgan Baley stumbled up the trail, a mile behind the rest and not caring. Her knees hurt now, though they had not when she fell on them crossing a rocky meadow this morning, making the others laugh and walk around her. You don't feel pain when Jesus is standing on the trail twenty feet ahead of you, laughing along with them and sorting through the crowd of girls so he can raise you, you alone, as the rest of them disappear shrieking into the woods. Smiling now, gentle, face dark and beautiful, hands as strong as some dark exotic wood, holding hers.

"Hello, Morgan."

"H ... H ..."

"Don't be afraid. I've been watching you for a long time."

"Me?" Lee was afraid all right, no matter what Jesus said. She was afraid she might wet her pants if she wasn't careful.

Jesus nodded. His eyes were kind, maybe a little tired. "You know, the other girls wouldn't laugh at you so much if you weren't so snippy with them sometimes. You could think about showing people unconditional love."

She hung her head, nodding. "I know. I can't help it. They're so... They don't seem like they think about anything but boys and clothes."

"Mm hm. Those things aren't all bad, you know. Boys, for example, God made them too. God and me, I guess, if you listen to that Nicene blather. Don't you think about them?"

"Well. Just not all the time."

Jesus squeezed her hands. She watched the cords rippling in the brown wrists and hands. She saw the marks of the nails, and that scared her worse than anything yet. Still, it didn't look like Jesus was worried about them, or much of anything else. He said, "I love you, Morgan. I'd love it if you could relax a little bit. You get very upset sometimes. I expect you know what causes that."

Lee nodded, watching the grass at their feet. She expected she knew, too. "Yes, sir."

Jesus laughed and laid a hand on her hair. "Oh, bless you, Morgan. You are such a gentle good girl. Your folks did a wonderful job on you, for sure. You know, though, we do have that one serious matter to work through. It's been quite a while, now."

"That is very hard, Lord," Lee Morgan Baley said. "It's too hard. When I think about it, it feels like death. Like it's me dying."

Jesus tipped his head a little to the side, and his smile the other way, to make up for it. "Dying, living. You'd never believe what a tiny difference there is between the two. Most of the time, they're pretty much the same thing. Still, you have a loving heart and a wonderful spirit. I have very high hopes for you."

Lee's eyes filled with tears, and while she tried to blink them away, Jesus disappeared as suddenly as he'd come. Between one blink and the next, the dusty pierced feet were gone from the meadow. A couple of grass stems straightened slowly. The wind flustered around her head, bringing birdsong and the cry of a hawk hovering, harassing small mammals in the grass.

Her breath hissed in her ears, and light fell through the blue air. She felt like, if she just lifted her feet from the trail, she would fly as easily as the hawk.

*

Highway Patrol Corporal Suellen Ransom settled in the "other" chair, the one troopers hated to be offered, because it meant the Commander was about to say something they'd best take sitting down. She put her Smoky hat on the floor, ran a hand through her buzz cut, and puffed a little breath at nothing.

"I got more than five weeks coming, last I checked. You were just on my case about how I wasn't using my leave time fast enough. OK, I'm using."

Commander Harold Hillemeier leaned back in his chair and bounced a pencil point on the desktop. "Which you're more than welcome to do, any time the governor's not coming through this district."

Suellen cracked a knuckle thoughtfully. "Fat jackass. Honest, sir, wouldn't it be a boon to the state if he drove himself off the side of a hill?"

"Long as it don't happen in my district. No other trooper in this district had the silly audacity to ask for leave next week."

Suellen perked up. "Leaves you well staffed, then, seems to me, sir. I can't think of a time, at least a couple of the guys wadn't on leave. Four or five, mostly. You got more than enough to pull him through that business."

Hillemeier's face turned a little pink, and a lot hard, and Suellen raised a preemptive hand.

"OK, sir, yes sir. All leaves canceled until His Excellency manages to cut a ribbon, which will probably take all day. May I be excused from immediate escort duty? Seeing you got such a runover plethora of better-looking guys anyways."

Hillemeier relaxed and looked out the window. Plethora. The flags of the United States and of the particular State of Tennessee hung like dishrags in the heavy air. As he watched, a patrol car came in off I-40 and parked by the barracks. Two troopers – regular male troopers, by God, with straight backs and straight attitudes, and about three arrests between them for the year, butts twice the size of Ransom's –

"Sir?"

"Yes, yes. You making any kind of progress on these disappearances?"

"Got a report of a suspicious vehicle humpin over I-40 into Carolina, sir. Somebody saw it leave the Welcome Center fast, same day the old lady went missing from there."

"That so? Left the Welcome Center fast, my. That's open

and shut. Go bust the sucker. Shoot if you hafta."

Suellen smiled, but her shrug was a throwaway. "Map lady says the dame was parked next to this car, and she saw her talkin to the driver, who had long black hair, a snake tattoo, and a leather ball cap."

"She saw this from the map counter."

"No, sir, she'd stepped outside on a break. Using up her leave time, I expect, like a good girl. Remembered both of 'em because the old lady made the redneck mad, blockin the line, takin up her time with questions about the best road into Carolina. Like there was any choice."

"Yes? And?"

"And I thought I'd go talk to the map lady."

"Where's she live?"

Suellen shifted restlessly. "Close to the Welcome Center somewheres. I'll find her. Doubt she commutes from LA. Or Charlotte, even."

Commander Hillemeier swiveled back from the window and stared at her. "Any of the other troopers in this district, they talked to me that way, they'd get busted to the car wash, trooper. Do you have any good idea why that shouldn't happen to you? Why I cut you so damn much slack?"

Suellen stood. "Sir, I suppose it might have to do with my number of cases cleared, which is fully sixty percent of the stats for the whole district, sir. May I go?"

"No, you may not, trooper. I cut you slack because you're a woman, that's why, and I've got that shitheel pack of femmes and lardbutts from Nashville, Smiley and her bunch, breathing down my neck about cop brutality and sexism in the Corps. If I disciplined you for this kind of smart-mouth crap, where it's my word against yours, I'd have another mark on that score. That's all that saves your little butt sometimes, lady. Don't you forget it."

Suellen hooked her fingers into her jersey and yanked hard enough to send buttons pinging and rattling off the furniture, the walls, and the stand-up picture of Hillemeier's family. She shucked it and threw it on the hat, exposing a ribbed muscle shirt and a 20-inch midriff.

"Why, then, sir, there is no further need for you to hold back, because I am not the kind of woman the lardbutts have in mind." She opened the office door, and turned back, lifting the muscle shirt to scratch a rib, letting the Commander's receptionist boggle all he wanted.

"You can tell Assemblyperson Smiley that you canned me because I was nothing but a goddamn dyke, and a insubordinate one at that. Good day, sir. It has been a pleasure keeping your ass out of the fire, temporarily."

"Ransom."

Suellen pivoted very slowly and looked back at Hillemeier. The receptionist snapped to attention and jumped to close the outer door.

"Sir."

"Keep your shirt on."

"Sir, I was not aware that there was a dress code for

civilians on this property."

"You ain't a civilian until I say you are, damn it! Come in here and put that shirt on. Then take it and your smart face out there, put them and your smart ass in a cruiser, and get over to that Welcome Center. Don't come back here without you bring back a solid lead, though, you hear me?"

Suellen smiled. "Might take me a couple days, I gotta actually solve the thing."

"I will await your reports, trooper. They better be good."

Suellen slouched in the seat of an unmarked cruiser and watched the speedometer flirt with 105 while she slammed past traffic that, to a car, slowed to about 40 and got themselves into the right lane as soon as they saw the flasher in their rearviews. Which, here on I-40 punching through the Smokies, was sometimes no more than a couple of seconds after she cleared the curve behind them. That would be the thing she'd miss about this job, she had to admit. Driving these cruisers, the power and suspensions designed for serious motion, that was the most fun since she left the Marines.

She spotted her alleged perp, his crappy yellow Honda spluttering up the off-ramp for Hartford, Tennessee, just as she got too far along to take the exit herself. Suellen swore, and began looking for a place she could cross over. But I-40 was split here, each direction negotiating the best line it could through the mountains, and it was a good three miles before Suellen could get across to the westbound lanes. She knew it was a fool's errand to go back to Hartford and poke around, but she really hated the thought of missing the jerk, and going back to the Welcome Center to ask the rest of the questions she should have asked the first time.

And would have, too, if they hadn't just had their till pilfered, and the map lady hadn't yelled, "Thur he goes yonder, while we're a-jawin!" Suellen had lingered to put questions she really wanted answered, but the map lady had gone into flustration, watching the little Honda go over the hill, with the State's money, refusing to listen to Suellen's assurances that she'd get the guy, and giving Suellen no further help on the disappeared lady. ("Listen, hyur," the map lady'd pled. "What kind a Welcome Center is it when folks get cussed out and their belongins took?")

The map lady managed to get a partial tag number, which the cruiser's computer added to the make and approximate year, and came up with three Tennessee cars. Two were from Memphis, way over on the Mississippi, and one from Sevierville. And since Sevierville was no more than twenty miles from the Welcome Center, she'd figured Ned Arlen Allmon of Pigeon Forge Road, Sevierville, was well within the Person of Interest category. Well, she would have a quick look in Hartford, and then call another trooper over to Sevierville, probably get there before Allmon did.

Smiling Fate gave her a break in Hartford. The exit ramp was higher than the town, and the yellow Honda stood out like a planet against the dark pines a half-mile across the valley, making fair time southeasterly on what she found was called the Waterville Road, when she got to it. Suellen relaxed, made some radio contact with backup, and started tailing Ned Arlen Allmon up into the hills. The knowledge that she could take him any time made her a little careless, though, and by the time she decided to pull him over, he slowed a little like he was going to obey, and then gunned it, veered to the left side of the road and waited for her, smirking.

"Hey there, Miz Cop. What can I do for you, this nice evening?"

"You can show me a license and registration."

He did. The license was from North Carolina, and had a woman's name on it, though the picture looked like the same jerk that smiled up at Suellen.

"Louise Barringer Allmon? That your legal name, Ned?"

"It's Luis. You cain't imagine how many fights I get into over that."

"I bet. Bout to get into another one here, you can't come up with your real license, Miz Allmon."

"That'n's it, officer. No foolin."

"Uh huh. Step outa the car, Mr. Allmon."

"Don't believe I will, officer, all the same to you."

Suellen stepped back, frowned, and put a hand on her pistol. "It isn't all the same, not even close. Step out the car."

"You got no grounds to give me no sucha order, lady. We ain't in Tennessee no more."

"That it? Think it matters to me what state you're in? Get

out of the car right now, jerk."

Ned Arlen Allmon started the Honda's engine. It sounded like somebody was running a sheet metal shop under the hood. "Officer, all the ground on the north side of the road here is North Carolina. You look to me like that dyke trooper from Tennessee, which is a state we done left about a hunnerd yards back, except for that National Park land across the road there. What I propose to do, see, is I'm gonna drive down this here shoulder to where you see that little sign, and I'm going to turn north into that little gravel road. Fifty feet up that road lives a fella that'll testify you done abridged my rights in a jurisdiction where your writ don't extend. You want me taken in, you gonna have to call somebody in the Carolina Highway Patrol."

"Think I was doing all the way up here, smartass? We watch on down this road, first thing you know, we'll see some flashers comin up."

"Funny. I don't see nothin. You better call them fellas again, tell 'em hurry it up, notorious Louise Allmon gonna slip outa your grasp."

Suellen opened the Honda's door and got a handful of shirt and an ear.

"Ow, shit," Allmon said. "You cain't – "

"You watch, Arlen. See'f you can slip out of this."

Suellen dragged him out of the Honda and frog-marched him back to her cruiser, her still button-less trooper jersey flapping open. She opened the back door and tossed him in, letting go of the ear last, so his head snapped back and he slammed into the opposite door face first. She vaulted into the driver's seat and slammed the cruiser into reverse, dumping Ned off the seat into the foot space. After a hundred yards of transmission doomsday, she lurched the cruiser onto the shoulder on the Tennessee side, hauled Ned Arlen Allmon out of the back and spread him face down in the middle of the road. She knelt on him and hauled his head up by the hair, to where he could watch a North Carolina cruiser rolling down the road, a shortish red-haired patrolman emerging after it stopped a couple of inches short of Allmon's head.

"Hey, Janklow," Suellen puffed. "Got a perp here, his top half's in your jurisdiction, and the better part of him, ass on down, is in mine. We want him for some petty crap at the Welcome Center. Other hand, computer tells me y'all had some questions for him about a post office over there."

Ned Allmon spluttered some hair out of his eyes, and spoke through a swollen lip. "Off'cer, we got a case of mistaken identity here. Plus, this goddamn dyke pulled me outen my car in your state, dragged me down here an' beat me up. I'm filin brutality charges, an' you're gonna be the first witness."

Trooper Janklow's eyes widened, and he grinned. "Neddy Allmon, damn. You done let a lady from Tennessee beat you up? You can't be no rightful son of North Carolina, matter how many post offices you stick up. Hey there, Suellen. I'll take the front half, you wanta keep the butt end."

"You take the good with the bad, pal. Want him, or not?"

"Oh, yeah. We'll find some use for 'im, thanks."

"Pleasure. Listen." Suellen kept a foot on Ned Allmon's back to pin him down, and jerked her head to bring Janklow closer. In deference to what she imagined Janklow's politics might likely be, she folded the floppy shirt over herself and tucked it into her jodhpurs.

"Anybody from Knoxville calls for me, you need me here a couple days, OK?"

He gave her a one-sided smile. "Takin' a little leave?"

"If I go back there tonight, I gotta do guard duty for the governor to cut ribbons for the new barracks."

"Holy shit, poor thing. But OK."

"I owe you one."

"We're even, we been lookin out for ol' Ned here a couple weeks. Gimme a rough contact, case they push."

"They won't. But, yeah, OK. Tucker Pardee, sheriff's office, Gabbro County."

"Got it." Janklow gave her jersey a parting leer. "Have a good time in the flats, sweetheart."

Gabbro County, Jesus. Suellen dreaded going back. Hated even being in North Carolina again, but there it was. She was loose for a couple of days, and the family needed her, they thought. But when she got back on I-40, and thought about the stretch of concrete from where she was to Gabbro, she couldn't face it.

When she cleared the Pisgah National Forest at Cove

Creek, she took back roads to Crabtree and Panther Creek, and from there into the real backwoods. The cruiser ambled up the grades and shrugged off the potholes in a little dirt track that led back into the Pisgah, and carried her up past the last of the farms, then the last of the shacks and trailers, and clearings.

On a ridgetop, she found a wide spot where a spur of the Appalachian Trail crossed the road. She got out, listening to the wind and the jays and the ticking cruiser while she locked up. A faded granola wrapper flipped weakly in the breeze, caught in the meadow grass. Suellen picked it up and crumpled it, tilting her head to the leafless trees, her eyes hot with tears. The sky was so blue above the oaks that it almost broke her heart. To the east past Crabtree Bald the land fell away, wrinkling and subsiding into the haze that hid the lowlands.

*

A small icon representing an airplane – this airplane, in fact – scooted a millimeter closer to the end of the flight path on the forward bulkhead. A text box above it decreased the Distance Remaining figure from 3,100 to 3,050 km. Altitude 11,900 meters. Airspeed 900 km/h. Exterior temperature -20. Francesco Bari Maryland looked at it and crossed his eyes with fatigue.

"How long's this piece of crap supposed to take?" he asked. He spoke Ladeinisch, the rough and ready dialect of the South Tirol, his language of choice when he was pissed off at life.

His mother smiled at him, unperturbed. "Eight hours, Cesco," she said.

"Four down, four to go," his father grunted. "You finish that book already?"

Cesco glanced at the book, now face down on the armrest. "Sucks."

Taylor Maryland shrugged. "*Peccato*. I told you to bring more than one."

"Yeah, right. There was this one and Travels in Nova Scotia, Dad. I told you I needed to go to Milan for stuff."

"Too bad about that, too. We were in Milan two weeks ago, and you were too busy dancing to go to a bookstore."

Giulia Bari-Maryland smiled at him. Her teeth were startling against the dense blackness of her skin. "Don't pout, Cesco. There will be books in Gabbro. All in English, too."

"I bet." Francesco looked out the window at horsetail clouds. He was half as dark as his mother, with sandy hair he inherited from his father and grandfather that made an odd counterpoint. "Sure, Hints from Heloise, The Farmer's Almanac. Successful Farming. Gabbro, Jesus. What kind of name is that for a town?"

His father looked at him, wary. Still, the kid asked. Always play it straight, the counselor said. Eventually, you will wear him down.

"Gabbro is black granite. They have a quarry there, used to, anyhow. It's a big hole in the ground now, with a lot of rust piles that used to be steam shovels and such. I'll take you to see it if you want. There's a mine, too."

"Woop-de-doo," Francesco allowed. But he'd switched to English, at least, if that is English. "This town's named for a quarry? Must be a jammin' place."

Taylor smiled, looking inward. "I thought it was the dumbest place in the world when I went there to live with Grandpa," he said. "But it turned out pretty cool."

" 'Cool?' " Francesco popped his eyes at Taylor, pretending with laborious strokes to write the word on his hand, K-O-O-L. "Father dearest, you gone guy. Is that something they said about stuff in your day, 1950, whenever it was?"

But he was grinning, so Taylor took a breath, and pretended to grind his fist into Francesco's nose. "No, it was Grandpa Hap's time, around 1066. BC."

Francesco's grin collapsed into wary sullenness. "Might as well be. He's dead, you know. Why do we have to go all this way to stand around and tell each other that?"

Giulia picked up the load. "He was wonderful for your father when Papa was your age. You have relatives you never met, that loved Grandpa, like your cousin Lee. It didn't seem right, he never had a funeral or a memorial service. You'd do the same for us, I think. No?"

Francesco stared at his parents briefly, picturing them suddenly gone, himself alone in Bolzano. No parents, no money for pizza or music. No house, living in an orphanage, poked at by a bunch of Tirolean nuns. His mother looked serene, sure that Francesco would put his ass on an airplane for eight hours to Armpit, Africa, wherever, and stand around singing hymns when she drowned, or mashed herself on the autostrada or went gaga and wandered off from the Home. The thought made him furious; he felt them pawing at him, trying to get him to say things he didn't want to say. He shrugged and buried his nose in the scorned book.

"Sure. Maybe."

Giulia patted her husband's hand. Don't, it said. Don't rise to the bait. He didn't. He picked up her hand and snuffled it, licking it gently with the tip of his tongue, knowing this would irritate Francesco.

"Yee, barf," Francesco said. "You guys wanna get a room?"

2.

Bethany Baley looked down the table. Considering everything, a pretty good spread. Maybe not the groaning board of traditional country hospitality, but solid stuff with a lot of choices and plenty of each. And, hell, it only took her two solid days to get together. With a little help from her daughter.

"Lee," she said. "Would you ask the blessing, please?"

"Morgan," Lee Morgan Baley said. "OK."

Francesco Maryland's faint snort of disbelief rang as clear as birdsong through the creak and rustle of bending necks. "Mower-gun," he mouthed. Lee blushed.

"In the name of the One Holy and Undivided Trinity," she said. "Amen."

"Cool." Francesco straightened and reached for the plate of pork chops. The words, "Please pass – " got out of his mouth before he caught on. His was the only motion around the table; the rest knew better. He shot a look at his father, got a raised eyebrow and a frown; and bent his neck anew.

"Dear Lord and Parent," Lee said, ignoring him, "our creator and sustainer. We gather in knowledge and fear of Your infinite love and mercy and in memory of Your servant our dear Grampa Hap to share these bountiful blessings from your holy Creation ..." And she was still at it four minutes later, having acknowledged and documented the unworthiness of anyone present to taste of these fruits of the Creation, and yet their wretched and absolute need of nourishment, throwing everyone present hopeless at the feet of God's infinite forbearance. She paused, looking for just the right scripture to close it out when her mother intervened.

"Amen," said Bethany firmly. "Thank you, dear."

Francesco blew air across his forehead. "Would it be in order at this time," he asked, "to petition a passing of the gravy?"

Suellen Ransom passed gravy, along with a wink, and cleared her throat. "Nice grace," she said. "Don't know that I've been this graced up in a couple years."

Morgan blushed again, and rose from the table. Her eyes were bright. "May I please be excused," she said. She stumbled from the room, while Francesco rolled his eyes, and the others – Taylor and Giulia, Bethany and her husband the Reverend Plummer Baley, watched either their plates or the pork chops, wondering when the two could be brought together.

"L – Morgan," her mother called. She shot a look at Suellen, *Thanks a ton, love.* "Come back and sit down, please. Aunt Suellen didn't mean – "

Morgan answered from the hall doorway. "I'm perfectly fine, thank you, Mother. I'm just not hungry right now." Stomp, slam, went the stairs, and a door at their head.

"My bad," Suellen said, putting her napkin on the table. "Lemme talk to her."

"Let her go, Suellen," Bethany said. "She's too sensitive

for her own good, these days."

"I can hear you, Mother. Kindly stop discussing me."
Slam.

Francesco yawned around a mouthful of pork chop.
"Sensitive," he nodded. "I used to be that way."

Suellen knocked at the closed door.

"What?"

"Hey, I'm sorry, Lee. My mouth – "

"That's all right."

Suellen tried to try the doorknob without rattling it, not
very successfully. "Can I come in for a second?"

Silence, then, "What for?"

"I haven't seen you for years. Last I knew, you had a
pacifier in one hand and my hair in the other. I'm still the same
loudmouth fool I was then; I just wanted to see how you've
come along."

Footsteps, very light; then silence. After a long half-
minute, the door opened.

"Actually," Suellen said, stepping back and squinting.
"You look pretty good, Lee. Might be a good idea to eat
something every couple days, though. Lose any more weight,
you're gonna float loose. What I come to say was, I'm sorry I
cracked wise down there."

The girl stood with one hand on the doorway, her quiet
face a little marred by a glaze of dried tears. "Morgan," she said.
"I'm going by Morgan now." She stepped back from the

doorway and, by so much, more or less invited Suellen in.

Suellen walked in, looked around at the room. The wall above Morgan's bed bore a small, dark-brown crucifix with drying palm leaves tucked behind it. The opposite wall bore a faint water stain, and that was it for decor. A window showed the back side of an azalea bush; a small desk or work table bore a Bible, the Book of Common Prayer, The Diary of Anne Frank, and a framed photo of Bethany and Plummer Baley holding a serious-looking baby. "Sorry," Suellen said. "Morgan."

Morgan sat on her tightly made bed, and Suellen sat beside her. "I forgive you, Aunt Suellen. Is that thing loaded?"

Suellen glanced at the Glock by her left hip. "Yeah, it is. Takes a while to get out bullets and load it when baddies shoot at me, so yeah. People take advantage, you slow yourself down too much. I'm always careful about the safety, though. How come you switched your name? Your grandmother Lee was a pretty cool lady. In her way."

Which, Suellen thought, don't ask me what her way was.

"I know. I'm not sure I deserve to carry her name. Also Jesus … well, nothing. Maybe people wouldn't shoot at you if you convinced them of your unconditional good will. Love."

"Maybe I'll try that next time."

Morgan blushed, and smiled. "Or maybe not, I guess. How come you're a cop?"

Suellen shrugged. "My pop was one. Not my real father, just the guy that brought me up. Plus, it's kind of fun, sometimes."

Morgan stared at Suellen, and gripped her arm. "You had a different real father?"

Shit, Suellen thought. You dumb dyke, whyn't you think before you talk? "Different from …?"

"From the guy that's married to your mother. Me too."

Suellen knew that, but couldn't imagine who'd been dumb enough to tell Lee Morgan Baley that the Reverend Plummer Baley wasn't her father. "My guy wasn't married to my mother," Suellen said. "Hated her, matter of fact."

Killed her, matter of fact, but Suellen wasn't going there. "He brought me up by himself, best he could. Fine guy and a wonderful cop."

Lee didn't say anything, just hung on to Suellen's wrist, and stared into her eyes. Suellen had seen looks like this from time to time in the course of her life as a Marine and a state Trooper. Mostly from folks she ended up testifying about. "What? Somebody try to tell you Plummer isn't your dad?"

"Nobody had to tell me. I knew it from when I was in the second grade."

Suellen stood up. "Yeah? Kids that age get ideas, sometimes. Make up their minds about something, get more and more sure it's gotta be so. You ever talk to your folks about it?"

"Huh uh." Morgan tipped her head at the photo on the windowsill. "Take a look at him, though. I look anything like him to you?"

Suellen looked out Morgan's window. Spring had been

slow this year, dawdling glumly from birdsong to cold rain and back. The azalea showed improbable colors to the outside world, and bare, moody twigs to the window. She looked back at Morgan.

"You look like your Grandma Lee, want to know."

"I know. Listen. Can you hear something and not laugh, and not tell anyone at all?"

Suellen smiled. "Is this something that'll get me in trouble if I don't report it to the Tennessee Highway Patrol?"

Morgan gazed at her, straight dark eyebrows over eyes so brown they were pretty much black. Straight, narrow nose, tight red mouth, no baby fat. She could have been a nuncio, listening with slight impatience to an old joke about the Pope.

"I expect it would get you fired if you did, and acted like you believed it. So, anyway, you look at Daddy. A real nice man, don't mistake what I mean. But a man with pretty strong features, wouldn't you say? Look at me. Look real good. Where is he? I look like my grandmother."

"Well, that can happen. I don't look much like my father, much as I can remember about him. My, you know, sperm-providing biological father."

Morgan stood up and looked Suellen in the eye. The top of her head came up about to Suellen's collarbone. "See, but you must look a little like him, even if you favor your mother. That's what folks say, I 'favor' my grandmother. I saw a picture of her once, when she was young, and I look <u>exactly</u> like her. I'm no relation to anybody else in the family. There's nothing else there. I ... sometimes I wonder if I had any human father at all."

3.

Taylor Maryland scowled at the lamplight that refracted through the bottom of his beer glass.

"For Pete's sake, Beffie. Why didn't you talk it over with me before you put him in a home?"

Bethany slid her hip onto the counter next to the coffee pot. "What, you were going to take him in, over there in Italy? Or move back here? Anyways, it's not a 'home,' like that sounds. Inglenook is a regular retirement facility, got all grades of ... of, you know. Independent, like you were in an apartment somewhere, down to Assisted Living, down to Nursing. And I didn't put him there, he went of his own accord the week after Paula moved out. Did all the research on it himself, signed the agreement, never told me a thing about it till it was done."

"Paula, jeez. I never liked that setup, either. I told you that."

Bethany gave him an asymmetric smile that remarked, without words, on opinions rendered from remote continents. "Paula was OK, and they loved each other, in their way. I don't think she ever felt at home with us, with Gabbro and all. I think she was just too young for him, finally. She got an offer from Harvard, what was she supposed to do? You don't turn down Harvard, not if you're a striving academic, anyways. Plus, it's not like they were married."

"She could give Dad a choice."

"She did. He didn't want to leave Gabbro and move to Boston as her, whatever ... dependent. He said it sounded like adult diapers suddenly."

"OK. So he went into this 'facility.' Still, he ended up hating the place, I think."

"Well, wouldn't you? It's built like a hotel, except hotels have bigger rooms. His whole life shrank down to this one room out on the edge of town. I done what I could for him, Taylor; me and Plummer and Lee." She sighed. "Morgan, I mean. You wont another beer?"

Taylor grinned. "You sound so country when you say that. Like Lee. Your mom, I mean. Sure."

Bethany slid off the counter and opened the fridge. "Anyways, he graduated to Assisted Living after a year. I went out there to see him about every day. In just a couple months of it, he started to slip, you could almost see it from one day to the next. Some days he'd be fine, read me funny stuff out of the Intelligencer and the Inglenook "Inklings," which was this silly little newsletter they put out. Some days, it's like somebody else was in there, or nobody."

Bethany held a bottle of pinot grigio to the ceiling light, and poured herself another inch. She looked beautiful doing that, Taylor realized. It was a shock to think of Bethany as a beautiful woman when it seemed like the last he'd known, she was a runny-nosed ten-year-old tomboy. Marriage to a Holy Roller seemed to suit her.

If she noticed his surprise, she made no sign of it. "He got depressed, I think, no place to call his own but that little room that was stuffed with books and papers and laundry and furniture. Morgan was real good to him, took him on walks out in the country. He'd be a changed man after he'd had a ramble, he called it, with her. Changed the scenery and got his blood moving, like. He'd shave, get dressed and all." She sighed and sipped the wine, made a face. "But basically, the story was pretty much downhill."

Taylor stared into the beer, watching bubbles rise and disappear into the layer of foam. You are a selfish snot, he thought. You let your Dad slip away while you were so bloody busy with proving you could be as good a Tirolean as the rest of your pals.

"Is there some chance he's still alive?"

Bethany put a hand on Taylor's arm. "We think we'd have heard from him one way or other by now. We keep hoping, but when it got to be a year, Plummer said, and I agree, we need to face up to the most likely thing, that he's out there somewheres, passed away. It's hard on us, of course, but he's at rest. And of course he did start to wander off by himself. Went AWOL, like, 'cause you're supposed to sign out when you leave. Morgan always had to remind him when they went out for a ramble. The head nurse would get mad at him, tell him they were gonna chain him to the bed. He walked in on the County Council in his pajamas and bathrobe to make a speech about the library budget. Thank God Tucker was there, and brought him back in the cruiser."

Taylor shook his head. "What kind of place is it to live, where you have to break out, or anyhow get permission, to go for a walk?"

Bethany nodded. "Good question. You always were right there with the good questions since you was Francesco's age. It wasn't 'permission,' you were just supposed to sign out and back in, let them know where you were, because they're supposed to be responsible. He didn't like even that much, what he called Big Sisterism. But it's what he chose, Taylor. Ever blessed step of the way."

*

Francesco sat up abruptly to silence and darkness at a tiny hour of the morning, slept out, his body clock still in some Atlantic longitude where the sun was well over the horizon by now. He was not quite sure where he was, or what was supposed to happen next. Rolling over, pulling the sheet over his head and thinking about girls didn't put him back to sleep. He felt dizzy but not sleepy, and definitely ready for some breakfast. He swung his feet over the side of the cot they'd given him, and scratched his ribs. Squinting at his watch told him nothing. Stupid thing wasn't half as luminescent as they showed on the web page where he'd bought it. Nothing was half as anything as people claimed, he'd noticed. Except sex, which was a hundred times more. What was the deal, anyhow?

Not that Francesco's encounters with Bolzano girls had robbed him of virginity. But the whole-body sweetness of his limited experience of necking had startled him, and left him ready for more. Which he was sure he'd been positioned to reap with a certain Arabella, if his parents hadn't yanked him off on this stupid trek to the cornball belt of pathetic America, whiling away his life waiting for a 13-year-old baby nun to run out of bullshit so he could eat supper. He couldn't remember where the light switch was, so banged his knee on the end of the cot groping his way to the door; and lit it up with whispered invective.

As he descended the stairs, they became darker; a light somewhere had gone off. That made it harder to remember the downstairs layout, and he walked nose-first into a hallway mirror whose paleness he'd taken for a doorway to the kitchen. This time he didn't whisper.

"Mother fuck," he grated, clearly.

As he turned back, a hand from the darkness closed over his extended arm, making him jump and yank it back, heart pounding in his throat.

"You would have an easier time of it if you kept your mouth shut and your eyes open," Morgan whispered. "Are you hungry or something?"

"What's it to you, More-gun? " Francesco snarled. "Come to the end of your rosary?" But as she'd whispered, he whispered back.

"I don't believe in rosaries, Chess-koe. Do you?"

"Not hardly. I thought you were training to be a bride of Jesus or something. What are you doing out of your Spartan cell?"

"Rosaries are a crutch. I can say the whole office from memory if I want. I got up to see if there was a pork chop left over, and there was. Want it?"

Cesco blinked. "Sure."

Morgan pulled him into the kitchen. "What a shame I ate it, then. But there's a chicken thigh from day before yesterday. I could nuke it for you."

Cesco scowled, and realized that facial gestures weren't going to count for much in this conversation. The kitchen was almost as dark as the hall had been, though a scattered constellation of LED's from the appliances gave enough light to see Morgan as a pale shape a little shorter than himself, shrouded in a nightie.

"Skip it. Where's the light? You got any cereal?"

"Nope. Let's leave the light off, OK? Granola bar and some milk?"

"Sure it's not too much trouble?"

Morgan opened the refrigerator. "Of course not. Why are you so hostile?"

"I'm not hostile."

She turned halfway back to him, a half-smile half-lit by the refrigerator light. "Whatever you say. Skim or 2%?"

Cesco couldn't help noticing that the glare filtering through her cotton nightie backlit a budding but certainly female human form. Not in much detail, the nightie wasn't the sheer kind featured in <u>Playboy</u> cartoons. But there were saliencies at about 11 and 4 o'clock. It was kind of interesting, and it kept him from answering right away.

"Uh ..."

"Skim's better for you." Morgan hipped shut the fridge, leaving her gestalt hovering in the sudden darkness. "Glasses are in the cabinet behind you."

He found one by touch, without breaking the others. "I can't see for shit," he whispered, holding the glass out. "You see in the dark?"

"Pretty well, I guess. It doesn't seem dark to me."

"Well – thanks." He took a bite of granola and a mouthful of milk. "I don't mean to be hostile. This trip wasn't my idea. You always wander around in your ... in the dark like this?"

Morgan nodded. "Thank God for things that happen to us that weren't our idea, though, don't you think? Our ideas are so far short of what there is." She nodded again, seeming satisfied with the truth of that. "I'm up at night quite a bit. The deep part of the night is my best time."

"Yeah?" Cesco found his response pretty lame, and tried to think of an improvement. "Yeah? So you like to let things happen to you in the dark?"

Morgan reached out and grabbed Cesco's arm again and pulled him to where the LED's would light her face. "Listen to me, Cesco," she said. She looked not so much angry as worried.

A spill of dark hair skirted the dark line of her brows, swaying in time to her speech. "That kind of sneering frivolity is like a childhood sickness that will keep you from ever becoming a man."

Her eyes widened; she'd startled herself. But she didn't take it back. Cesco stared at her, knowing even in his anger that she was right, but far from ready to let her get away with it.

"Well geez," he said. "Ex*kyuse* me. You could work on not being so snippy. I thought Christians were supposed to be full of unconditional love."

Morgan narrowed her eyes at him, then sniffed. "The trick to that, of course, is to love the sinner and hate the sin. Nevertheless, there is something to what you say, and others have said it. I will work on 'snippiness.' And you?"

Cesco shrugged; remembered her perfect high breast and slender little butt, sketchily x-rayed by the refrigerator. Christ, why did women have to be so perfect, and so lethal? Still, she was communicating now, like a serial killer asking to be caught. "Yeah, OK. So, what do you think, More-gan? Shall I work on frivolity first, or sneering?"

"What do you think, Chess-coe?"

He laughed. "I think if I knocked off one of them, it would take care of the other one automatically. You think snippiness and love might work the same? Like, if you loved the sinner you wouldn't be so snippy about the sin?"

"Why is it men call women 'snippy' when they mean truthful and forceful?"

Cesco put down his milk so he could gesture without spilling it. "Because they're <u>being</u> snippy, that's why. Truthful and forceful, bushwa. Look, that Suellen? The cop? She looks pretty forceful to me, and she talks straight. She's not snippy, though, by a mile, cripes."

"Yes? What is snippy, then?"

"Just exactly the way you just asked that question. Play it back, you'll see."

Morgan was silent for a moment, and then asked, "Where do you live, Cesco?"

He sipped his milk and shrugged. "Bolzano. It's this kind of city in the Italian Alps."

"That sounds exciting, I must say. It's a city, though? With traffic, lights on all night, and so forth?"

"Do we have lights on at night?" He gestured at pitchy Gabbro beyond the window. "<u>Most</u> places do. Why?"

"Let me show you something."

"What?"

Morgan, maybe hearing the effect she sought, smiled in the dark. "Oh, maybe it's nothing to you. Come here. Give me your hand, or you'll bang into something, and say something barbaric."

"Like M-F? I apologize about that, Morgan."

"Really? How un-frivolous of you, Francesco. Thank you."

"Yeah. Next time, I'll use Ladeinisch so it doesn't hurt your little virgin ears."

She didn't answer, but led Cesco to the back door. "Shut your eyes," she said. "Don't worry, I'll keep you safe. Careful, step up so you don't – "

"Ow! Sfacim!"

" – Shh, stump your toe. I'm sorry."

They walked together into silence and chill, and deeper darkness. She whispered, still. "Was that ... whatever? Laddishen?"

"Regular Italian. It just means, sort of, 'darn it.' Why am I keeping my eyes shut? I'll prob'ly break an ankle next." He reached for her voice, to put an arm around her shoulder, see if she was shivering, offer some warmth if so. She turned away from the groping hand.

"You're going to see God. Just a second. Stand right here." She put her hands on his shoulders and turned him a little to the left, lifted his chin with a gentle finger. "OK, open your eyes."

Francesco was more than ready to see God, if anyone meant by that, achieving the promised land with a willing girl. And if this little thing wanted to be that girl, he could see no reason to refuse her; it's not as if they were real cousins. When he opened his eyes, though, what he saw was not Lee Morgan Baley naked and smiling, as he'd been optimistic enough to hope, but heaven, blazing with the thousand stars of late summer, though it was chilly April. Libra, Taurus, the Seven Sisters, and Virgo ascendant above all, all resplendent in silent majesty close enough to touch. Cesco could see how a pious virgin might call it God.

"Oh, Jeez," he whispered. And, with some calculation, "Oh, sweet Jesus. How beautiful!"

The fact was, Cesco had seen stars as dazzling on hiking trips in the Dolomites. Still, it would be a stupid barbarian indeed who would say so to a country girl who might have other wonders to reveal, if she were encouraged by just a little show of appreciation early on.

Morgan whispered something that Cesco didn't catch.

"What?"

"Nothing. I'm glad you like it. I'm cold and sleepy. I'm going in."

What she whispered was this: "Really? Or is he just the best You could find?"

4.

The front door of Inglenook Village was inviting enough, Suellen thought. Not obvious about keeping undesirables out and clients in, though well set up for that, too. It looked like the entrance to a moderately well gated nest of condos. She was eyed doubtfully by the fluffy, fragile-looking receptionist inside.

"May I he'p you?"

Suellen, who'd buffed up her trooper suit and sewed on some dime store, kind of military-looking buttons for this, flexed enough to make her belt creak, and leaned on the counter to loom over the receptionist. Carolyn Albright, said her nameplate. "Hope so, Ma'am, Miz Albright. Who would be the person that would be like a social worker or a head nurse, like that? Works with the clients face to face."

The receptionist cocked her head to one side, as if this was such a good question, she just had to enjoy it for a bit.

"Why, that would be Ms. Welles, I believe. Whom shall I say wishes to speak with her?"

Suellen smiled down at her. Meem, honey. "Ransom, Tennessee Highway Patrol. This isn't anything real official." But Suellen handed fluffy Ms. Albright a card:

STATE OF TENNESSEE
Highway Patrol
Cpl. Suellen Ransom, District 11

And figured that would look plenty official to get her going.

Ms. Albright rose from her chair with satisfactory speed and gave Suellen a nervous reassuring smile as she exited, hands flared from her hips, fingers curled, Suellen's card between two immaculate knuckles. Ms. Albright's left hand sported an engagement ring too large for her finger, but no wedding ring. Just planning the wedding had gaunted her, Suellen thought. Don't blame her.

Suellen occupied herself with close inspection of the hunting prints on the walls to keep from thinking about Hap Maryland living here, tippy-toeing past Ms. Albright in his PJ's and a raincoat to make a spectacle of himself downtown. Nodding and smiling like a loony, exiting with little Lee Morgan Baley for one of their rambles. Beaming at Morgan, maybe toward the end seeing the older Lee, the namesake that she so resembled, thinking he was running off with the great love of his life. Grandma Lee, who'd irresistibly, comprehensively loved Hap to the horrible day of her death, and still had betrayed him, almost killed him with her rueful, offhand, cain't-hep-mahself infidelity. Maybe that's why little Lee wanted to be called Morgan.

"Yes?"

Suellen turned from the now blurred hunting scene, blinked to focus herself, saw at her elbow a Xerox copy of Miss Albright. Slender, fluffy, but with a bronze name pin that read, "Judith A. Welles LPN / Resident Affairs." Could be Albright's sister, Suellen reflected. Though on second look, maybe somewhat steelier.

"Er'm," Suellen said. "Thank you for taking the time to meet me, Miz Welles." She looked behind Ms. Welles at a couple of clients hovering at the counter, trying to catch Miss Albright's elusive eye. "Maybe what I have to ask you is something you'd just as soon keep confidential, Ma'am. Could we ..." She leaned in the direction of the open door behind Miss Albright.

Ms. Welles appeared to weigh whether to cooperate, or call Suellen's bluff. She turned halfway toward her office, then turned back. "Very well. I must warn you, my time is quite limited today, and it is difficult to imagine just now what I might have to discuss with the Tennessee Highway Patrol."

"Yes, Ma'am. Maybe nothing at all. Still, I don't know that you'd necessarily choose to discuss losing one of your residents right out here in front of the others. The survivors, so to speak."

Ms. Welles spun on her stacked heel and walked to her office door, where she turned and sent Suellen a brief look before going on to her desk. Come on in, it said. Or be damned. Suellen followed her in, taking the opportunity to mug "Hold her calls" at Miss Albright. Miss Albright smiled, and pretended that she hadn't.

"Now then, Corporal Ransom. Please tell me what makes you think we "lost" a resident?" She cocked her head and shrugged. "Of course, we do lose a resident from time to time, as they pass away in the course of nature. Our residents generally enter Inglenook at an advanced age. We are far from practicing the kind of negligence your remark appears to imply."

"I'm sure you are, Ma'am. Perhaps I misspoke. Thing is, we've had a series of incidents over Tennessee, where elderly folks flat disappeared. First couple of 'em was from I-40 rest areas in Tennessee, so the THP has been the lead agency in figuring out what's going on. Course, any time you got a population of older folks, you're going to have a percentage of them that just take a notion, wander off, forget to tell anyone, and a percentage within that, that'll get in some kind of trouble, or lose their orientation, and never show up again."

Suellen waved a hand. "Account for all those, we still have a residue of unexplained disappearances, and since two of those were our rest stop patrons, we're still in it. Now, we coordinate pretty well with the North Carolina Highway Patrol, other law enforcement agencies over here, so we thought we'd see if this was a regional problem, so to speak. One of the folks we've learned about was a Mr. – no, I'm wrong, it was a <u>Doctor</u> – Harper F. Maryland, known as 'Hap,' last known residence and location the Inglenook Retirement Community, Gabbro, North Carolina."

Suellen looked around the office, out the window at a smiling greenscape with benches and bird feeders, as if to confirm her presence at that very spot. "Nice place."

"Thank you. Just a moment."

She rose and walked to the door, murmured to Carolyn Albright, and returned with a ring binder, which she put on the desk. "Assisted Living L – Q" said a plastic-window label on the spine.

"Dr. Maryland became a problem, in his last weeks with Inglenook," Nurse Welles sighed, turning pages.

"That so? A problem for ... "

"For those whose responsibility he had become. The staff, certainly. His family. For Inglenook in general, and for the larger community. We make every effort to provide a restful and pleasant environment at Inglenook. In the Assisted Living facility, we take seriously and literally our responsibility to *assist* our clients in their *living*, you see. Beyond such old-fashioned amenities as our landscaped setting, a fully trained staff, appealing, balanced and nutritional meals, spotless and proactive housekeeping and so forth – which any assisted living facility worth the name must provide – we also use the latest in lucent and auditory techniques to promote a restful ambience."

Suellen cocked an ear at the auditory technique. "Blue Skies," drained of bounce, dribbled from hidden pipes. "Lucent?"

"We use ..." Ms. Welles looked a little awestruck. "The ceilings of common areas and living quarters contain closely spaced polychromatic LED's," she said. "Residents may choose from a menu of illumination themes, all of them professionally composed to promote a harmonious and restful tone."

Suellen puckered as if to whistle. "And Dr. Maryland wasn't … restful with these techniques?"

"He began calling on some of the oldest residents during what were supposed to be rest periods, and attempting to engage them in … in painful and inappropriate discussions. He attended a meeting of the Gabbro County Council without taking the time to dress appropriately, to say the least; he was half-naked. He constantly evaded the amenities Inglenook provides for wholesome, quiet recreation. And he was constantly taking off on his own." Ms. Welles found the page she was looking for, and began to read from it.

"February 14: Absent overnight, no signout. March 9, the same. March 16-18, absent without signout. There was a very severe storm on the night of March 17, and when he was found the next morning, it was evident that he had been out in it all night. It is a miracle he didn't pass away of hypothermia." More page-flipping. "He was sometimes abusive to floor staff, more frequently toward the end of his time with us. He was last seen on April 3 of last year, at evening vespers. We had a particularly beautiful service that evening, with the Bozlee High Glee Club." Ms. Welles lifted a shoulder and closed the book.

Suellen carefully unclenched her jaw. "Sounds to me like the kind of thing you must get pretty often from old folks. Don't play ball with the staff, make a nuisance of themselves."

"It was the deception, Corporal Ransom. We are prepared to help residents who do us the courtesy of playing fair with us. It is difficult to help one who actively schemes and dissimulates in order to evade ..." Ms. Welles glanced at the benches, the birdbaths, the overhead glow. "The amenities we offer."

"So when he went AWOL after April third, you figured it was just more of the same?"

"We contacted his – mm, family, of course. Mrs. Baley, who acted as co-guarantor of his account was not, of course, immediate family. We attempted to contact his son and his former wife, both of whom live in ..." Ms. Welles shrugged, smiled faintly. "In Italy."

Suellen decided to squeeze a little, pulled out a notebook, flipped pages filled with entirely different matters. "That'd be Miz Bethany Baley of Good Hope Road? When I talked to her, she said she considered herself his daughter. Didn't he marry her mother?"

"That is true. Our policy is to notify blood relations before stepchildren and other ... attachments. We did call Mrs. Baley when our attempts to contact Mr. Taylor Maryland and his mother were unsuccessful."

Suellen gave that a nod and a smile, like a dean hearing of a particularly stupid fraternity prank. "You have a person right here in Gabbro – and if my notes are accurate, Ma'am, a whole family in fact – that considers themselves related and responsible, and you waste time trying to call Italy? What did you suppose they were going to do?"

"We considered that their business. Our responsibility is to contact next of kin when there is any issue involving a resident. We did also, of course, contact Mrs. Baley."

"So you said. And when was that?"

Ms. Welles reopened the ring binder with a small sigh, flipped, read, and closed it again. As she drew the binder into her lap, her hand slipped from the desktop and out of sight. Suellen heard a faint buzzing from the direction of Ms. Albright's desk, and knew that her remaining moments with Judith A. Welles were numbered.

"April tenth," Ms. Welles said. The telephone on her desk gibbered. "If you will excuse me, Corporal. This is a call I've been expecting."

*

"Sure," Taylor said. "She called. She called every time Dad went missing. Left a message with our landlady this time, which came through pretty garbled, you can imagine. To the extent we could make any sense of it at all, it looked like it was more of the same, Dad wandering off like he'd done a dozen times in the last couple of months before then. Always turning up again. We got back from Innsbruck four or five days later, there was just the one message. I called Bethany, and found out it was a panic here, he'd been gone for days by then. She knew that, not because goddamn Inglenook told her. She knew it - "

Taylor opened a hand toward Plummer and Bethany.

Plummer Baley shifted in his chair, recrossed his legs. "Because we doggone near lost Lee, the same time."

"Morgan," Suellen said.

"Morgan, uh-huh." Plummer dipped one eyebrow in faint remonstrance at a cop instructing him on his child's name. "Anyhow, it was a Sunday afternoon, April the fourth. L – Morgan always took him out for a walk on Sundays, any kind of good weather. It was good weather, we had a early spring last year, a lot of rain and warm weather, and this was the first sunny weekend seems like since before Christmas. Lee talked all morning about getting Grampa out for a good hike. She'd used to ride out there on her bike, and take him out'n the country, through the woods, all that. Give him a good healthy walk, make him talk to her, tell her stories and such. We encouraged it, as a way for him to get some variety – get a chance to use his mind, really – and to be something to somebody. And for her to learn about getting old. This time, apparently, they run across a canoe tied up at the edge of the swamp out there, and she says Hap says to her, You ever heard the story of the lost princess of Indian Girl Swamp? So she says, No, tell me. And he says, I can do better than that, I can show you."

Plummer held up a hand. "I know you're gonna say, what were we thinking about, lettin a young girl go off in a swamp with an old fella maybe isn't as sharp and as strong as he once was. Well, these Sunday walks were a big thing to those two, seemed to do Hap a world of good. Not that we were there to be consulted on it in any case. Off they went, Lee - "

"Morgan," Bethany said.

"Morgan, yes," Plummer said, a little abruptly. "And him. What happened out there, seems like it's a long story, but Morgan says they got separated, and she like to never found her way out on her own. She come home way past eight that Sunday night, wet and crying how she'd lost Grampa. We were fixing to get worried about her – she'd often enough stayed out to Inglenook for dinner after one of their hikes, didn't always call, but she was usually home by seven thirty, eight at the latest. Here it was past dark by that time. We run out to the swamp with Tucker Pardee in the county cruiser, but it was just flat dark as a coal mine in there, but for once in a while a, a ... what're those things, Hon?"

"Will-o'-the-wisp?"

"That's it. 'Course Tucker had his big flash, and we called and hollered. Morgan tried to show us where they'd been, but I'll tell you, you get back into one of these cypress swamps, there's not that much that distinguishes one tree from another, nor one stretch of water and duckweed."

He shook his head. "Got on toward midnight, then some, and we'd of got lost ourselves if Tucker didn't had his little GPS unit along. But Morgan was getting so upset, I made the judgment we needed to get her home to bed. It was a warm night, thank the Lord, and we just prayed and decided to trust in the Lord's mercy to keep Hap safe out there."

"Which, it turned out, didn't happen," Taylor said.

"Doesn't seem so. Mind, no one's laid eyes on Hap or his remains since that day, spite of a lot of hard looking. It ain't every time that what we want and what the Lord's got in mind comes out to the same thing."

Taylor gave that a curt nod. "I see, right. If God wanted Dad to make it, he'd find his own way out, and if not, tough beans. Like one of these trials by ordeal. Lets you off the hook, doesn't it?"

Giulia put a hand on Taylor's knee. "I don't think Plummer meant that, caro," she said. "Just, if people do all they can, and the problem is still there, ..."

"Then they do something else, seems to me. They don't go home and say, Hey, your turn, God."

"No," Plummer said. "Not that you've painted a flattering picture, but it isn't accurate, either. We had Lee there, she was like to come down with hysterics. Somebody had to get her out of that setting and into some comforting and shelter. I could see we weren't doing a doggone thing out there hollering. You ever go out in the middle of a swamp and try calling somebody? Sound bounces off'n the water and the trees, you got no idea where it's from. If he'd <u>had</u> of called back, it still would have been the devil to find him. But we never heard a sound but our own voices coming back at us from a million directions. You can't even use dogs in a place like that. There wasn't nothing for it but to come back in daylight and search by eye. And that's what we done, the next ten-fifteen days, dawn to dark and past." He turned a hand, and looked sorrowful. "It's a pretty big place, and it all looks the same."

"Helicopters, too," Bethany said. "From out F'etteville. Out there for hours on end, back and forth over the swamp, nobody could have missed them. It's like Daddy took it in his head to disappear and stay disappeared."

Suellen leaned forward and cleared her throat. "Do we know how they got separated? Hap and Morgan?"

Plummer cocked his head, as if this was the last thing anyone had ever worried about. "I never was real clear on that. Didn't seem the most important thing at the time. Morgan explained it, something about his needing to, to pee. Sending her off out of sight, I guess that surprised me a little; didn't seem like Hap, really."

*

Francesco, having slept not at all the remainder of the previous night, passed a restless and humdrum day getting a tour of the campus of Gabbro College (with its one-of-a-kind Museum of String Dolls) and finishing the book he'd brought for the trip. He saw nothing at all of Morgan, since she left at ten that morning for a debate tournament in Durham, returning long after Cesco succumbed to jetlag and went to bed. Still, hoping to recover something from the day – hoping, really, to revisit the tender, alarming sight of Morgan in her cotton nightie – he set the alarm on his night-luminous watch for 2:30

in the morning.

But he slept through the alarm, and woke at daybreak to find the watch blank-faced and dead. He barely stopped himself from smashing the damn thing underfoot, remembering at the last instant a troublesome and repeated dream about a hornet drilling into his wrist

"Shit," he snorted. He felt a little dizzy from oversleeping, still not perfectly reconciled to this laggard and stumblefoot time zone.

He met Morgan on the stairs under a slant of daylight. She gave him a formal good morning and passed upward, her feet firm on the steps, not tarrying. She wore a featureless jumper of ivory denim. Her hair was smoothly pinned back, her face the same. The virginal swellings that had seemed tender, poised and accessible by fridge-light looked as dull as plaster in this flat morning glare.

"Hey," he said, wanting to ruffle her.

She turned without speaking.

"I slept in," he said at last. "I wanted to see you again."

"Here I am, then. Was that all?"

He started to speak, and stopped. What he wanted to say, would later thump his forehead for not saying, was, No, that wasn't near all, chickie. Francesco Maryland blushed, shrugged, and descended to the kitchen. Over his bowl of Gran-Pomegranate Crunch, he snorted, shot a glance at the hall doorway, and snorted again. Little nun, Jesus.

Assisted Living

*

Suellen Ransom stood in the Walden Wing of Inglenook, outside a door that bore a miniature brass knocker with the nameplate, "Ms. Faye Bynum." The door was half-open, and a faint tang of lilac and ammonia drifted through it. Suellen switched a potted tea rose to her left hand and operated the little knocker.

"Yeah." It sounded like something from a broken bellows.

"Miz Bynum?" Suellen opened the door and put her head around it.

The tang got a little richer, the ammonia settling toward urine, the lilac withdrawing altogether. Bluish areas crawled the floor of Faye Bynum's room, shadowing the passage of golden lightclouds across walls and ceiling. On one of the walls, TV mimed excitement with the sound off. On the bed, a woman of great age and negligible mass reclined in a fluffy wrapper. Her hair was sparse and magenta. Her face was as thin and skeptical as a hawk's, and the hands and feet that emerged from the wrapper were garnished and corded with blue veins.

"Who're you?" The hooked beak wavered at Suellen's uniform. "You come about that ticket from 19 an' 65? Well, you're too late. I'm damn near broke, the car's long since down't Mercer's for junk, and I'm not going to your JP for trial. You try and yank me outa this bed, parts'll come off in your hand."

Suellen grinned. "Heck, then, guess I'll hafta shoot you

right here, Miz Bynum." She bit her lip; maybe that was a dumb thing to say to a lady who might have lost a step in repartee.

"Oh, honey, would ya? Only thing, you'll have ta use a mighty small charge. I ain't up to stoppin no bullets, and as for these partitions, I think they bought 'em off Japs. Shoot me, you'd hit six other senile wretches between here and the first brick wall. Not that they wouldn't thank you too, far's that goes. Where do I know you from? Wait, don't tell me."

"I'm Suellen Ransom. I'm a friend of – "

"Don't tell me, I said! Christ Almighty, is everybody under sixty goddamn deaf, or just slow? You're a friend a Bethany Morgan, married that skinny preacher. Baley. Thought you were supposed to going to be some kind of scientist."

Suellen felt a little pulse of satisfaction: a reliable witness. "I never could get excited about that," she said. "I went in the Marines for a while, then the Tennessee Highway Patrol. All that time, I don't think I met three people that could remember one conversation from fourteen years ago like you just did."

Faye Bynum shook her head. "Honey, you overestimate the pace a life around here. I prob'ly had three conversations in that fourteen years that was worth remembering. It was right after I took my stroke, in the Total Care wing of Gabbro Memorial, that's been shut down ten years now. It was a Tuesday in July. Probably middle of the month, I know it was a pay week. You were there with Bethany and her daddy. What was his name?"

Suellen pursed her lips. "Hap Maryland. I thought you

knew him pretty well."

The skinny shoulders twitched under the wrapper. "There ya go. Some things are clear as day. Other stuff, you gotta remind me what foot goes in my left shoe. If I ever wore shoes. Anyways, yeah, him. He was around here for a while, ya know."

Suellen walked into the room, looking for a place to put down the tea rose. "Uh huh. Guess I did know that, Miz Bynum. I was fixing to ask if you ever talked to him, knew what was on his mind."

Faye Bynum emitted fizzing noises and held a tissue to her face. Suellen figured she was laughing, or maybe blowing her nose.

"Mind," Faye said. "What there was of it, you know. We're all half loony here, and them that come in not so loony, you watch, they'll be along in a week or two. Hap Maryland ..." She trailed off, maybe having run out of thoughts, maybe seeing something on Suellen's face.

"Didn't you live with him for a while, Honey? What was that about?"

Suellen waved a hand. "He put me up for a little while, after I broke up with ...the person I'd been living with. There wasn't anything, you know. To it."

The hawk face regarded Suellen as if she were a meadow mouse caught in the open. "Broke up with young Bethany, now I think on it. What was that like?"

"What do you mean, what was it like? It hurt. Could we

get back to Hap Maryland?"

Faye Bynum reached an arm across the distance between them. It reminded Suellen of a chicken's ankle. "Good for you, Honey. I meant living with Bethany. I can't tell you how I wished I'd had the guts for something like that, back when I was twenty."

"Like what?"

"Moving in with a woman. Sleeping with one, you want to know. Sit down here."

Suellen sat down. "Turns out," she said, and looked at Faye Bynum's nightstand. It held a pile of used Kleenex and a small silver clock that said **Faye Bynum, in gratitude for 55 years at The Gabbro Intelligencer**. "Turns out not that different from ... whatever. The big difference is living with somebody, not what kind of somebody it is. I wasn't too good at that."

"Funny thing," Faye sniffed. "Hap said you were fun to have around the house. His exact words."

The same Hap, Suellen reflected, whose name escaped Faye not three minutes ago. This was going to be something. "Well," she said. "I guess with Hap, it wasn't a sex thing."

Faye sniffed again. "Maybe not. He never let on, one way or the other. I never took it to mean you played Parcheesi with him."

"Nope. Never did that. What was Hap up to around here?" Suellen figured she'd better make what questions she had as blunt and as fast as possible.

Faye drew a breath and turned pale, patting her chest

with a parchment hand. "Honey, slip one a them pills out the drawer there, would ya? Tighten my grip on things a little."

Suellen had the bottle out and open in four seconds. When Faye fumbled with the pill and dropped it into the folds of her wrapper, Suellen shook out another one. "Under your tongue?"

Faye nodded. The blue lips opened, and Suellen tucked the tablet under Faye's tongue. Faye lay inert, scrutinizing the middle air while her breathing deepened, and the lips reddened toward purple. She sighed, and hitched herself straighter against the pillows. "God damn it," she slurred. "I talk big, but when I get a chance to slip away, it's 'Honey, shoot me the nitro.' What am I hanging on for?"

"I'm making you tired," Suellen said.

"Seventy one years of Gabbro, North Carolina is what's made me tired, Honey. I could tell you things about this little town that'd put you to sleep, the Seven Trumpets of the Revelation couldn't wake you up on judgment day. What was it you asked me when I took my angina?

Suellen considered, watching the light show as it simulated an Arizona sunset. Maybe thinking about Hap had brought on the angina. Maybe she would be doing well to let this old woman rest quietly here, waiting for the one that a nitro pill wouldn't fix. She found the missing pill on the edge of the bed, and capped the bottle again.

Damn it, no. Faye Bynum was a human being, not a child, and not a Ming vase, either. She deserved respect, and that meant being treated as a capable adult. Suellen shut the drawer on the bedside table and squared around to face her.

"Do you know what Hap was up to around here? Why he checked himself in here, and then did everything he could to slip away and … I don't know. 'Evade the amenities,' is what Miz Welles kept calling it. I knew Hap pretty well, and it doesn't sound like him. Did he ever talk to you about this place?"

Faye Bynum looked at Suellen with suspicion. "Hap who?"

5.

Tucker Pardee leaned back and cocked his head at Suellen. Remembering, Suellen thought, the couple of hard times she gave him when she lived in Gabbro. Like the photo she got of him stumbling over De Loris Potter, Gabbro's first-string prostitute, after De Loris caught her heel in the welcome mat at the Holiday Inn and Truck Stop. Suellen grinned, hoping Tucker remembered it too, not too bitterly. She needed a favor from him.

"Got your camera with you, Trooper?" Tucker asked.

"Huh uh. I burned that picture, anyways."

"Yeah, after USA Today turned it down."

Suellen shrugged. "They were already over budget on cop brutality for that year. I tried to get the Enquirer interested in just the part with De Loris's panties sticking up, but they said the whole thing or nothing, so I kept you out of it. I need a little favor."

"Do you, now. Shoot, any ways I can accommodate a fella officer. Even if she ain't a fella. Strictly speaking."

Suellen let that pass, because she didn't want to get Tucker's back up. But she didn't exactly forget it, either.

"I'm on semi-official leave from Knoxville District, really so I can help with Hap Maryland's memorial service, but s'posedly tracking down a lady that went missing off I-40, maybe with a fella that come across this way. I'd appreciate it, you'd back me up on that – check it out with my boss, of course, I'll give you the contact – anybody asks you. And if Hillemeier calls looking for me, tell him I checked in with you, an' you'll pass on any message." Suellen took off her Smoky hat and spun it between her fingers. "And don't be in an awful hurry about passing it on, see what I mean."

Tucker shook his head. "Too late."

"What?"

"It'd be too late, if I was to be in a hurry. Commander Hillemeier awready sent you a message. He says, Good job grabbin this fella Allmon, and your missing lady turned up at her daughter's out'n Iowa. Says she can't imagine for the life of her why folks didn't know she was going there, she'd about told everybody in Pigeon Forge. Hillemeier says, you keep that cruiser out past tomorra, it's unauthorized leave. Past the weekend, it's felony absconscion with state property."

"Absconscion?"

"I believe that was the word he utilized. Wadn't in my dictionary, but 'felony' sure is. Hey, don't … Dang it, Suellen, put that shirt back on."

*

Two bicycles wavered and chattered along the shoulder of North Carolina 73 north of Gabbro. Francesco Maryland didn't much like not leading, but he didn't know where they were going, and he contented himself with watching Lee Morgan Baley's tight backside and legs propelling her ahead of him. Her preppy little Oxford shirt showed a hint of darkening in the groove of her back. Sweat, by God, that offered a new perspective on Our Lady of Gabbro County. And a box with sandwiches and lemonade in the rattletrap basket in front of her, that was kind of promising too.

Cesco was sweating himself, of course. The modest dawdle of spring had kicked into a hot and headlong gallop for summer. This day, now barely past noon, was already at 88 and ambitious for more. Birds, taken by surprise after weeks of huddled fluffing and recriminations, were yelling about whose tree was whose, matched by bugs that the birds were letting live, for now. Dark forests brushed the road where land was too low and swampy to plant, holding coolness and faint menace. Cesco watched Morgan's pony tail blowing in the wind of her passage, and once in a while caught a faint scent of her sweat, a vanishing citric tang that might have been the lemonade leaking for all he knew, but he hoped not. He promised himself that in exchange for a chance to learn which, he would clean up his act, would ravish her with un-frivolousness. Hoping a week of that might be time enough to lead to other ravishments before it was time to fly to Italy and Arabella.

Cesco didn't know what more he exactly wanted from Morgan, except that it should if possible involve facial expressions not so other-worldly and amused as what she sent him most of the time. Adoring was probably out of reach in the short time he had, but he'd settle for interested. Or willing. And a few buttons.

Morgan stopped her bike at a track that wandered across a waste and ticking meadow, and waited for Cesco to catch up, turning back toward him to reprise the three-quarter profile of twisted waist and high breast that had slain him in the night kitchen. Cesco sucked a breath through his teeth, slain again, murdered by the pony tail and the sturdy smooth legs splayed across the bicycle. A bird sang from the meadow.

"It's in here," Morgan said.

"Good."

Morgan tilted her head. A half-smile and the dark diagonal of her eyebrows compensated, the way Jesus did it. "Getting tired?"

"Not hardly," Cesco lied. "It's hot, though. This place better have nice cool water."

Morgan smiled at him. "Oh," she said. "It's cool. I believe you'll find it right adequate to cool you down some."

The Gabbro River here emerged briefly from forests of gum and cypress that brought it from higher-up snowmelt in the Smokies to mix with chill seepage from the Coastal Aquifer, carrying a year-round guarantee of exhilaration, but never more than in this season. The late and rainy spring had done nothing to warm it from the extra chill of winter; Morgan was looking forward – in a way that she knew was sinful, but which she couldn't help – to seeing Mister Alpine Hiker Maryland get the shock of acquaintance with a good lowland blackwater river.

She dismounted and began pushing her bike up the loose sand of the track that led into the forest. Cesco, of course, took that as a challenge to pedal his way in, but had to give it up after fifty feet.

"Sheesh," he gritted, when Morgan caught up with him. "You guys ever heard of paving?"

Morgan shrugged. "We don't choose to pave over the whole world. What's your rush?"

"Aren't you hot?" Cesco glanced at her shining face and the patches of darkness on her shirt. "I bet you are."

"This isn't hot."

But it was, and the tick and whirr of bugs confirmed it for Cesco. "Compared to Hell, maybe." *Frivolous.* "Not that you're likely to visit there, course."

"I hope not." *Snippy.* She was silent until the track entered woods, and the heat and soft sand gave way to shade and damp earth. "Unless there's such a thing as Deadly Snippiness. We're almost there. Down there is Riverbend."

They stood in a grove of pine. At the foot of a modest slope, the river emerged from a tangle of alder and gum, broadened and slowed. Following some aqueous imperative, it bent into a curved and dappled pool before it tumbled over a dike of black rock. The plunge of water below the dike echoed from the cypress swamp around it, sounding like the blather of a crowd. Cesco thought he heard words, Italian and Ladeinisch mixed with South-softened English.

He scowled, and spoke before he thought. "Spooky."

Morgan watched the forest, solemn and silent. "Kids have drowned here," she said at last. "Ignorant people say it's them you hear."

Cesco laughed, a little tentatively, and started kicking himself out of the clothes he wore over his trunks. "Let's give them something to talk about," he said, not quite sure what he meant. "Last one in's a rotten corpse."

Morgan shot him a look. "Don't be flip, please, Cesco. Those were – "

"Yeah, yeah. Sorry. How's this for flip?" He dashed for the water, meaning to do a handspring into it, skidding to a stop when he saw the snake swimming toward him. "Whoa, shit."

"Pretty flippant." Morgan bounced on one foot, yanking at a stuck shoelace. "Slow down, for heaven's sake. What's the matter?"

Cesco gritted his teeth and peered at the snake. "A snake," he said. "A cotton-head ... what's that kind of snake you guys have?"

"Moccasin?" Morgan came up beside him, bare feet rustling in the silent grass, assessing the narrow head at the point of the ripples. "Nope. It's a plain old black snake. He's headed for the woods, see? But you can thank him for your life, cottonhead. See that?"

"Nope ... Oh." A foot below the surface of water dark as tea, a snag nodded in the current, a blade of rough wood that disappeared into the blackness of depth. Cesco shivered a little.

"I would've missed that. Why's the water so brown? Polluted?"

"Tannin," Morgan said. "It comes from the pine needles and stuff. Plus, it's dark because it's really deep here, and you can see way down. If it was muddy, you wouldn't see down into it like that. Then you really could rip yourself up on snags, if you wanted."

She stepped out of her shorts and laid them next to her sneakers. Straightening, she unbuttoned her shirt and stripped it off with a gesture that about stopped Cesco's heart. A black one-piece swimsuit wrapped an immature but, Cesco thought, handsome little shape.

That shape ran past Cesco and jumped over the snag, well into the middle of the pool. The water that splashed back on him was cold, but Cesco didn't let himself think about it. Giving the snag due respect, he dove into the spreading ripples of Morgan's impact. He had an instant to see himself, a jagged form against the sky in the dark mirror of the water. Nice form, he thought. See how she – Ah! Shit!

At first he thought the water was electrified, or possibly carbonated. The cold was so profound that he had no way to classify it. He emerged from the dive, trying to climb into the air.

"Holy sha ..." he yelled. "Wha ... " He had trouble getting enough breath to finish words. He looked around. Morgan was already on the bank, grinning, jumping from foot to foot.

"Like it?" she yelled. "But you can't lie around in it like

that. You get in and you get out. You'll get used to it after a bit."

Cesco began to flounder toward the bank, whooping. "Why dinchoo ..."

"Warn you? I told you it would be cool enough for you. If I'd told you it was cold enough to freeze your hair off, maybe you'd have chickened out."

Cesco wallowed straight over the snag, finding it massive and multifold. "Chickened out? I'll chick you out." He cleared the sunken tree and grabbed for her, but she was gone into the water again, splattering him with liquid ice. God, he thought. Do I have to?

But it wasn't so bad this time, and the third time it was almost OK, really. They chased and hooted and played Marco Polo for ten minutes, slipping in and out of sunlight that sent wavering pillars of gold far into the champagne depths. Cesco submerged himself, yanking Morgan's ankle down to join him, and let the current carry them through one of the spots of sunlight while he clowned in slow motion to a silent house of brown and frigid darkness. When they rose with it into air, Morgan shook the water out of her eyes and told him he needed to warm up.

"I'm fine. What, you getting tired?"

"No, I'm not. But your lips are as blue as my Aunt Faye's, that's got heart failure. You ready for lunch?"

When Cesco was toweled off and fed, sitting in a spot of sunlight, and when the bumps on his arms had flattened out, he lay back, listening to blood fizzing in his belly.

"Jesus Pete," he said. "Oh, shit, I'm sorry. This feels so good, though."

"Doesn't it?" Morgan said. "Makes you more alive than you ever were." She looked down at him, and pivoted to face him. She'd buttoned the shirt over her wet bathing suit, and it was darkened at a few places by the touch. Strings of damp hair clung to her forehead, skirting the blackness of her eyes. Her lips were as red as the dark current that careened in his chest .

"What do you want from your life, Francesco?"

Cesco scowled a little. He'd asked himself that, in a half-assed kind of way, and given up on it. He didn't know what he wanted, that would make any sense to discuss with her. He wanted an Alfa, all the books and movies he could read and watch, a zillion euros, and a girl. Three girls. He wanted Morgan to take off her bathing suit, maybe keep the shirt on just to give him something to work with, and tell him she was cold. He sighed.

"I want to quit being a kid. I want to know what I want. What do you want, Morgan?"

She looked across the pool and into the forest. The voices of the waterfall spoke, and a little breeze ruffled her drying hair, making her shiver. She smiled. "One of the things I've wanted for a while is for someone to call me Morgan, like you just did, without … you know, like little quotes on it. Thank you."

"You're welcome. That was your life's ambition?"

She looked away. "I just wish people would take me

seriously."

Cesco puffed a little air through his lips. "Far as I can see, people take you very seriously. I don't, of course. But your mom and dad are completely intimidated."

"Poo." But she looked a little abashed, maybe a little interested. "You want to swim any more?"

Cesco shivered. "I don't know. Does it feel this good the second time you get warm?"

"Nobody would blame you if you wanted to stay dry."

Cesco snorted, and rose to sprint for the water. As he hurtled from the bank, he yodeled like manic Tarzan. He forgot the sunken snag again, until he was about to impale himself. Morgan heard a little yip of alarm and effort from him, and a shallow splash truncated by the shuddery thunk of wood. Cesco hit the water awkwardly on his back, sending a sheet of golden water into the sunlight. His foot stayed above the water for a half-second, oozing blood, and disappeared.

*

Suellen Ransom slammed the cruiser into District 11's marshalling yard, jumped out, and opened the back. From the seat, she yanked a folding bicycle, not much worried about the skid of grease the chain left on the seat. She unfolded it, locked it in riding position, and banged it out of the yard. Harold Hillemeier watched as she rode down the steps onto the walkway that led to the barracks. Though she never looked back, she flipped a bird over her shoulder just before the bike went out of sight behind a chinaberry tree. Hillemeier had no doubt that she meant it for him. He sighed, and went to his intercom.

"Sarge," he said. "G'on over to the barracks and see what Ransom's up to, will you?"

The intercom hummed, and the receptionist's voice came from it. "She faxed a resignation while you were over lunch," it said. "Want me to ax her for the hard copy?"

In the barracks, it took Suellen no more than five minutes to clean out her locker, throwing half the crap it held into the trash, stuffing clothes, a couple of Thelonious Monk CD's, a copy of The Poetics of Space, and four Mars bars into a duffel. When she left the barracks, a citation for extraordinary diligence and bravery was impaled on the screen door hook. A half hour later, she bungee'd the duffel, fatter now by some leather and spandex, a somewhat respectable, crushable chiffon dress, a toilet kit and changes of underwear, onto the back of a flame-red Triumph Speedmaster, and blatted east toward I-40.

*

Francesco Maryland looked down on the State of North Carolina from a height of five or six stories; though the place he surveyed was at least fifty miles from any building that tall. At about his altitude, the tips of a few loblolly pines and cypresses nodded in yellow sunlight, and a minor cloud of midges danced away from the predations of a cardinal.

Things seemed a little strange to Cesco. For one thing, he had no feeling in his fingertips nor – he feared – any fingertips. Or other appendages. He was a point of view without a container, and he found that his point of view was not controllable, but sank slowly earthward through the sun-laced needles of the loblollies. He drew an impatient sigh, and found that breath was another thing missing from the point of view. Downward, only downward was all that he could accomplish, and that with the lazy reversibility of thistledown. The turbulence from a passing horsefly sent him into a helpless arabesque a foot, two feet, west before he began to sink again.

Below the trees, something was happening that concerned him, but he couldn't get a fix on it. He glimpsed pale sprawled skin, a towel, a slender form bent over them. A zephyr whispered in the tree and carried Cesco up again, far above the trees into darkening air. It was long minutes, weeks perhaps, before the point of view fell back to the treetops. He heard an intermittent rushing sound, like someone shoveling loose wheat, grunting with the effort.

Tangles of foliage drifted upward like sea grass around him, revealing more and more of the scene below. The sprawled paleness was legs, one bent and one straight, both limp as bloody linen. A twitching hand, a flank with a streak of blood across it. A person, then, though the bent form blocked its face. Cesco sank toward a delicate head plastered with black hair. The wheat-shoveling sounds grew louder, and matched themselves to the bending of that head over the sprawled victim. The point of view moved, and became a line of sight.

The shoveling sounds stopped, and the wet black head lifted. Francesco's terrified line of sight identified the still, bluish face beneath it as his own. From the girl bent over him came a sob of effort as she forced her stiffened arms against his chest, hard, again and again. Water dribbled from his mouth, and then there were wheat sounds again as she bent over his face. The line struggled, skidding sideways to see, generating a plane of inquiry, a flat window that framed the girl's head. Each hair became a moving point of blackness as the window sank though it. He reached the scalp and penetrated her skull.

He saw her then as if through some feat of clinical technology. Convolutions appeared and grew, slice after slice of her brain and spine, eyes, tongue, the papery complexities of delicate bones, of windpipe and jaw, the flesh that wrapped it clenched in a scowl of concentration. Cesco gasped, fascinated by the gristly living tangle that held the girl, and was the girl.

And by solid lips that pressed against his. The wheat-shoveling sound became breath that crowded through them and into his, past his tongue and into the spaces of his chest. Whoa. Red lips jammed against my mouth, not such a bad thing. Is that her teeth?

Assisted living. Breath poured into him. Burning, crammed with time and feeling, teaching him the sweetness and unity of breath, of lips and life. The sweetness of life, he thought. That's what it is. When he'd held Arabella's breast, that limpid desperation, the sweetness of sex, was just the sweetness of living itself gathered into a peak. And when the peak passed, leaving him with a little moist spot on his khakis, that sweet soreness was life too. And he saw the great lesson: So was the simple drawing of breath, it was the very same sweetness, and it rose somehow from that tangle of bone and brain, tongue and lips, cavities and organs and wetness.

This is an important thing, Cesco thought. I will never forget this for as long as I live. He clenched and spasmed, and felt himself cough river water into the mouth that was pressed to his. And he drew a great, shuddering breath. I must not forget this. Never forget.

"Thanks be to God," Morgan Baley said, and wiped the acrid warmth from her mouth.

"'Msorry," Cesco answered. "Barfed."

6.

The motorcycle trip across North Carolina gave Suellen a chance to think, try and figure what the hell she was doing. She'd lasted eight years with the Marines and three with the Highway Patrol, not throwing tantrums like this. Something was bothering her, more than she'd known. Something about the whole setup down there in Gabbro, about Hap, wasn't right. It was not, she thought, the unsurprising wandering-off of a confused old man, not even that sorrowful kind of right. She was not going to get at it by getting mad at Hillemeier. She should, she knew, try to keep her shirt on. She should face up to what it was about Hap Maryland's disappearance that ached and loomed at her, and threatened to break her heart.

Whatever the bothering thing was, its message was as thin and delicate as silk, just visible but evasive and damn near transparent. If she thrashed around and yanked at it, it would tear and she would lose it. And once lost, she thought, it would never return even to the edges of her vision. Let it settle and firm up. It had taken her so long to understand why people said, and maybe once, even meant, that they would think about things. Not at them. The goddamn marines, that's all they did, was attack problems, and it took her years to get over it.

All she really could say for the Marines was, they'd brought her into the presence of a woman in Kurdistan who taught her not to think preemptively. The body is wiser than the will, she said. And the will is wiser than the mind. Listen to them all, but remember which is wisest. Suellen turned off Thelonious Monk, memorized the empty road as far ahead as she could see, and then looked at the sky above it with half-shut eyes, letting paint lines and grooves in the concrete become a weaving dance of light and dark. What was it? Her asking was shy, offhand, as if she were a sweat-faced boy at the drinking fountain, and the bothersome thing a glimmering girl.

And she waited for an answer, while the interstate rushed at her, and the drumming machine under her butt made lines and structures of fatigue and mild pain radiate from the place she broke, getting out of Kurdistan. I am 35 years old, and that's old enough to feel it when I act like a jerk kid. The thought was dispiriting, but it was also part of the gauzy troublesome thing, and she didn't dare not think it. What? Please, what is it?

*

In a shadowed and pungent room at Inglenook, Faye Bynum took a nitro tablet with a shaking hand, and pulled a book from the shelf by her bed. Spiritual Sojourns in the Near East, With Biblical Gazetteer, by Austin Mayfair, M. Div. She opened it as the orderly appeared at her door, smiled at her, and turned up the room lights. Golden cloudlets on the ceiling sprang into being and commenced a gentle stampede toward the LED sunset on the west wall.

"You'll strain your eyes, reading in the dark, Honey," he said.

"Got this memorized," Faye sighed. "Know it by heart. Ha ha."

"Heh, heh," the orderly acceded. "They's any God's amount of books in the library, Miz Bynum. Won't you like me to drop by and pick you some new ones out?"

"Then I'd have to turn on the lights, wouldn't I? Cut 'em down a notch, would ya?"

The orderly hesitated, and twisted the dimmer a judicious three or four degrees. The drifting sunset faded as if by the approach of night. "Like me choose you a different theme, Ma'am?"

Faye shrugged. "Seen 'em all. What's that first one I had?"

"Midwest Morning. Lots of residents love that. You want to try it a while?"

"Wrong time a life, Sweetheart. This'n is more my time. Is that old McLain I hear? Whyn't you drop by the library, pick the old fart out a songbook."

The orderly cocked an ear down the hall at a whiskey baritone belting "Cry Me a River," just that one line, over and over.

"I'll just see what he's after," he said. "Don't you be trying to read in the dark, now."

"Thank you, dear." Faye Bynum waited until "Cry Me a

River" swelled with the opening of old Rayford McLain's door. She got herself to the door with patient minimal steps; shut it and dimmed the Arizona Sunset to a glow. In bed again, she opened her book and flipped its pages.

Spiritual Sojourns in the Near East was a printer's error that Faye found in 1965 in a used book store in Maine: 314 numbered pages, dove-white paper, handsomely bound, generous format, perfectly blank. She'd meant to use it as a diary, and there were a few pages at the beginning that bore the self-conscious beginnings of one that ran as far as Vietnam and the Nixon disgrace. But Faye Bynum was a merciless editor who'd never tolerated half-assed writing in the Gabbro Intelligencer, and she found it impossible to ignore in her own journal. The last of these pages bore her vow of silence: *There is no fool more perfect than a scribbling spinster. Shut up shut up, Shut. Up.*

That page was followed by fifty blank and silent ones, which may have been meant as a buffer between the diary and any other use, or possibly a back-handed venue for its some-day continuation. And then a page that began,

21 September. Hap Maryland has given up and moved into Paradise Limited. This ought to be fun.

Succeeding entries were spaced generously by weeks, then by days.

Maryland dropped by to talk. We did, about Inglenook and age and death. Next morning he brushed past me in the Refectory, pissed about something.

Maryland very much schnockered on stiffened cider at Hallowe'en party. Don't think Welles knew or intended cider to have that capability.

HM brought grandchild to Refect. for dinner. No blood relation, I believe. Solemn little thing, and pretty. Image of the late Lee. My God, to be that young and clear again. I'd do some things otherwise next time around.

Shut up.

and

HM and Welles in catfight after Evensong. Something about pressure, or who knows? He can't be out of money already.

Faye closed the book on her finger and lay back on her bolster with fluttering eyes. She wasn't perfectly clear about what to do with this thing. The day wasn't that far away when the room would host some strapping kid EMT, shaking his head and packing up his defibrillator. When Wegeman's had come and gone – while the survivors were asleep or at dinner was the usual protocol – the next guests would be a couple of snuff-chomping janitors with black garbage bags to pack up her things. Faye had no next of kin that she knew of, and the book would go to the landfill. Or, God, maybe into the Inglenook library if they were impressed enough by the binding; then some day, somebody would open the thing, and there would be her hideous self-revelations. Not to mention the later stuff about

Hap. Some kid, probably, visiting his Grandma, bored silly, sent to the library. Stealing it, reading it out loud to his kid friends at recess.

"Blood-red October makes my heart ache." Ow, ow, mine too, hee hee. *"Summer wind stirs tremors on dark water, and in my soul." "Maryland very much schnockered,"* snort, giggle. "Daddy, what's schnockered?"

Burning the stupid thing wasn't an option because they don't allow matches at Inglenook. But she'd ought to tear it into confetti and flush it down the commode. She knew she wouldn't; the dead are immune to shame.

*

Suellen Ransom rolled into Gabbro in a warm rain. Her back and hips felt like she'd been on the rack for six hours, not a Triumph. She stopped at the Pick-Kwik on 73 Bypass for local cuisine (chili dog, coke, Little Debby) and re-mounted, grunting with stiffness, her butt close to rebellion now. She'd evolved part of a plan, and the first part of that took her to Hap and Lee Maryland's old place on Swamp Road.

It was locked and dark, waiting for Bethany and Taylor to agree on what to do about it, but Suellen had lived there for a time, and knew its permanently locked front door and its hidden weaknesses. She parked the Triumph where it wouldn't be seen from the road, and listened to the bugs and the drip of leaves in the fading light. A car approached on Swamp Road, and its passage was without pause, a doubled blur of light and noise, a thump of music, and gone. Suellen opened the back shed that once housed Covington the mutt on warm nights like this, found and dragged a lawn chair under the kitchen window whose lock never quite fit. In twenty seconds, she was coming out through the kitchen door. She un-bungee'd the duffel and brought it into the house, moving in darkness without hesitation. She dumped the contents on the bed she'd once shared with Bethany, took off her wet clothes, and brushed her teeth. She found a desiccated sliver of Dial soap, and showered briefly in cold, rusty water. There were towels in the cupboard; Suellen wrapped herself to pad through the dark house and stand on the screen porch where she and Hap Maryland had shared beers on rainy nights.

Lights showed on the campus of Gabbro College a half-mile across Lake St. Luke. Suellen knew the place. She had studied there, and Morgan's grandmother Lee had been its president. Hap never admitted that Lee's infidelity had damn near killed him. He housed and fed Suellen instead, because she was a wreck after Bethany, and much too young and needy to admit it. That was more than a dozen years ago, almost forgotten and long healed; but coming back to this house showed her how much pain was still down there, if she really wanted to dig around for it.

She dropped the wet towel and walked onto the porch, welcoming the soft air on her sore butt. The screens, drowned in honeysuckle, admitted only the lightest of breath, staining it with bubblegum sweetness, and a dribble of leftover light from a farm a half-mile down the road. She laid the sleeping bag on the floor, and sat on it to stare at the honeysuckle shadows on the wall. They were as faint and jumbled as the troublesome thing that nagged her mind, the thing that she dared not think about directly. She wondered if just staring at the pattern of darkness while her body dried and her fingertips brushed light circles on her knees might help her hold on to the thing, neither tearing it, nor letting it fade as her mind faded into sleep.

She woke cold and stiff at some silent hour to crawl into the sleeping bag and pursue the delicate thing that nearly revealed itself in a dream of great and terrible age. Faye Bynum, she nodded, as she fell again into darkness. Faye would tell her what it was.

7.

Suellen woke when a cardinal started yelling, "Birdie, birdie" in the honeysuckle next to her ear. She pulled the lip of the sleeping bag over her head, not managing to shut the thing out. She reached up and slapped the screen. Goddamn state bird of North Carolina, isn't that enough? The cardinal scrammed, but it was too late. Suellen pulled the bag down far enough to expose an eye.

The pattern of shadows on the porch wall was gone because everything was the same neutral gray now, light from time when you couldn't tell whether you'd slept in on a rainy day, or were up with the birds on a clear one. Bird, though, she thought. Also, no rain sounds.

She dragged herself out of the sleeping bag in a little puff of body scent, arching her back to help the Triumph kinks sort themselves out. Hap and Lee Maryland's house and yard were filled with the silence of abandonment. No dog snuffling and shaking its brains loose, no fridge noises, water running, clocks ticking and bonging. Just the soft padding of her own feet to the bathroom, the gush of urine, flutter of the last dusty squares of paper on the roll. Suellen began to spook herself because she was the only source of sound in this silent place, as if the house were listening to see what noise she'd make next, and put it in quotes. "Flush," said the toilet.

Suellen found the main gas tap and turned it on. She looked at the ancient and complex water heater and decided not to risk it, but put a kettle of water on the stove and searched through the mouse-desecrated cupboards for anything to eat. By the time the kettle was screaming, she'd found a fairly clean tea bag and some sugar in a screw-top jar. She took the tea and the rest of the hot water into the bathroom and gave herself a sponge bath while daylight began to fill the window. Shivering, she fished a disposable razor out of the toothbrush rack and shaved her legs, gritting her teeth, lubricating the flimsy blade with spit, sunblock and the grudging lather of Dial. She hoped to hell Judith Welles, LPN, would appreciate the gesture.

*

At Inglenook, Faye Bynum was awake. She always woke early, usually in the dark, but she'd had angina around midnight. Taking a nitro, waiting for it to work, and then finding a position that didn't pipe the mutter and rustle of her heart through the mattress to her ear kept her awake for an hour. It was dawn and then some before she woke for good.

"Or ill," she thought. This whole business of being a frail old lady sucked, had sucked from the day she looked in the mirror and saw herself so, and had only gotten worse. 'Old age is not for the fainthearted,' that cliché so beloved of the editorial staff of the Inglenook Inklings, made her furious every time she saw it. Old age had made her heart faint, and would stop it entirely before long.

Well, it was high time to wrap things up. There was a chance, still, for something to be done about Spiritual Sojourns in the Near East, but not a lot of time. A heart beats a million times in ten days. Did her heart have a million beats in it still? She found it difficult to believe. She would have to call Hap's daughter, though she hated the thought. The business about Lee would be hard for her to read.

Faye was beginning to look for the breakfast tray when she heard a tap at her door. New nurse, evidently, none of the regulars knocked, or stood on anything but the necessity of getting the plates out fast so they could have as much break time as possible before pickup began.

"That my breakfast? Where the hell you been?" If it was a new nurse, it was none too soon to get her good and alienated, before she started talking about "87 years young," that kind of shit.

"No ma'am," Suellen said. "It's me again."

"For crying out loud," Faye said. "Great. Perfect. Get your butt in here, great God, is that a dress? What, the smokies fire you, or you working vice now?"

"If vice is work, I don't do it," Suellen said. "I'm not a cop any more."

"Their loss. You lookin to hook up with a older woman, now you're retired?"

"Nope. I'm looking for a conversation about Hap Maryland, and don't pull that 'Hap Who?' baloney on me again."

Faye Bynum cackled. "See, though, when the old lady's only half there at best, they's no good way to tell, is there?"

"No'm. So I'm just going to figure you're kidding me all the time. Look, Ma'am, Faye. There's something about all this that doesn't seem to sit quite square, see what I mean. Hap put himself in here, and then the next thing anybody knows, he's – "

Faye Bynum held up a hand and cocked her head toward the hallway and the rattle of a handcart. "Awful good a you to bring that little rose th'other day. Look there, they put it in the winda for me, and it's not dead yet. Not even talking to itself, hardly, been here two days."

The breakfast cart banged the door jamb behind Suellen, and a well-knit black orderly entered with a covered dish that smelled like an IHOP parking lot. "Hey there, Miz Bynum," he said, twisting the room lights to full blast. "Got company awready today, my stars. Can I bring you anything else? Cup a coffee for you, Miss?" He put a hand in his pocket and gave Suellen an admiring survey. Suellen, regretting the coffee, gave him back a look she used when Marines and state troopers got that way. It was more than enough.

"OK, yeah," the orderly said, and dropped the dish cover on the floor. It bounced off his foot and rolled under the bed. Suellen turned to the window to miss the butt cleavage she figured was coming when he crouched to pull it out. The tea rose looked dry, so she took it into Faye's bathroom for a drink. When she came back, the guy was getting to his feet, looking flustered.

"You give me a call, anything come up, Miz Bynum," he said. "Bye, Miss, enjoy your visit."

"You bet," Suellen said.

Faye turned her cheery goodbye wave into an imperative, palm-down hook of fingers. She fingered a remote, and motors under the mattress raised her to a more conspiratorial position. "Get over here, Hon," she whispered. "C'mere close. I need somebody to take something for me, that's got some guts and a brain or two. I was gonna give this to little Bethany, but if you're telling me you got some concerns about Hap Maryland, you might be the ticket. Here."

Faye dug under the covers and brought out Spiritual Sojourns in the Near East. "I need," she said, and her face started to sag. "I need somebody to look at this, see if I'm a crazy old bat, and won't tell nobody if I am." She thrust the book at Suellen, and Suellen took it, lips puckered.

"Spiritual Sojourns?" Suellen looked up to find Faye Bynum poking a plastic spoon at her plate of Egg Beaters, looking as if her life had come down to a lukewarm mound of spayed and tinted protein.

"If I muck these around enough, it looks like I ate some," she said. Suellen thought Faye's irony held back something else, perhaps tears.

"You could just, you know, eat some. Or how about you tell me what you wanted to say about Hap?"

"You'll enjoy that, Hon. Don't let the cover fool you."

Suellen flipped open Spiritual Sojourns, and hit the blank stretch of fifty pages. She looked sharply at Faye, and saw Faye shaking her head. She was crying openly now.

"There ya have it, Hon," Faye said. "My life's an open book, mostly blank. There's other things there, though, if you look. You want to talk about any of it, come on back. When you're done with it, promise me, burn it. Call that boy to get my plate, will you? I'm tired."

Suellen went into the little bathroom and wet a washcloth with warm water. When she got back to Faye's bedside, she wiped her face, wetting back the magenta straggles of hair, smoothing the ancient skin, drowning the tears in tapwater.

"Damn, Miz Bynum," she said. "You were a looker, weren't you?"

The faded eyes opened and Faye blushed. "You need glasses," she said. "I was plain as a pot."

"Let me be the judge," Suellen said, and gently kissed the purple mouth. "Get some sleep, OK?"

Faye put a hand to Suellen's cheek. "That's the kind of judgment you got, Honey, we're done for."

Suellen turned at the door. "I'll look at this and we'll talk tomorrow. That be OK?"

"Make it first thing, I could be out dancin after lunch. Turn them silly lights down, would ya?"

*

Suellen spent the rest of the morning on a lakeside bench on the campus of Gabbro College, reading through Spiritual Sojourns in the Near East. Not taking notes, trying not to think too hard about what she found there. Stopping once in a while to watch the martins that had come in for the summer to flit over the water and eat bugs, watching the ducks that hadn't made up their minds whether to start the haul north to breed, or just maybe have another tadpole and take a nap.

Knowing she shouldn't, Suellen read Faye's youthful diary and tried to imagine the one who wrote it. It was hard going, the blood-red Octobers and the tremoring dark waters, and many another Edgar Guest-ish image - *My heart is three ripe apricots,"...* really? scattered through with occasional winners, like " *'Gabbro' may just be a kind of black rock, but Oh! How it fits this blathering little burg."* But she figured Faye would expect that she would read it, so maybe there was something there for her. What there was, was Suellen's own dismay at a smart kid telling herself so viciously – probably echoing a world that didn't care to hear from another sensitive girl, thanks – to just shut up. And obeying so thoroughly.

When she got to the entries that began with *"21 September. Hap Maryland has given up and moved into Paradise Limited,"* she stood and sought out a vending machine. Chewing corn chips, she began to walk around Lake St. Luke, reading and smiling, once in a while grunting with surprise or speculation. Maryland dropped by to talk. Maryland schnockered. HM and Welles in catfight. And more, recording Hap's doings and suspicions along with what looked to Suellen like trivial gossip, right up to a few days before he disappeared. Though other Inglenookers came in for a share of Faye's commentary, Hap Maryland was the only one it denoted by initials. And his going put an end to the log.

Completing her third circle of the lake, Suellen stopped at the college library and called up a search engine to check some of what Hap thought he'd got onto at Inglenook. What she found didn't help her much. She went back to the lake, walked around it, and climbed through whispering deep grass to the ridge of dunes and pines that separated the campus from Swamp Road.

A hundred yards away, Hap Maryland's house snoozed in the sun, silent, waiting for someone new to own it and live there, or to tear it down and plant cotton. Not, as far as Suellen could see, pining for somebody to stick their nose into Hap's disappearance and stir up a lot of heartache. Finally, she went back to where she'd parked the Triumph and rumbled herself out to Bethany's house to see if Bethany wanted to kick things around over a decent lunch. Suellen was starved.

She walked in on a gathering of Bethany and Plummer Baley, Taylor and Giulia Maryland, a brace of Plummer's fellow clerics, and two recent arrivals to this post-hypothetical-mortem assembly: Taylor's mother - and Hap's ex - Ginnie North, and Ginnie's Mafioso consort Silvio.

"Hap never was what anybody'd call a through-an'-through believing man," Reverend Sam Wainwright said. "Even when he was a Elder with us, you always had the feeling, he was holdin something back."

"Holding back his hard-wired and God-given skepticism," said Farnell Hastie of True Foundation AME Zion. "Brother Hap wouldn't rather of said nothing, than put on any kind of a show. Not that I mean to suggest being an Elder in your excellent church has any taint of the street-corner supplicant to it. Far from it."

"Point taken, Brother Hastie," Sam nodded, unruffled. "Just, I meant to suggest that his memorial service hadn't ought to imply that he thought of himself as Jesus' own, just itchin to meet The Lord in the middle of the air, like that. We need to set a tone of appreciation for one of Gabbro's adopted sons that was generally a credit to this town and a help to his fella man. Person." Correctness still came hard to Sam Wainwright.

Bethany sighed. "You're right, Sam. It still just kills me to be talking about a memorial service. Legally, he's still alive, until we find evidence otherwise, or he walks back in here. Not that I think that's going to happen, mind. Daddy's gone, all right. It's just so hard, not really knowing, just having him disappear, never saying goodbye."

Ginnie North grunted and scratched her chin. She looked like she was about to say something, caught a look from Taylor, and shut up. Ginnie was – reluctantly – pushing 70 now, Suellen figured. Suellen had heard a fair amount of damnation from

Hap about her over the years, but never met her, so actually seeing her was an event of sorts. Ginnie had apparently once been wiry, maybe even muscular, in a flyweight kind of way, and now was simply bony. She wore an assemblage of silver-beaded turquoise scarves with no detectable structure that somehow managed to coalition a garment among themselves through shaky compromise. She'd evidently done a couple of runs down the re-assembly line herself, that had left her with the China-doll look of the frequently worked-on.

Taylor sighed, and tossed a hand. In his late 30's, Suellen realized, he was starting to look like a mild and slightly unformed version of the fortyish Hap she'd first known.

"It's tough for me too, Sis," he said. "And I wasn't even here to have some recent memories. But I don't think we're doing anybody any good by not facing it, and putting it to rest. Plus, the house is just going to sit there and deteriorate, get vandalized, if we don't do something about it. It'll get broken into one of these days, and maybe set on fire."

"Already been broken into," Suellen said. People turned toward her. "I spent last night there. Everything looks pretty good, so far. I came to ask if anybody minded, I camp out there for a couple days."

Ginnie North's surgically widened eyes narrowed, with some difficulty. "And you would be ... ?"

"Corporal Ransom, Tennessee Highway Patrol, Ma'am," Suellen said. Anyway, used to be, she thought. "I was ... I rented a room out there, ten-twelve years back."

Ginnie shook her head, and the silver beads murmured. "Hap was quite the one for these brief liaisons, wasn't he? Have we heard from his last girlfriend yet?"

"Asking me?" Suellen said. "That'd be Paula Vanek. I lost track of Paula when I got deployed overseas. She even know he's missing?"

"Yes," Bethany said. "They stayed in touch. Paula doesn't think he's dead, she says. She's in the running for Dean of Arts and Sciences at Harvard, or she'd be down for this."

"What a shame to miss her," Ginnie said. "That was the whore, wasn't it? One of them. How like Harvard."

"Her research field was prostitution," Suellen said, calmly enough. "She was to hookers what Dian Fossey was to gorillas."

Ginnie smirked, and Suellen gave up on nice. "Paula and Hap had a wonderful relationship," she snapped. "I don't know what led them to break it off, but I expect Hap decided he didn't want to tie her to a geezer, when her career was taking off. Sure, he said he didn't want to leave Gabbro, but it was more than that. Hap was a generous, decent, loving ..." Learn from Faye Bynum, she thought. Shut up.

Ginnie sniffed. "I'm not sure we're talking about the same person. He murdered his own – "

Taylor's hand slammed the table, and he ripped a line of rough-tongued Italian at Silvio. Silvio pulled a face and rose with courtly menace.

"I believe Geenie and I make a little passeggiata, just

now," he said. "Be so good as not to take final decisions until we can join you again. Venga, cara."

Ginnie put on a look that might have last been seen on one of Emperor Nero's domestic panthers whose chain had been jerked, and rose, her silver beads flashing constellations of ill omen. When they were gone, there was a general throat-clearing among the clergy. "Is there," Sam Wainwright asked, "any real doubt that Hap has passed on?"

The table was silent until Suellen's stomach growled. Nobody, she reflected, wanted to kill Hap by confirming that there was no hope at all of finding him alive. The next thing that was said was by Bethany.

"Suellen, we're about to sit down with some lunch. You got time to join us?"

8.

Suellen wrapped an apple in her napkin and pushed back her plate. "Here it is," she said. "According to Faye Bynum, Hap got a kind of a thing about Inglenook, after he'd been there a while. Like they were sucking out people's life savings and then killing them off as soon as they went on Medicaid. He got a notion about they were controlling the clients with drugs or some kind of – I got to admit this is a little vague – hypnosis. She gave me her diary, where she kept track of what he said. Some of it's just plain … well, it doesn't make much sense."

Taylor looked up from his linguini. "Not that I'd ever doubt a place like Inglenook is out for what they can get, processing oldies through like beef cattle. Still, they couldn't hide actually killing people off. Could they?"

"Listen to this," Suellen said, riffling through Spiritual Sojourns. *"HM and Welles in catfight after Evensong. Something about pressure, or who knows? He can't be out of money already."*

"He had that all covered," Bethany said. You pay Inglenook by the year in advance. He'd just paid for the second year, and he had plenty to go on with."

"OK," Suellen nodded. "So even if he's right, they wouldn't be ready to kill him off yet. But listen: *'HM in this morning, out of breath. Forde Morgan passed away, and left all he had to Inglenook. I could have told him Forde was a lazy cluck without one brain to rub against another.'* And the next day, *'HM says Forde changed his will.'*

Bethany shrugged. "Forde promised Mama a big chunk of his estate for the college, I remember that. It was the first big gift she ever got. Course, it was what they call 'Deferred Giving,' meaning Forde had to pass before the college got anything. Forde was Mama's uncle twice removed, something like that. He was right proud of her being the first president after the college went private. Daddy could've known about it from when he took over when Mama was sick, or maybe she just told him, she was so tickled Forde came through like that. Time he passed, it wasn't worth so much. Still, …"

"Still," Suellen said. "Maybe that was what the 'pressure' business was. Or I guess not, the dates don't fit. Maybe it was somebody else, though."

"Maybe," Ginnie North said, re-settling herself from her cooling-off, "it was all a lot of moonshine. It wasn't some conspiracy that sent Hap to a county council meeting in his pajama bottoms. The man was losing his marbles. It wouldn't take much to get him going on some crusade that didn't amount to anything real." She glanced at Taylor, and stuck out her chin. "I know you don't want to hear this, Taylor, but your father was always unstable, ever since he – ever since your sister died. He drank enough alcohol in his life to float a battleship, and he was well over seventy. It simply caught up with him in the end."

Suellen raised an eyebrow at Bethany. "What about that,

Beffie? Are we just dealing with dementia here?"

Bethany sighed, and got up to clear plates. "There may have been a series of small strokes," she said. "The kind of thing where you can't be sure whether he's just being forgetful, and maybe something really serious is going on. He'd had a brain scan, didn't show much."

Ginnie North grinned. "I could have told them that, saved them the trouble."

"Forgetful like staying out overnight, and nobody knew where?" Suellen tried not to sound accusatory.

Bethany tried not to sound defensive. "Before he started that kind of thing. It was just tiny little slips at first. The sort of thing they used to call 'senior moments.' Starting a sentence and never finishing it, not remembering why he'd gone into a room or a store downtown. Heck, I've done it too, but in Daddy's case, it kept on. He knew it was happening and it got more serious, like these blank spots in his life, which that visit to the county council was one. I expect that's why he let Paula go to Harvard without him, though it pretty much killed him. And why he put himself in Inglenook."

"Yeah," Suellen said. "God, this is painful. OK, listen to this. *'Hap thinks it's Delta Dawn that's the worst.'* What's that supposed to be? Some kind of perfume?"

"A song," Ginnie said. " 'Delta Dawn, what's that flower you got on?' It was a big hit when I was pregnant with Taylor."

"Mm. Sound likely to anybody, he'd be critiquing 70's pop at this date? And Faye Bynum thinks it's worth writing down?" Suellen pocketed her sequestered apple and stood. "Maybe I'll stop back and ask her about it. There's a couple of other funny-sounding things that don't seem to make much sense." Not to mention, she thought, the part about Hap and Lee, that would be hard for Bethany to read. She needed to talk to Faye about that before she showed it to anybody else.

Suellen was at the door with Bethany when Francesco appeared at the head of the driveway on a bike he'd borrowed from one of Morgan's friends, and skidded on loose gravel. Bike and boy collapsed in a cloud of dust, limbs, and sun-glint. Suellen could see a tear in the elbow of the shirt next to the ground, and figured on some scraped skin behind that.

"Mother of all mother-fuck!" Cesco yelled. He rose limping, and came toward the door. His left foot, that he'd lacerated in his swimming accident, was dragging a little, and he swung himself along with a rolling pace that seemed awkward even for an adolescent boy.

"Boy's got a tongue on him," Suellen murmured.

"It's been awful the last day or so," Bethany whispered. "Poor Giulia is at her wit's end. I guess he's restless and all, here with a bunch of strangers. I can't help wondering about drugs, though. They're not that hard to find here any more."

Cesco came up the path to the door and Suellen thought she could see the beginning of tears. She started to say something, and decided *Shut Up*. Cesco climbed the steps and floundered into her, scraping his arm on the door jamb, and snarled, " 'Scuse me, damn it," impatiently.

Giulia's chair scraped, and she called a reprimand in an angry and fearful voice.

"Mom, jus' go fuck yourself," Cesco muttered, and limped toward the stairs. From what Suellen could see, he looked as shocked and scared as Giulia.

*

Suellen stopped at the Hallmark store on her way to Inglenook, looking for something – anything – that would be less mortal than a flower. She finally settled, in view of the recent passage of St. Patrick's day, on a remaindered ceramic leprechaun holding a sign that said, "Trust me, I'm Irish." Faye could always put it in the pot with the tea rose, or throw the whole mess out the window. On the way out to Inglenook, she met the county ambulance loafing toward town, siren off, an EMT's arm out the window dangling a cigarette.

The Inglenook Choristers were practicing "Gaudeamus Igitur" when Suellen opened the front door, voices quavering or booming. One of the things Hap had fulminated about to Faye, and Faye reported with amusement, was the phony spin of the translation in the Chorister songbook supplied by Nurse Welles: *"After jolly youth and matur'ty's mirth / We shall all possess the Earth."* Got that one exactly backward, Faye had noted.

Suellen kept a low profile passing the reception desk – in view of what she'd found in Faye's diary, she thought maybe the Fluff Sisters might take a second look at repeat visits from an officer of the law. The dress – now getting a little rumpled – and the shaved legs were supposed to deflect that kind of suspicion; still, Suellen didn't want to push it.

Faye's door at the end of the Walden Wing was open, which made Suellen frown. Faye kept it shut except when she had company, and Suellen didn't want to have to out-wait some social worker. She put the leprechaun on a hall table and pulled her dress into shape, brushing off some bugs that had landed on it after losing a collision with the Triumph.

In Faye's room, the lights were on full blast, and not the sunset theme, either. What blazed from the doorway was a uniform off-white radiance, with a faint bluish tinge. The sort of lights she used to see in sterilizing cabinets in Iraqi barbershops, Suellen thought. She walked in, and a soft explosion of dismay rose into her throat. The bed was empty, the mattress rolled and tied, sitting endwise on the complex mesh of springs, wires, and little electric motors that had kept Faye Bynum comfy for twenty years. A pair of black trash bags sat by the door, waiting for disposal. The tea rose was gone from the windowsill, and the window gaped, letting in air that smelled of earth and farewell. Suellen walked into the room, mouth open in protest, tears springing. "Oh," she said. "Oh, shit, no."

She looked at the leprechaun, and it leered back. *Trust me*, it winked. Suellen slammed the stupid thing to the floor and watched the pieces scatter across the tiles. And in a half-second, she was on her knees at the side of the bed, craning to see where all the wires went.

She'd just found the extra one when she heard one of the trash bags rustle. The breakfast orderly was at the door, having a good-natured look at her butt while she groped under the bed. Suellen turned, and let the movement hike the dress up her thigh.

"I …" she said. "Is Faye, is she …" Suellen opened her knees a little, sprawled there on the floor, and lifted an elbow to the bedframe. The effect was satisfactory; the orderly quit looking at where her hand had been, groping along the extra wire, and concentrated on legsville.

"Miz Bynum done passed very suttenly, over lunchtime," he said, in a voice that seemed to come from kilometers below the Earth's crust. "She a relation of yours, Ma'am?"

"Just my very best darn teacher ever," Suellen wailed. "I was a intern at th'Intelligencer while I was in college here. Miz Faye just taught me everything I know about the news business. She was the … the most…" Suellen lifted the hem of her dress and bent to dab her unfaked tears with it, giving the orderly such cleavage as she could muster to compete with the new stretch of leg. She wished she'd bothered with a bra. "I brought her this little leprechaun, and it was such a shock I …Oh, poor Miz Faye, I cain't stand it!"

"There," the orderly nodded. "There, now. I don't expect she suffered hardly none. We heard the page and come in here, found her nitro pills all spilled, and her awready gone." He nodded regretfully while Suellen stood and smoothed her dress.

"Hardly none at all."

"Do you happen to know what the ... you know, the Arrangements will be?"

"No, Ma'am. Bit early for that, really. Wegeman's done took her. I expect Miz Welles is working on that end of it."

Suellen bowed her head and gave him an upwards look. "You reckon I could spend just a couple minutes here where I saw her the last time? She was such a wonderful lady."

The guy looked doubtful, and Suellen didn't blame him. As far as he knew, she showed up for the first time this morning, and now she's a lifelong disciple of the old lady.

"Miz Welles axed me, turn the room over right quick," he said. "Got a long waiting list, new old fella coming in before supper yet."

Suellen blinked, and tensed her pectorals a little to maximize the meager cleavage. The orderly nodded, possibly in appreciation, and picked up one of the black bags.

"I got ta run this out' the dumpster," he said. "You might stay a little. If you was gone when I come back for the other, I'd have no way to tell how long you was here before that, would I?"

"No sir, thank you," Suellen mewled. She gave him a tearful little smile as he turned away, and was gratified to see that he bumped into the door frame on his way out. She dove under the bed to confirm what she thought she saw, and had time for a quick check of the second trash bag before she heard the door creak at the far end of the corridor.

Suellen stopped at the Pik Kwik on the way back to Swamp Road and bought some food and a pack of Pilsner Urquells. When she had the Triumph stashed again, she got the hell out of the dress and into a pair of boxers and a tee shirt as quick as she could. On the breathless honeysuckle porch, surrounded by the muttering and tuning-up of afternoon bugs, she popped an Urquell and lifted it in a useless toast to Hap Maryland, who'd persuaded her that no better beer existed. She hoped that wherever Hap was now, he'd found something twice as good.

"All right," she sighed. She stretched, rubbed the sweating bottle across her forehead, and cocked a leg onto the arm of the rusty old glider. Damn it, she'd just got Faye Bynum to trust her, and now Faye was dead. Suellen would have to make what sense she could out of the diary without her help, or her friendship, for that matter. She was a sweet, sharp old woman, a self-sufficient femme, and Suellen already missed her.

Suellen groaned and rubbed her eyes. Sweet or sour, her bed had included a small microphone, hidden among all those wires that raised and lowered its sections, controlled the TV, and summoned help for the dying. Was that a standard feature of Inglenook, one of the countless amenities along with the spotless and proactive housekeeping and the lucent techniques?

Suellen shook her head at an early gnat that had worked its way through the honeysuckle. What, it's a facility with maybe three hundred old folks, and every one of their beds is bugged? Who listens to all that creaking and muttering, the snores, the jangle of dropped spoons, the soft rain of incontinence? No way. If they were listening to Faye, and therefore maybe to Hap, they had a special reason to. Or, OK, all beds had microphones, but they were only tuned in at random, to make sure there was no widespread evasion of the amenities.

Suellen grunted, and sat up. <u>Or</u>, they were off most of the time, and turned on when somebody had a reason. For example, by an orderly who dropped a plate cover and had to fish around under the bed to find it. How long had Suellen been out of Faye's room, watering the tea rose?

She grabbed the Urquell and stood. Walked to the screen and put it on the sill-like frame. Picked it up and started counting. She took six or eight steps to the right to put herself in Faye's bathroom, pictured water running into the flowerpot while she counted seconds. Remembered getting the bottom of the pot wet, and she wiped the bottom of the Urquell with an imaginary washcloth so it wouldn't make a ring on the windowsill. Rinsed crumbs of potting soil out of the washcloth, wrung it, and hung it up. By the time she walked back to the screen with the surrogate tea rose, she'd counted slowly to thirty.

And the guy was just getting to his feet when she came back in the room. Almost half a minute to retrieve a plate cover? Suellen didn't think so. He'd done something else under there – activated the hidden mike, surely – while Suellen was out of the room. Wouldn't Faye have noticed that, though? She was no dummy, to be taken in by a clumsy charade.

And she wasn't taken in, Suellen realized. She'd whispered the few things that had any meat to them and might alert someone; the rest of what she'd said was innocuous: read this, let me know what you think. My life's an open book. Come back tomorrow, we'll talk about it. Yes, Faye, please talk to me.

And then there was the postcard, her one trophy from the unguarded black trash bag, snatched at the last minute before she walked out of Inglenook, waving her ass at the orderly. A cheap color photo of the statue of Paul Revere in Boston, with the message, "One if by hand, two if by me. You'd love this place. Love, H."

Great. Either Hap Maryland had sent Faye a slightly raunchy postcard during a visit to Paula, or some other person named H had. Or maybe M, you could read the scrawl either way. She tried to remember Hap's handwriting, and found that she couldn't. And what was with the message? Suellen snorted. It sounded like a sexual boast: you can do it by hand, but you'll have more fun, or get better mileage, with me. Is that something Hap Maryland would conceivably have said to Faye Bynum? Or maybe what she read as "hand" was just a scrawled "land." Had Hap even gone to Boston in the last couple of years? Well, sure, maybe with Paula when she was getting ready to jump to Harvard. She would have to ask Bethany next time she saw her. And if he had, so what?

She finished the beer and tucked the postcard down the

waistband of the Umbros by her bare flank, where it scratched and tickled her while she walked back to the kitchen to decide between another beer and scrambling up some hash and eggs for supper. It was self-evident, suddenly, that she would do a better job on the hash and eggs if she had a cold beer in her hand.

It was while she was scraping her plate into the sink, thinking what a shame Covington wasn't around to lick it clean that the thought entered her mind, *I'm too goddamn dumb to figure out any of this. And there's nobody who will care if I do.*

Suellen took another Urquell, the last of the 6-pack, onto the screen porch and settled on the glider with a notepad and *Spiritual Sojourns in the Near East.* Maybe nobody would care if she figured out what Hap had been up to, and what happened to him. She would care, and that was all she had any control over anyhow.

She sketched a time line on the notepad that began with September 21 and ran nineteen months to April of the second year, when Hap disappeared from Inglenook and the journal stopped. Using a superfine 0.2-millimeter lead pencil she'd copped from the Marine mapping office, she wrote in the events Faye had thought worth recording: Hap and grandchild, HM schnockered, HM in catfight.

And on to the tougher stuff:

July 1 Poor Hap brought back to Paradise in the County cruiser in his PJ bottoms from County Council.

July 11. Hap sedated after scene in Refectory in which he suddenly stood with tears in his eyes and announced that Lee, his beloved wife of many years, had been truly repentant for cuckolding him repeatedly with Tim Summerton.

July 12. HM dropped in on me, asked me what he'd said about Lee in the Refectory. Remembered getting up to propose a simple toast to love, remembers nothing after that. When I told him – who am I to lie to someone who wants the truth? – he left without a word.

August 14. HM moved to Assisted Living, which is good one way, it brings him closer, but awfully hard on him.

Nov 30. HM's 71st birthday. Bethany, The Rev. Mr. Bethany, and little Lee Morgan out for the celebration. Hap appears pleased, maybe a little behind the curve on it. He is too young to be so confused. Bethany stopped by, asked me about Hap's crusade on the lights.

Feb. 12. HM gone overnight, no sign-out.

March 4. HM out with little Lee on Sunday, came by my room, had shaved and spruced himself for a change. Seemed happier, in a sad kind of way.

March 15. HM tells me, Lee coming for him again this Sunday, she's so charming when she wants to be. I told him I thought her charming *all the time – Yes, he says, "but you know she cheated on me something awful."*

Suellen put the pencil down and ran her hand through her hair, trying not to think about that. And when she was finished, she kept her hand over her face and didn't think about anything at all.

When she woke from her doze, she was drained and exhausted, draped over the glider like a Victorian floozy. Something else I can't do any more, she thought. Ten years ago when even life as a Marine was easy, she could pull all-nighters five nights in a row, drink a sixpack and never feel it. Now, a little restless sleep one night, and she was ready for jammies at nine o'clock.

*

Lee Morgan Baley knelt by Francesco's bed and offered a quick and earnest prayer. She put a gentle hand over his mouth to keep him quiet, and whispered, "Are you awake?"

"What the fuck?"

"Shh. I thought you liked having things happen to you in the dark. I need you to be awake."

He grumbled and muttered; Lee closed her heart to the vileness of his language. Francesco was, she knew, not responsible for it.

"Please stop that, Cesco. Listen."

"What?"

"I want to pray with you."

"Yeah? We gonna see God again? Or are you gonna show me your – "

"Hush." Lee was near tears. This was her fault, all of it, but if he didn't stop the dirty talk, she didn't see how she could go through with what it would take to fix it. "Listen, Cesco. Something has happened to you. I'm afraid it happened when we … When you had your accident, at the river. I'm going to pray for you to be healed."

Cesco drew back. "Lemme alone. As if that'd do any good, even if. 'Snothing wrong with me, God damn it. Go fuck yourself." His eyes widened. "I didn't mean to say that," he squeaked. "I say things I don't fucking mean."

Lee could see that he was starting to cry, and it let her cry too. "Of course you didn't," she whispered. "What can I say that will let me help?" She looked at him with sudden seriousness. "Would you stay quiet and help me pray, if I took my shirt off for you afterwards?"

Cesco came alert. "Bra too?"

"I'm not wearing one." She took his hand and pressed it to her chest. "Here. See? But you have to promise to help me pray."

Cesco smiled in the darkness. "Shit. OK."

Morgan moved his hand away but held it firmly. She knelt by his bed and laid her other hand on his head. "Jesus, our heavenly Counselor," she whispered. "You know what is in our hearts before we say it. Guide and guard your servants Morgan and Francesco in what we will do and say tonight. We pray with all our hearts that the evil spirit that dwells in Francesco Maryland be banished forever."

*

Suellen was sitting on the toilet, not clear on how she'd got there. She rose, feeling stiff and dizzy, entertaining the notion that six Urquells might have been a little much on an almost empty stomach. Uncertain moonlight filtered through the stained bathroom curtain and showed her a dark shape in the mirror over the sink. She knew it was her own reflection even as she gasped with fear. The shape was too dark to have a face, but when she moved, it moved.

"I think not," she thought, and headed back to bed. As she entered the hall outside the bathroom, she added aloud, "Therefore I am not." It seemed a profound and funny insight, and she snorted with amusement. The hilarity carried her into the kitchen, where silent utensils watched her pass. You never washed us, they said. You're gonna catch it.

"First thing tomorrow," Suellen said, and giggled at her rusty voice in the dead silence of the house. "Not."

Feeble light, a cellar smell of earth and dampness, greeted her in the dining room, with the muted sound of crickets. She felt air on her shoulders, a chill. The dining room furniture crouched and wavered in the dimness as if it were fathoms deep in the fluid earth.

As she entered the porch, she saw two people sitting on the glider where she'd dozed off over her notebook. Hap Maryland said, *Here she is* and Lee Maryland, sitting next to him on the glider said *Oh, good. Hi, Suellen. Come set with us a bit. Scooch over, Hap.*

Suellen sat between the dark shapes, smiling, trying to see if they were smiling too. If she faced straight ahead, she could see them, middle-aged and handsome, the way she remembered when she first knew them. It made her glad to see them looking so good. See, she thought. What was the big deal? But when she turned to look at either of them directly, they were only blackness and silence.

"Hi," she said. "I'm glad you're here, you two. We really need help."

The shapes didn't move. *We can't help,* Hap said at last. *Lee needed to tell you something.*

Suellen smiled at Lee. "OK."

Silence, and a restless faint breeze in the honeysuckle.

Suellen leaned forward and tried to look at Lee. "What is it, Lee?"

Lee sighed soundlessly from her darkness. *It would have … This is hard to say. But, well, it would have been all right.*

"What? What would have been all right?"

You know. If you'd decided to sleep with Hap, after I … you know, after I passed.

"Oh," Suellen said. "Well, thanks. I don't think it

occurred to me. No offense, Hap."

None taken.

I know it didn't, Lee said. *Not until later. When it was too late.*

Suellen put an arm around each of their shoulders, meaning to say something like, "I'd never want to ..." But they crumbled under her touch. Something began to catch and build in her throat, and she felt herself floating an inch above the glider, lifted by a freezing wind of fear that stole her breath. A car passed on Swamp Road, and pale light swept the porch. The two dark shapes beside her were faceless, vaguely human mounds of earth. Suellen's heart exploded, and she tried to scream.

She threw herself to the floor to get away from them. The glider lurched under her and slammed back against the wall with a rusty bang that made a dog bark a quarter-mile down the road. An Urquell bottle spun and tumbled across the floor, scattering drops.

Suellen dove into her sleeping bag and crouched with her back against the screen to stare at the swinging glider. It took her a long time to calm down while the rhythmic creaking slowed from the slam-bang syncopation of outrage to sulkiness, to reproach and resignation, skipping a beat, then two; dying into squeaks and whispers quieter than her own sobbing.

When dawn came, and the cardinal began to sing in the honeysuckle again, Suellen pulled the sleeping bag down far enough to send a mistrustful glance at the glider. It sat motionless in a beam of buttery sunlight. When she remembered the two who had shared it with her, the wind of fear swept through her again, nearly as deathly cold as in the dark of her dream.

The Kurdish woman warned her that bad dreams have a message that you ignore at your peril. "Ask it, always," she said. "Ask what it wanted. If you don't, if you laugh at it or try to shake it off, it will come back, each time worse. The will is wiser than the mind."

Suellen closed her eyes against the sunlight. "All right," she said aloud, while the cardinal boasted and preened above her. "What was the message?"

9.

Saturday morning, Bethany Baley looked out the kitchen window and saw Plummer's car pull into the bare tracks that served as a parking lot next to the turkey oaks. Evidently his Bible class had called it quits early; it seemed to Bethany she'd just got him out the door before she settled down with the church and business accounts.

When Plummer entered, he kissed her tenderly – and, really, he was a hell of a kisser, Bethany thought; they must learn that in the SEALs, because she'd never seen any sign of it at Indian Girl Pentecostal Holiness Tabernacle – and looked at the checks she'd lined up for him to sign.

"Shoot," he sighed. "I was hoping you wouldn't have that ready for me just yet. Some days I get kind of sick of that little place. Where is everybody?"

"Morgan's gone to Ella Jean's for the weekend. Ever'body else is in town at the lawyer's except Cesco, who's still in bed, I guess. You're home quick. Didn't they wont to think about Salvation By Grace this morning?"

Plummer looked at the clock, which was crowding up toward noon. "Pretty much a regular class. Jenny Dial wanted to know, 'Well, if Jesus can save you without regard to your merits an' good works and all, and He's too good to let us go to hell, then what's the point?' I don't believe a year's gone by that some kid didn't ask that. What's for lunch?"

"I don't know that a day goes by somebody doesn't ask that. You hungry already?"

Something about the way she asked told Plummer that there might be benefits to skipping a time and temperature report. "Hungry? Why, that little word don't begin – "

Bethany stuck out a lip. "Time was, you'd talk that way about me."

Plummer got a hand on each hip and turned her so he could twinkle at her. "Why, Bethany, Hon! What did you think I could be talking about? Some weenie and mayonnaise sandwich?"

Dropjaw blush, maybe a little over the top. "Why, of all the … rotten, dirty-mouth talk from a so-called man of the cloth! I am going straight to the Deacons if you don't start to behave yourself." She sighed, and put her mouth to his ear. "Soon as I get dressed."

The marriage of Bethany and Plummer Baley began as one of rushed convenience, starting as it did seconds before the birth of Lee Morgan Baley and remaining unconsummated for a considerable time after that. When Plummer's patient wooing at last established the sexual dimension, their first essays were pretty much by-the-book, missionary ventures. That was fine with Bethany; for one thing, the brutal rape that created Morgan had more than enough of the exotic in it to last Bethany for the rest of her life. But primarily, she never saw any reason to experiment beyond Page One. After the first hesitant and tender trials, she and Plummer had never failed to use the plainest of materials to build structures of such blazing delight that Bethany really wondered whether her constitution would survive anything fancier.

This time was no exception. Plummer, murmuring to her accelerando pulse, agreed with touch and small gestures that he and Bethany, their love, and this very coupling, lay at the center of humming concentric spheres of notice and applause that encompassed themselves, their clan, and all of humanity, not to mention the oceans with their leviathans, the spinning planets, the galaxies and dwelling places of the Most High; and that as she approached the far end of that journey, her cries of amazement were echoed and dissolved in an angel chorus of hosannas that swelled bright and comprehensive, through this universe and through its cheering sisters in unguessed parallel dimensions and all spirit worlds.

Bethany was never sure how this worked. The half-articulate murmurings they exchanged spelled out nothing. And they didn't always go this far; in fact no occasion in the thirteen years of their marriage had yet been in every way the same as any that had come before. Sometimes their lovemaking was just about itself, and had no wider message. Sometimes it touched more on the inwardness of things: on their love for Morgan, on the duality of their union, or on the small sadness that Bethany had not conceived again, than it did on the timeless vastness of Creation. But what she called in her heart the big cosmic universal scroogies were always Bethany's favorites.

When they had reluctantly separated (and Bethany shivered one last time at the feel of his going) and they had re-clasped and tangled and assured each other that it was a delight unto the Lord of Hosts, when two of his children got it on so spectacularly, and had yawned mutual praise and devotion, and when they had dozed until somebody's tummy growled, Bethany said, "I should go and poke that lazy boy and see if he don't wont some lunch too."

"You change your mind about going to the Deacons?"

Bethany looked at him, cross-eyed with love. "I reckon you're safe. If I told them poops what a delicious man you are, they'd make me come up with a extra thank offering. Why don't you go wake up Francesco, and I'll put together lunch. BLT be all right with you? Or – " She leaned over to nuzzle the base of his belly, still fragrant of herself – "I could make you up something out of milk and honey, raisins and apples and pomegranates and the fruit of every tree, each according to its kind from every corner of Creation. If you wonted."

"I'll go with the BLT, I guess. Some of them corners are right distant."

"Aw right, then."

Bethany was in the kitchen, concentrating on slicing tomatoes so she wouldn't moon back over the bed episode and slice her finger, when Plummer came into the kitchen, buttoning his shirt cuffs.

"You sure he didn't come through during the morning?"

"Who? Francesco?" Bethany thought back. The house had been quiet all morning as she sat in a moving sunbeam and worked on the slender books of Indian Girl P. H. Tabernacle and the more substantial ones of Baley Cabinet Works. "I'm sure not. Why?"

"Well, he's not in his bed, nor the bathroom. Sink's dry, and the shower, and you know he never goes anywhere without forty minutes in the shower."

Bethany considered. "Well," she said. "I wouldn't swear he didn't go into town with his folks first thing, or maybe tooken off with Ginnie and Silvio. I just wish people'd tell me these things."

*

Suellen learned little from holding herself open to whatever message her nightmare held for her. The best she could come up with, and she distrusted this to its bottom, was to recall a time when Hap was drinking and getting himself into a depression about Lee's infidelity and death, and she lost patience with him and told him that he needed to get laid. Conceivably, Hap was returning the favor, getting Lee to carry the can for it by giving her permission.

The most heed she could imagine paying any such message was to plan a trip to Chapel Hill to use the engineering and psychology libraries to see what they might have that the Gabbro College library and the Internet didn't, about the bee in

Hap's bonnet. And if she succeeded – best, if she succeeded after a long and diligent day reading goddamn science journals – well, she would certainly have earned a beer and burger at the Trigonal Rose, where she might see some old friends from PFLAG, and if that led to somebody getting laid, well … Suellen shrugged. Well, hey. But there would be no question that the trip to Chapel Hill was for the science, and not the humanity.

And at a quarter to six that afternoon, when Suellen slapped shut the last copy of <u>Operational Psychology</u> she could bring herself to open, she felt she had earned the beer, if not the burger. It was possible. It was just possible that what Nurse Welles called the harmonious and restful ambience she served up with cyber-controlled LED's could be toughened into something altogether more hypnotic and predatory. As if you could pipe a nice restful tinkly fountain into your garden, and get it to cast spells on the bystanders.

Suellen smiled. Already done: every tinkly fountain in the world was paved with the pennies and dimes of people it had suckered into chucking money at it. OK, but could you do it with lights, and for serious money? So Hap had thought, and such, just possibly, was the state of the art in commercial interior decor, at least for a population group with certain susceptible brain rhythms. And that group, she found, was heavily weighted toward the elderly.

Suellen stood and stretched, making a crew-cut boy blush and return his eyes to his notes. God, though, could this sort of thing go on regularly, and be kept quiet? It seemed awfully unlikely. Some architecture student would get an attack of conscience and go public with it, there would be exposés in the press, and Congressional hearings. Suellen snorted, and headed for the Trigonal Rose. God damn it, why do paranoids have to be so crazy?

First of all, it was hot in the Trigonal Rose. And loud with the cries and blather of infants, twenty-somethings who'd been lisping their ABC's when Suellen first came here as a PhD candidate in chemistry. The only face Suellen knew was an old jerk on the Duke faculty who trolled Chapel Hill when everyone in Durham and Raleigh had gotten sick of him.

"Suellen, dear girl," he beamed. "What ever have you been doing with yourself? Wait, no, don't tell me."

Suellen, remembering Faye Bynum with a pang, didn't. But that wasn't what he meant, this time. "Didn't somebody say you were in the SEALs?"

"Marines. That was a while ago."

"Dear girl. Is it right, what they say about Marines? Grunts of passion, all that? How hot does it get in the desert, dear?"

Suellen dealt with him by turning her back and walking away. He cooed, piercingly, "Simper Fi, darling," so Suellen shot him a bird over her shoulder. And walked straight into the breakfast orderly from Inglenook.

He didn't seem to recognize her in the first instant, so she turned her head and brushed past him. But it wasn't quick enough.

"Hey there," he said, and did a graceful little glide across her trajectory. He was not a hair less baby-faced than Suellen remembered, but maybe his eyes were a little sharper than she'd thought. "Wait, lemme see. The lovely little intern, wasn't it? With the legs and the cute cleavage an' all?"

"Do I know you?"

"Harve, from Inglenook," he said, and his smile was genuine, and so white. "You do now. You here with anybody?"

Suellen considered, swallowed irritation, and said, "Well, Ah was sposed to be, but it'd look like she gotten held up. You wont to buy me a beer while we wait, see if she gets here or don't?"

"My pleasure," Harve said. "What do you favor?"

"That Pilsner Urquell, or anything else they got from over there Europe. Not Heineken's." Harve might as well pony up for something decent.

"You got good taste," Harve nodded. "Want fries with that?"

"Why, yes. Yes, I do."

When he elbowed his way to a table with a basket of fries and a pair of bottles, Suellen cocked her head at him. "Good taste for a country white girl, that what you meant?"

Harve smiled and shook his head. "Miss," he said. "You are not no country girl, and there's no friend coming to meet you here, or I am the Pope of Paducah."

"You lose, your Holiness," Suellen said, and pinched a

spray of fries from the basket. "I grew up in F'etteville an' Gabbro. You can't hardly get n'more country than that. Also, not to waste your time, I'm a regular here, and this is a gay bar."

Harve gave her a gentling pat on the arm. "That's all right, hon," he said. "Me too."

"That right? You sure were having a good time watching my butt yesterday."

"I appreciated the little show you put on. Far's that goes, I got nothing against women, they got behinds as handsome as your'n, which is but rarely. But mainly, I had to kind of take my hat off, how hard you were working to get me not to think about what you were up to, down on that floor. I admire anybody that's got a quick mind and a good solid body, that they'll press into service for a cause."

"That right?" Suellen felt the encounter slipping away from her into some kind of revelatory momentum that might carry them both farther than they'd planned. It seemed to her that Harve had more to lose from it than she did, so she took a shot of beer, holding the bottle close to the top to look tougher. "You gotta admit, I was a little quicker on the draw than you were with that silly dish cover."

He laughed easily. "Dang switch stuck on the mike," he said. "I was down there so long the old lady started laughing."

"That why you looked so flustered?"

Harve shrugged. "Blood rushes to your head after a while."

She grinned. "Don't it, though. What's 'Delta Dawn?' "

He shrugged again. "Delta what? Some kind of commando unit? Or a movie?"

Suellen shifted her eyes a little, let his face float off-center while she examined the beer. He didn't look like he was lying about that, not that you could always tell. Truth was, she realized, he looked kind of ... well, shoot. Like if a buff and dark brown girl were playing a pants role in Two Gentlemen of Verona. She looked over his shoulder at the door. How far down this road could shrewd and lonesome keep company? When it came to a fork, which would she stay with?

He followed her glance. "Lemme guess. Why, there's ol' Margie now, all in a lather she kept you waiting. Nope, dang it, she's got some dyke drill sergeant with her. Or was it Sarge herself?"

Suellen grinned. "Man, you are pure merciless, aren't you? Listen, you having a good time here?"

"Better now, than I was. You got another idea?"

Suellen gave him a good, wide-eyed stare that got to him, she could see that. She felt a little lance of sorrow for her dead mother, otherwise a shitty parent and a no-good, betraying bitch who had, though, taught her that particular look and its uses. "Don't you know someplace a little quieter and more ... grown up, I guess?"

Harve opened his eyes and nodded. "I do, for a fact. You like Thelonious Monk, some early Brubeck, Johnny Desmond, that kind of thing?"

"Man," Suellen said. "Nobody even knows about those

guys. Where is this place, the Smithsonian? What made you think I'd care about them?"

He smiled. "A hunch. You look, if I can just be frank here, like that kind of woman. Which, I hasten to say, is a pretty damn superior kind. See, you can't possibly know who they are, and that they're all of a kind, without you like them. Friend of mine runs a little place outside Carrboro, which he keeps open because he plays bass in a quartet that covers Brubeck and Monk, you shut your eyes, you couldn't tell you're not back in 1950. He don't make much on it, but it's real friendly. Sound good?"

Suellen considered. "Maybe. What's he serve?"

Harve leaned back and cocked his head at Suellen. "Beer, wine coolers, top hemp, Special K, and 'ludes. Thing is, I can't show up there with somebody, I don't even know their name."

"My name," Suellen said. "Oh ... call me Suellen."

"OK, sure, 'Sue,'" he said, waggling his fingers on either side of a grin as charming as Christmas in Vermont. "Your car or mine?"

The Xanadu Bar and Grille occupied the basement of a veterinary hospital and pet boarding operation next to a good-sized pond at the far west edge of Carrboro. Suellen didn't see how the guy could be paying more than fifty bucks a month for it. To get in, you walked around behind the kennels and ducked down a concrete stairway that was gritty with cat litter. Every patron who entered did so to a chorus of yaps and barks; even so, there weren't enough to interfere that much with the music.

Suellen and Harve picked up a couple of beers (no Urquells here; you wanted exotic, you got Genesee Cream Ale), and things looked up a little. The basement itself was more of a warehouse, jammed full of liquor, veterinary supplies, and feed. For the music, you followed a raised boardwalk over the boxes, out a side door, and across a shaky bridge to a Samoan cabaña kind of thing on a woodsy little island in the pond. The band – a keyboard the size of a short one-by-eight, a couple of drums, sax and bass – occupied a platform that cantilevered out over the water, next to a wavering strip of moonlight. The hour and the body of water had tuned the day's heat down to a mildly tropical shade of balm, the differential heat capacities of kennels and pond water generated a small breeze, and a phalanx of smoldering citronella coils and a high-tension bug blaster were knocking down the mosquitoes. The smells of woods, water, and citronella worked like SSRI's, without the side effects. As soon as Suellen heard the sax weaving the husky melancholy of "Here Lies Love" through the frog songs, she began - oh, my - to relax.

"This is OK," she sighed. "How come I never heard about it?"

"Look around you. Everybody you see told all the people who still like this stuff, and they all brought their buddies, before you know it, a couple dozen people could show up, and the place'd be a madhouse."

"I hate bogus math," Suellen sniffed. "And I'm not sure

how I feel about guys who claim they're gay and then lay this slippery charm all over me. But the music is great. Also, it's been ten years since I had a Jenny Cream. I appreciate being invited."

"Well," Harve shrugged, and leaned back with his eyes half-shut, digging the sounds. "I appreciate your accepting the invitation. I figured you for a superior type of person the first minute I seen you in there with Miz Bynum. Rest her soul. And gay folks can be - if this isn't bragging - can be charming if they just plain like who they're with. Maybe we can break some new ground here, gay guy and lesbian lady, got the alliteration market cornered, whatever. Maybe find some new ways to charm each other."

"That what turns you on? New dimensions of charm that no cave man in the last million years ever thought of? Assist each other's living, that's your game anyhow, isn't it?" Suellen sniffed. "Find new ways to hurt each other, more like."

Harve sighed. "Could be, which I for one would regret. Le's just let the music roll, see where this gonna go."

"If anywhere."

Harve smiled, shrugged, and said nothing more. "Here Lies Love" was followed by others, all subtly nuanced, and all killer favorites of Suellen's: "Let's Do It;" "Perfidia;" and "The Girl from Ipanema." After a couple of sets and six or eight beers, and possibly at a request from Harve while Suellen was behind the bush marked "*LADIES*," hemp was brought by a barefoot waitress with an attitude and a pin that said, "CALL ME

HONEY" and a towel around her waist, from which she fished four wrinkled paper slugs and a pack of matches.

"Thanks, Honey. Blow?" Harve asked, taking two.

Suellen raised her eyes to a bank of cumulus that was nuzzling the flanks of a setting moon. Some issue was getting worked out in its belly that involved a lot of indirect lightning that lit vast inner courts, dimming the moon for milliseconds, then leaving it to shine on. For a time, Suellen had been having trouble distinguishing the scenery from the sound track. Recognizing that she'd had enough Jenny Cream to hold her for another ten years, and recognizing also that it and the creamy music and this unlikely moonlit paradise in Orange County, North Carolina had her heeled on a slippery sloop over three-sheet water, she took one of the joints from Honey the scowling server, and kissed good sense goodbye. "I'll be sorry in the morning," she sighed, "but it won't be the shit. It'll be the goddamn Jenny."

Harve said, "Yeah, but listen to the sax man."

The bug blaster lit up with the death sizzle of a good-sized moth. " 'Fare Thee Well, Annabelle,' " Suellen hummed. "Fare thee well, Faye Bynum. She was a very, ver' sharp old femme that missed the boat by a couple decades too soon. That make sense?"

"All kinds," Harve said. "I'll miss her too."

Suellen nodded. "Know her buddy Hap Maryland?"

"No," Harve said. "Who she? At the Home?"

Even at the time, Suellen knew that was overkill. But she

was pretty far along now, and her cop radar was on break. The band had turned down her request for "Fugue on Bop Themes," and Harve said he thought he had it on the Fantasy label Brubeck Octet from 1950, vinyl, mint condition. She let it go, promising herself that she would examine Harve and his dark and slippery charm really carefully – mercilessly – some time in the next 18 hours. Or so.

At the latest.

Forty minutes later, while the fugue tumbled lithe and languid from his speakers and warm rain rattled his skylight, Harve parked the roach in a Nutella lid, helped her slip the tee shirt over her head and asked, "If a hundred – Whoa, nice ink, just lovely. That a rose, or what? – if a hundred percent gay guy has regular straight sex with a hundred percent lesbian lady, would that make them even one percent straight?"

"I don't know," Suellen sighed. "Might make one of 'em as much as a couple percent happier, though. For a while."

10.

Every patch and crack on North Carolina 73, flashing past at 75 miles an hour, jarred the Triumph like a New Jersey pothole. The Triumph had no way not to pass the suffering up to Suellen, who made no effort to avoid the bumps, but gritted her teeth and endured them. For one thing, seeking out smoother concrete would have needed better vision than her hung-over sunward squint could manage.

For another, she knew she had some suffering coming to her, and if it came through her sore and wayward tail, well, that was a zone that had some amends to make. She jammed the throttle forward and looked for tar patches. Stupid mall-rat behavior, to hook up with Harve like a goddamn sophomore!

But when she had parked the Triumph behind the Swamp Road house, when she had slammed a big cook pot from the kitchen tap to the stove and brought it to a boil, and thrown that and a handful of baking soda into a tub of rusty bath water, and when she had eased herself into the steam and it had lapped over the aching loins and covered the rose tattoo with stinging heat, it was of Harve that she couldn't help thinking.

Of the body: smooth walnut, nicely muscled. Of the hands, deferential as bellhops, that had gone about opening her windows, checking switches and taps, turning down covers, wishing her a pleasant stay, and accepting with practiced surprise the currency she offered; and of the voice that spoke the language of the South in the key of minor amusement and the register of a ten-foot organ pipe.

Harve, damn his ass, was a terrific lover; versatile, inventive, and passionate without losing his sense of humor. He was the only partner – indeed, the only living creature – Suellen ever met, who seemed to understand as she did the inexhaustibility of sex and the negotiability of role. They had batted the initiative back and forth, switching from male to female, straight to gay, top to bottom like a pair of strolling mummers determined to act every part in the First Folio.

They arrived again and again in the neighborhood of ache relief, only to ease at the last second onto another track: suitor and bitch, Othello and Desdemona, nymph and shepherd, Stein and Toklas, Bonnie and Clyde, Hoover and Tolson; Tinker, Evers, and Chance. They swung from one role to the next along looping catenaries of in-between; they made hash brownies from a Denver mix and fed them to each other, slow-dancing naked to Thelonious in the flare and rumble of the rainstorm. The sharpening of skylight spatter to a flickering downpour cued him to the light switch, calling down the fires of heaven to animate Suellen's stitched-together Frankenbride, and the obligingly timed bang of thunder scared them both into a new start as sex researcher Ingemann and her monstrously inhibited subject. ("Und how often does your husband require zis electrical assistance, Frau Stein?") And all along there was Harve, singing along with Brubeck, fluffing her pillow, lighting her toke, nodding at her talk, spinning worlds of words and notions and nonsense while his eyes – his bottomless blast-your-eyes – told her that no one had ever heard these things before, that she had opened doors and thrown switches in him that left Harve himself astounded. There were times a-plenty in which Suellen - completely stoned on Genny Cream, hash, music, Harve, and those towering cumuli of interior moon-lightning - lost track of which of them was herself and which was Harve, somehow voodoo'd through her skin and onward, into gardens where grew flora that were both of them and neither in particular, and might or might not lead them someplace farther, still forbidden.

When the storm gave way to birdsong and hints of dawn, they at last allowed themselves to for God's sake get it done. Suellen smiled and blushed a little, remembering the wall-banging from the neighbors at a quarter to five in the morning before she piped down and collapsed across Harve's sweating torso like a crash dummy. She opened her eyes now to wrinkled fingers, tepid water, and a pink and sodden body full of peace. So much, she thought, for merciless examinations.

The day started late, and the bath ate another big chunk of it. By afternoon, she was still wrapped in a towel in the kitchen, peeling new potatoes into slick little spheres for supper. She had no particular schedule, and something she'd thought of in the bathtub had made her laugh. She began sticking the slippery potatoes together into little triangles with toothpicks from the junk drawer:

She went back into the bathroom and rattled through the medicine cabinet until she found what she knew must be there: a bottle of old-fashioned tincture of iodine. In the kitchen, she dipped a toothpick in the brownish fluid and scratched the initials F, G and R (for Female, Gay, and Ransom) on one of the trios of potatoes. Within seconds, the brown letters reacted with the potato starch and blossomed into intense blue. On the other triangle of potatoes, she wrote M, S, and H for Male, Straight, and Harve.

She giggled, remembering the tedious crystal and molecular structure labs she'd lived through in her first year of graduate school. These things had some practical application after all. Tongue between her teeth, Suellen pinned the R-G-F set onto the H-M-S set, so that each potato nestled down between the slick roundness of two neighbors, and each pair

(Ransom/Harve, male/female, gay/straight) were at opposite poles:

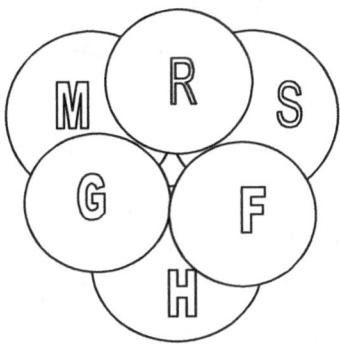

She regretted that she had used "Gay" as a label for both herself and Harve, and considered changing it to "Queer," but decided not to waste another potato.

Suellen rotated the little cluster of starch in her hands, letting one trio of potatoes after another show on the top: {R-G-F}, {H-S-F}, {R-S-M}. Standing, of course, for Ransom the Gay Female, Harve the Straight Female, and Ransom the Straight Male. There were eight possibilities in all, none of them more likely to turn up than any of the others. The tumbling of the potato construction echoed their tumbling exchanges of role and position in Harve's bed. She smiled and flipped her little six-potato creation around the table, remembering an episode or two of role-playing and garden exploration for each flip.

And still, it dawned on her as the various combinations appeared, that these polarities might be just the extreme ends of a continuum of options. Was she entirely gay or entirely straight? Not from the evidence of last night, Lord. Nor entirely female, in spite of the unambiguity of her equipment. With Harve, she felt free to be as female or male (-ish, she conceded) as felt right in relation to Harve, or in response to what she at any given moment in the hours of their sporting transactions, wanted, or needed Harve to be.

All right, then. There's no male or female, but a sliding scale, a continuum. Same with straight and queer, she guessed. A logical thinker, she couldn't help edging her mind toward the third polarity. Good God, was the R-H toothpick telling her something unbearable about her identity? Was she even entirely herself when she was with Harve, or was she part Harve, with yet a third continuum stretching between the two of them? Is that what losing track of her boundaries was about? Suellen felt invaded, diluted, transgressed upon. She pictured a lineup of Suellen-Harve cocktails, from 100% Suellen all the way to 1% Suellen, 99% Harve, all options within her mind, body, and will. What would a 50-50 mixture look and act like?

Like if we for Chrissake had a kid, she thought, and the horror of it woke her to berate herself *(Hey, why not practice writing "Suellen Harvey," or "Mrs. Edward Briggs Harvey the 596th," with a lavender fountain pen, you moony fucking idiot?)* when she heard Bethany calling through the front door.

"Suellen? Cesco?"

"What?" Suellen rose and padded toward the door. "Beffie? Hey, sweetie, look at this."

"Suellen? Oh, thank God. Is Cesco with you?"

"Huh? Of course not. Hey, look at this."

"Suellen, listen. Cesco's – Yikes, honey, you better get some clothes on. Tucker Pardee's outside in Car Ten, fixing to poke around with his flashlight. Thing is, Cesco's gone missing. We've about looked everywhere we can think of."

Suellen shrugged, still amused by her potato construction. "Well, isn't it kind of a relief to have him out of your hair for a while? I mean, where's he going to go, around here?"

Bethany shook her head. "I gotta admit it was, for a while, but Taylor and Giulia are worried, so I am too. You know how he was acting the other day."

"Well, that's what I meant. They think he's going to hold up a bank, or something? Hey, Tucker, what's up? Speaking of holdups." Suellen undid the towel tuck and walked out on the porch drying her hair, allowing the sun to pick out random stretches of skin for Tucker's entertainment. Tucker turned sideways, made nose-clearing noises and spat in the grass.

"Hey there, Suellen," he sniffed. "Hear you ain't a cop no more. Might have to run you in for public indecency."

Suellen grinned. "This isn't public, for one thing." She bunched the towel and stretched in the sunlight. "An' what do you see that isn't about the decentest thing you ever saw?"

Tucker grinned. "Little skimpy up top for my taste, you wanta know. C'mon, now, wrap up. What do you know about this Maryland kid?"

Suellen pushed out her mouth and cocked a hip, just to

keep Tucker bothered while she thought about it. And Bethany, truth to tell. "Saw him day before yesterday, I guess. Wasn't that it, Beffie? When he came in and skinned his knee, something, on his bike? My stars, he let out a string. Who's seen him since then?"

"Well, family, off and on. He and Morgan have gone places together. They got into a kind of scrape, swimming at Riverbend, that Morgan pulled him out of. Anyways, they were out on their bikes night before last, come in about eight-nine, had some dessert, and Morgan went to do some homework she'd been putting off. Giulia looked in on Cesco about ten, found him asleep over a book, so she got him tucked in, and that was the last anybody saw. Taylor and Giulia let him sleep in, the next morning while they went off to talk to a lawyer in Raleigh about having Hap declared deceased. Ginnie and Silvio left early to go to Myrtle Beach for the weekend, and I was at home all morning. I'd have seen or heard him if he came through the kitchen, which he sure would have."

Suellen shrugged. "We know for sure he didn't go off with Ginnie and Silvio?"

"We called them yesterday afternoon. They're by themselves."

"What does Morgan say?"

"She says she took him in to town the evening before, introduced him around her youth group, and he seemed to get on OK. I think Cesco's kind of exotic for some of these kids, but he and Forde Morgan's grandniece seemed to be hitting it off.

They were talking about getting in touch the next day."

"And the girl says Cesco never called."

Tucker cocked an eye at Suellen. "What makes you think that?"

Suellen grinned back at him. "Cause if he had, you'd have been all over her, instead of floundering around like this. You looking for some help?"

Tucker shrugged, but Bethany said, "You bet we are, Suellen. Anything you can do, we'd be right thankful. In't that right, Tucker?"

"Lady got herself a reputation as a man hunter, over'n Tennessee," Tucker said. "Don't know if that works for boys. I s'pose if she was to hunt bare-butt like that, she'd catch a few."

Suellen smiled. She didn't want to get stuck scouring Gabbro County for a wayward boy, but she was still mellow from Harve and the potato game. And having an official reason to snoop around for a day or two might come in handy. "Y'all could do a better job keeping track of folks around here, seems like. Hold on a second, lemme get my detective kit." She swung the towel over her shoulder and swivel-hipped her way back into the house.

When she reappeared in a tank top, cutoffs, and biker boots, Tucker hawked again in relief and quit looking at the porch ceiling. Suellen winked at him.

"You interested enough to deputize me, Tucker? I could show you a fistful of commendations from the Marines and the governor of Tennessee."

Tucker shrugged. "We got reg'lar procedures for that. Download a application from Gabbro.gov, submit by fax or e-mail, along with a government-issued pitcher ID, and we'll get back to you in due course. Meanwhile, raise your right hand."

*

Suellen looked from Taylor to Giulia, trying to decide which to tackle first. Giulia looked a bit more together, even sniffling into a hankie.

"OK, then. First of all, I expect Tucker already asked you a lot of questions, and I apologize if I'm going over the same ground twice. Still, sometimes it's useful, and anyways, this way I don't have to get my information second-hand. You saw Cesco the last time, when exactly?"

Giulia wiped her nose. "About ten o'clock, I think, night before last. Maybe a little later. Before eleven, I know."

"How did he look?"

"Looked asleep. This is his first long trip east and west, so jet lag hit him pretty hard, I think. He still gets sleepy after supper."

"But Morgan took him in to her youth group after supper, and he seemed OK then."

Giulia shrugged. "Well, yes." Suellen thought she was about to add something, but she didn't.

"Yes, but ...?"

Taylor shook his head. "He's been a little hard to live

with the last couple of days. I came down on him pretty hard about it, maybe that has something to do with this." He put a hand on Giulia's thigh. "I should be more patient with him, I know. He's fifteen, which is a tough age for anybody, plus being from a mixed family is still a problem in Italy. Also, we're not Catholic, so there's another thing. Thing is, he began to get lippy, run with a ... well, not a <u>bad</u> crowd, just a bunch of guys without much respect for authority, law and order. He's a lot like me."

Suellen raised an eyebrow. "Meaning?"

Taylor smiled and shrugged.

"Stand up for himself, don't take bullshit," Giulia said. "It's the first thing I like about Taylor."

"I see. Well, a lot of fifteen-year-old boys are like that, aren't they? Were when I was in high school. Has he run off before?"

"No," Taylor and Giulia chorused, and Giulia went on. "Never. This is just not something he's ever done. I think he knows which side of his bread has the butter. He knows we take care of him."

Suellen turned a hand. "And anyhow, whatever troubles he had in Italy would hardly have come to a head over here, would they? What did you mean, he's been hard to live with lately? Like the other day, when he fell down on his bike?"

"Like that," Taylor said. "Acting like he's a little bit – I don't know. Drunk, or stoned."

"Well, what about that?"

Giulia shook her head. "Hard to understand. Not drunk, for sure. We have no evidence he took drugs in Italy; his bunch of friends weren't that depraved. And here, he's only been away from us when he's been out on bicycles with Morgan. You don't see Morgan as a pusher type, I think."

Suellen snorted. "Nope. How about withdrawal? 'No evidence' of drugs isn't the same as evidence against. Any chance he was habituated, and now his supply's cut off? That can give you some funny behaviors." And hey, I ought to know, she thought. She remembered eyes, voice, and herbal smoke, and yanked herself back with an effort. Taylor and Giulia were falling over each other to quash the drug suggestion.

"No way," Taylor said. "Parents are famous for kidding themselves about this kind of thing, but if Cesco was into drugs in Verona, I'd say it was something that causes absolutely no changes in behavior compared to what you'd expect from an adolescent kid."

Suellen nodded. "And anyhow, the point is, where is he, not why's he gone. Have you talked really seriously to Morgan?"

"Bethany did. If she knows anything, she'd tell Bethany, I'd think."

"What was this scrape?"

Taylor cocked his head. "Scrape?"

"At Riverbend. Bethany said she'd pulled him out of some kind of scrape."

Taylor grimaced. "Just that, I think. He jumped in on top

of a snag, and cut his foot some. It wasn't bleeding by the time they got home. His foot was pretty sore for a day, and he stayed off it."

"Did he need stitches, or anything?"

"Nah. It really was just a scrape, I'm pretty sure. Giulia?"

"Not serious," Giulia said. "I looked at it. A little dirty, not deep. I clean it up, put antibiotic cream, big band-aid. Next day, no inflammation, already start to heal."

"Giulia's a nurse," Taylor said. "And very serious about Cesco's health."

Suellen sat back and ran her fingers through her hair. "So why did he need to be rescued? You said Morgan pulled him out of a scrape."

Taylor frowned. "Manner of speaking, I guess. He was a little upset about it, bleeding, and all. I think she might have pulled out a splinter. Giulia?"

Giulia nodded. "Not out of the question. There was no splinter when I saw the wound, but there might have been. There was some dirt down in, that I got out."

Taylor shuffled a foot, and tapped it once on the porch. "Why is this important? Our son is missing, and Tucker Pardee is actually looking for him, not asking a lot of first-aid questions. This country needs carabinieri."

"Highway patrol's the closest thing we got. Did Tucker ask you about Riverbend?"

"No."

Suellen smiled. "See?"

11.

Morgan looked up at Suellen, and back again at her biology book.

"Mind if I come in?"

"Of course not, Aunt Suellen. I've got a lot of homework, though."

"I thought you were on spring break."

"Think that matters to Mr. Frogface Phillips? We got state exams coming up on May 15th, and if we don't all pass, he doesn't get paid next year."

"Uh huh. Mind if I ask you about Cesco?"

"Mom already asked."

"So I understand. I sort of thought maybe I might accidentally ask something she didn't think of, and that might remind you of something you forgot. That happens a lot with cops."

"I heard you quit."

"I did quit. But Tucker asked me to help out with trying to find Cesco. Don't you want to help with that? I thought you and Cesco were getting to be pretty good friends."

Morgan turned to Suellen, and her eyes were glazed with tears. "Sure, if ..." She turned a page, and didn't say any more.

"If?"

"If I could. I have a feeling you might do better talking to somebody else, that's all."

"Well, for example?"

"For example, Jennifer McLean." Morgan bounced her cupped her hands about three inches in front of her small breasts.

Suellen grinned. "She's the, uh, the girl from the youth group?"

"Yes."

"Tucker tells me she didn't see anything of him, after the meeting where you introduced him."

Morgan shrugged again, and turned a page. Suellen let the silence go on; people with something to say have a hard time not filling a silence, she'd found. Apparently, though, Morgan had nothing to say, except, "Cesco's OK. I hope. I just don't see what I can do to help find him. I have to read a hundred pages of this and make an outline with at least three levels of organization."

"Man. Tell me about what happened at Riverbend."

Morgan sighed, and shut the book on her pencil. "Mr. Stupid Francesco was showing off, and he jumped in on this big snag, that I'd already warned him about twice, and tore up his foot."

"Was he scared, or anything? Anything else happen?"

"He was bleeding a lot, and I had to put a moss compress on it and tie it up."

"Really. Good for you, Morgan. Were you on bikes?"

"We don't drive, and it's too far to walk."

"So how did he pedal home with a hurt foot?"

"We got a ride. I went out to the road and Reverend Hastie was coming along in his rattly-trap pickup. He brought us and the bikes home."

"Uh huh. Lucky break."

"Uh huh." Morgan opened the biology book. "A biome," she recited. "A biome is a major unit of ecology, defined by its climate, vegetation, and soil. Examples are prairie, rain forest, and desert."

*

Farnell Hastie was crouched next to a six-foot granite obelisk in the little cemetery behind the True Foundation AME Zion Chapel when Suellen found him. When her shadow fell across it, he put down his crowbar and mopped his head.

"My goodness," he said. "Evening, little Sister. Certainly was a treat to see you again, out to Sister Bethany and Brother Plummer's house the other day."

"You too, Rev. Give you a hand there?"

Farnell hesitated, then handed Suellen the crowbar. "When the blessed remains of our departed get tired holding up six foot of wet dirt and another six of granite after a long life of lifting dirt and rocks, they seem to feel like they're entitled to let down the load. I don't blame them, mind, but it can let the headstone sag in a kind of unseemly manner. Ain't respectful, the aggregate of them begins to look like a crowd of drunks, people got to tilt their heads to read the departed's final greeting. I try an' keep them plumb, but it's got to the point where Brother Body don't always want to pick up the loads I give him. Gonna quit altogether, one of these days."

Suellen braced her arms against the obelisk and heaved it a little past upright. "Whyn't I hold her in place," she grunted, "you shovel some of that gravel and dirt under."

And when he had done that, and Suellen had let the massive stone down and they stepped back to judge its new plumb-ness, Farnell looked at her and shook his head.

"Sister, Sister," he said. "That chunk of rock has got to weigh three ton, if it's an ounce. Where's a little thing like you get off, lifting that kind of weight?"

"Power of prayer, Rev," Suellen panted. "Plus, I didn't lift it, I just straightened it up a little."

"I am most grateful to you," Farnell said. "Not to mention the family, that's been on me about this here obelisk for the last month or more. How can I return the favor?"

Suellen wiped her hands on her shorts and sat on a tombstone. Little bright specks were swimming in the grass at her feet, that she thought probably only she could see. Maybe Wise Sister Body was getting ready for a job action of her own.

"I understand you gave a lift to Lee Morgan Baley and her cousin the other day."

"I was happy to do them kids a favor. They stood in some considerable need."

"So I hear. Though I guess it turned out not so serious as

it looked."

Farnell Hastie pursed his mouth and tipped back his fedora. "The wound was bloody, no doubt, but little Lee had put a compress on it, that stopped the bleeding. I was more concerned about the boy's global state of health."

"How's that?"

"I have to say, he didn't look good to me. He was kind of sucking air, and he looked very pale and weak. I had to bring the truck just about right down to the edge of the river to pick him up. It was beyond him to much more than climb in."

"Really. From a little scrape on his foot?"

"Would make you think there might have been more to it, wouldn't it? Yet by the time we'd loaded up the bikes and got them home, he was looking some better. I would have a professional bias toward believing that the girl's prayers had something to do with that."

"She prayed over him on the way home?"

"We both did. The Lord is gen'lly pretty much indifferent to whether one of his children is on their knees in a church, or on the seat of an old truck. What matters is what's in that child's heart."

Suellen nodded. "Highway Patrol works like that, sometimes. Would it violate a confidence if you were to give me some idea what she said?"

"Well, Ma'am, it was a matter of petitions pretty much straight from her soul to Jesus. So, reluctantly, yes, I'm afraid it would."

"OK, then how's this? Do you ever have any reason to think there's always a lot more to that girl than she lets other people see?"

"Some folks would take that as presumptive evidence for the immortal soul."

Farnell Hastie sighed, and looked across the cemetery for a moment, letting his eyes rest on one headstone after another; men and women he had known, counseled, scolded, comforted, and buried. "But I understand what you're asking me, and I will say this: I was present when that little girl was born. The first thing she did, she let out a holler that would crack your fillings. On that occasion, certainly, she spoke straight from the heart. If she has since grown in the ways of silence and subtlety – well, don't we all do that?"

*

Suellen stood for a moment before the bathroom mirror, the tap laboring and shuddering and bringing forth a tapered thread of cold water, toothbrush forgotten in her hand, and looked over what showed behind it. *Little skimpy up top for my taste.* Yeah, well.

She shrugged, and started brushing. OK, maybe she was a little streamlined. What there was, was right where it ought to be, not down around her belly button. Far as that went, she never came on as Dolly Parton, and nobody complained; Harve, for example. She scowled, the toothbrush became brisk, and slowed again for further inventory. The knockout days, when just looking good had been effortless and looking killer had been fun; those days were pretty much gone. The cropped blonde hair showed sprinkles of something less sunny now. There were lines around her eyes that had nothing to do with sunlight, and what had once been smooth and merry hollows defining her cheeks were starting to look deep and permanent. She still had the body of a twenty-year-old athlete, but her face looked thirty-five, she thought, or maybe forty, and tired. The body is wiser than the will. She wondered as she shrugged into a tee shirt, how old Faye Bynum had been when she realized that she was getting middle-aged.

In the kitchen, she stopped to pull a beer out of the fridge and walked toward the screen porch. When she thought of the glider, quiet as a coffin against the wall of the house, she stopped and headed for the back door with a chilly line of fuzz erect in the hollow of her spine.

Behind the Swamp Road house lay a stretch of grass that, thanks to the house, the surrounding greenery and a low hill to the north, was invisible from anywhere but directly overhead. It was there that Hap Maryland used to sit with Lee, when neither was yet a mound of earth. And for the time that Suellen lived here, after she split up with Bethany and after Lee was gone, she would sit out there with Hap while he looked for Lee's profile in lunar maria.

And it was there that Suellen took her beer now. From the shed she extracted and dusted off the folding aluminum chaise she remembered from those days. She set it up in deep, gone-to-seed grass and a yellow slant of sunlight, and eased herself into its frayed embrace. With most of the grass topping out over the chaise, she figured she was pretty much invisible now. She stripped off the tee again to catch the breeze that impending sunset had sent to ripple the grass around her, delighting her as it played across her ribs.

She acknowledged in her bones what the mirror said: she was tired. Tired from her late night, tired from chasing around Gabbro County on the Triumph, and tired of being jazzed, misled, lied to, and stiffed. It was time to consult the only human on the face of the earth she trusted: herself.

First on the agenda had to be Harve. Disinclined as she might be, she needed to face up to and figure out what the hell Harve thought he was doing, giving her this bareface stuff about "Who's she," when Suellen mentioned Hap's name.

Suellen snorted, and drained the beer. Harve could be a dear fellow, but he was a fellow, after all, and it had taken some effort for Suellen to put aside her feelings and relax into what had been ... she sighed; all right, a first-class and deeply satisfying boff. If the message of her nightmare about Hap and Lee was that she just needed to get laid – well, she had done so, in real-time broad-band high definition polymorphous alpha wave Technicolor. Maybe what had let it work for both of them had been the slight smooth effeminacy that overlay the depth of his voice; his blackness that made him twice an outsider. Her reciprocal tough lesbian manner meant that neither of them had been forced to come all the way across the Green Line into the alien camp. The continuum had turned into a smooth pathway to the Emerald City. So if a hundred percent gay guy has a whole range of arrangements up to and including regular straight sex – if you could call it that, she admitted – with a hundred percent lesbian lady, did that, or did that not, that make them what percentage …

Stop it! Christ, what a schoolgirl! The body is wiser than horseshit. Suellen sat up, straddling the chaise, and her suddenly focused weight popped one of its weather-rotted straps. The guy lied to her about Hap, and could be trusted about nothing. Assume that he lied about Inglenook, he lied in the surprise with which he greeted her, lied about sex. Probably lied about liking her tattoo, for Christ's sake. Lied about – well, no, what he said about Brubeck and Thelonious was true enough. Suellen lay back, her fingers absently tracing the course of the rose tattoo from root to blossom. Harve had …

Suellen hurled the empty beer bottle, its hoots of farewell dopplering forty yards into the brush and turkey oak that backed the Swamp Road place. Her eyes narrowed and her teeth gritted. If Harve thought she was fooled and seduced, he had a little surprise coming, she thought. The first thing would be to get a line on him, see what his real name was for one thing. Then get at him from behind, even if she had to – or, she guessed, could get Tucker to – subpoena the Inglenook personnel files, see who his boss was, see if his duties included shadowing and diverting people who might be asking inconvenient questions. And then, by God, to get the weasel by himself somewhere quiet and private, to browbeat the truth out of him and then, just for the satisfaction of it, beat the living –

"Your name really Suellen, in't it, you tricky lady?"

Suellen sat up. "Harve? For – "

" 'Call me,' " he said in a Suellen voice, wiggling his fingers, "Edward Briggs Harvey, ma'am, at your very substantial service." Harve walked out of the sunset, a gold-gloried black cutout without a face, though with a smile in his voice. "You gave me your real name, and implied it was a fake. The least I can do is reciprocate. Do you mind if I join you?" He held up four stubby bottles, sunglare refracting merrily through the glass. "I found a place that has Jenny Cream."

Suellen started to bounce to her feet, already targeting the scruff of his neck. But pushing down on the chaise broke the next strap, and then it was the domino theory played out in sun-rotted polypropylene, and her butt was on the ground with the rest of her sticking up out of the chaise wreckage like a begonia in a raffia pot.

Harve chuckled a little, looked sympathetic, and extended a hand. Suellen took it, and as soon as she had her feet on the ground, pivoted Harve to clear the chaise, yanked him toward her, put a foot in his groin, and vaulted him over her head to land with a crash in a pile of weathered and rotted tomato stakes. Two of the Jenny Creams smashed, and the others bounced across the grass, promising future eruptions.

Suellen rolled to her feet and pounced on Harve before

he got turned, hooked an arm under his chin, tangled her legs around his, and yanked his arm behind his back so that he collapsed onto his belly again, whooping with pain and looking for breath to whoop again.

"Wha – ?"

"Talk to me, Harve," Suellen crooned. "Tell me about Hap Maryland and Delta Dawn, you rotten liar. They send you after me? They figure I'd be an easy target for a guy with your natural charm and your collection of fifties jazz?"

Harve sighed, and got to his feet, Suellen riding along like a lion bringing down a buffalo, except that it seemed to be running backwards, the buffalo bringing up the lion. Harve plucked Suellen's arm from under his jaw and spun out of the hammerlock while Suellen's feet flailed at his legs, trying to keep him tangled up. She succeeded well enough that he fell again, but he fell on Suellen, and she found it hard to get a breath. Harve stepped back, wiping at a bloody scrape he'd got on his wrist from falling on the tomato stakes while she huffed and retched and reconsidered her strategy.

"Jeez, Suellen," Harve complained. "You don't know where them tomato stakes have been. I could get infected. Could we talk about this, whatever's botherin' you?"

Suellen got up, a little bent over, and said, "Sure ... thing, Harve. You talk first, or I'll make you wish that scrape had Novocain in it."

"Oo-wee. You scare the crap outa me, you know? What's your issue, anyhow? Looka this, you broke your share of the beers."

"Yeah?" Suellen couldn't figure out what to follow that with, so she dropped into a crouch and advanced on Harve.

Harve circled to get the sun out of his eyes, and smiled at Suellen. "You are some tough cookie, I suppose. You could prob'ly make me ache for a week, we go on with this. On the other hand, think about this: what if we cut to the chase, ask me what you want to know, I decide what I want to do about that, we share a little refreshment. Tell you what, you can have one of my Jenny Creams. You want a second to put that shirt back on?"

Suellen relaxed, shrugged, tossed a hand in Harve's direction and, when he reached out for it, got Harve's elbow in an old-fashioned whizzer and yanked him past herself, neatly cutting his feet from under him. Harve hit the grass again with a whoosh, and Suellen landed on him hard, knocking out the rest of his breath. She didn't muck around with hammerlocks this time, but whacked the side of his head with the palm of her hand, wanting to make his head ring. Shock and awe, she thought. Never worked that well in Iraq, but maybe –

No, it didn't work here either.

"Aw right, Goldilocks, damn it, this the way you want it," Harve gritted, and timed the next whack well enough to grab Suellen's wrist and roll her under himself. She took a couple of good licks that made her eyes cross before she escaped, and they both got to their feet, breath whistling and eyes staring,. Then they had at it close in, circling on trampled grass, grappling and slapping, knees to groins and elbows to ribs and heads until their noses and mouths were swollen and their ears were ringing. Suellen took a stunner to the cheek and hit the ground on her back. She came up, mad and scared, tasting the coppery tang of blood when she gritted her teeth. She found she was holding one of the remaining beers, and took that as one of those lucky breaks that happen to people who are about to win a fight. She slammed it against Harve's head in a chaos of glass and suds, and watched as he lurched backward and then slumped forward with a bloody cut on his brow.

It was a ruse. Harve tackled her and they fell into deep grass together clawing, ripping cloth and skin, ducking fists and feet until Suellen got Harve from behind in a figure-four death hold, grabbed a handful of his hair and pulled his face back against hers while she listened to the singing in her head and considered how to get out of this without getting killed.

There was a moment of puffing quiescence, and then Suellen got a cramp that compromised her leg-lock long enough for the rest of him to turn to face her. Harve took the chance to get an arm free and clamp it around Suellen's neck. They lay side by side in the suffocating grass, gripped in unbreakable holds that neither dared release, glaring across an inch of buzzing air, gasping and snuffling and turning their heads to spit blood and tooth chips over each other's shoulders while they ached and itched and struggled not to breathe gnats.

After a while, Harve said, "Ain't gonna be no re-match."

"Don't want no re-match," Suellen said. She smiled

bloodily. "Rocky One, right?"

Harve nodded. "Good for you. Listen, think we could work out some other way of relating? My goddamn clothes were a mess already, and now I got a wet spot in my jeans."

"Pff. Aren't you the hottie? Didn't do that much for me."

"Yeah? What you think set me off but that tender moment just now, you stiffened up and squeaked in my ear? You about tore my hair out."

Suellen sniffed. "I got a cramp in my leg."

Harve laughed, pleased by her and by himself, by their sweaty, itchy stalemate. "Yeah, the kinda cramp folks get, down where that tattoo grows out of. You always bite folks in the neck when you got a leg cramp?"

"Sometimes it helps," Suellen said. "Look, if I let go of you, will you tell me some truth for a change? Or do I have to beat you up again?"

"Try it. Maybe I'll pull some jackass trick like you done when I was extending the right hand of friendship just now."

"Right hand of a goddamn liar."

Harve sighed. "Gold- ... Suellen, listen. I admit, I followed you into that bar, because I figured you were jiving me about the old lady, so I kind of jived you about some stuff right back. Thing is, sometimes it's kinder to feed folks a little jive than tell 'em what they think they want to know. Understand?"

Suellen snorted, and unclenched the handful of hair. It hurt to straighten her fingers, and a fair amount of his hair floated loose when she did. "I was looking for kindness, I'd write to Mister Rogers. How about you just answer a couple of brief questions to the best of your knowledge and belief, for a change?"

Harve slowly loosened his choke-hold on Suellen's neck and let go of her arm, flinching and ready to grab it again, depending on what she did with it. "Aw right, then, shoot," he said.

Suellen untangled her legs from his and sat up, combing grass seed and bugs out of her hair with skinned fingers. "Say we clean up and split that beer first?"

"I could do with a shower an' a band-aid, for a fact. You feel like sharing?"

Suellen started to grin, but stopped when her bloody lip objected. "Sure, but you won't. There's no hot water here."

A half hour later, they were gingerly toweling their banged-up heads, blue-lipped, in the last rays of sunset. Harve wore wrinkled Jiffy-lube coveralls that Suellen found in a drawer of stuff Hap Maryland hadn't bothered to pack for Inglenook; Suellen her last clean tank top and her Umbro shorts.

"This is nuts," Harve said. His teeth were chattering, and his skin had turned a bluish bronze.

"Nobody has to know," Suellen shivered. She felt a little better, probably because the cold water had numbed most of the real damage.

"Know what? I meant trying to get clean in ice water."

"You're clean enough." She slanted her head at the nest

of trampled grass. "I meant, if this gets out at the Trigonal Rose, neither of us can ever go in there again."

"Oh, yeah. The love that dare not speak its name," Harve said. "Swear you'll never tell."

"Don't worry, believe it. Who said anything about love?"

"Not me. I don't love ladies, as a rule."

"I do."

"There you go, then."

"Yep."

They were silent for a few minutes, passing the surviving Jenny Cream back and forth, sipping carefully through puffy mouths, before Harve sighed. "OK. You want to know about Doc Maryland and his light crusade."

12.

Bethany tapped on Morgan's door gently, but with enough force to push it open. Morgan was sleeping at her desk, dark hair spread across 21st Century Life Science. Bethany swallowed a lump of fear and tenderness, and crossed the room to rub Morgan's shoulders and rouse her as gently as she could.

"Honey, it's almost midnight," Bethany whispered. She brushed wisps of damp hair from Morgan's eyes as they fluttered open. "Let's get you to bed, sweetheart." Morgan looked about seven years old, rubbing her eyes, pouting, yawning, letting her mother lead her to the closet to trade her tee shirt and shorts for a cotton nightie, stumbling to the bathroom to stand pigeon-toed at the sink to brush her teeth, squinting against the light until Bethany turned it off.

When Bethany tucked her in, she reached up for a goodnight kiss and murmured, "Did they find Cesco yet?"

"Not yet, honey. Tucker's got the State folks in on it now, not to mention Aunt Suellen. The State folks say if he doesn't turn up in a day or two, they're going to call in the FBI."

"Are Uncle Taylor and Aunt Giulia OK?"

"They're right worried, of course, honey. Don't you worry, they'll find him before long. Don't cry, sweetheart."

Morgan brushed away tears. "I can't help it, Mom. I hate that Aunt Giulia is so worried. I heard her crying after supper."

Bethany nodded. "Well, you can't blame her. If it was you, I'd be in an awful state."

"Would you?"

"Of course, honey. You know Daddy and I love you more than anything there is."

"Jesus would take care of me, if I was lost."

Bethany sighed. Sometimes she got plain fed up with Jesus. "I'm sure that's so. But until I was holding you in my own arms, it wouldn't be as much comfort."

"Please tell Aunt Giulia not to worry, Momma. Tell her Jesus is watching over Cesco, and surely will bring him back. If I say that to her, she won't pay any attention, but she would if you did."

"All right, honey. I'll tell her. Go to sleep, now."

"OK." Morgan closed her eyes. After she heard the door click shut, she kept them closed long enough that she did in fact get a little mixed up about where she was, and what time it was, whether there was time to get to Biology if she still couldn't find her good yellow #2 pencil to fill in all the little ovals in the test, which anyhow was printed in Hebrew. When she woke, the house was quiet.

Morgan slid out of bed, keeping her feet on the rug to be as quiet as possible. Grandma Lee's grandmother's cousin's clock gritted and huffed and bonged endlessly while she pulled her shorts on over the nightie. Late, oh Jesus, please let it not be too late.

*

Harve paid for the beers, though Suellen resented it. On the other hand, he looked a lot more beat up than she did, and counter kid at Nik's Pik smirked while he handed Harve his change. As they left, Suellen heard a voice behind them say, "Loser pays, huh?" Harve pivoted, snarling a little, and Suellen yanked him back around toward the Triumph, and the sight of Tucker Pardee easing up to a gas pump in Car Ten.

"You go in and dust off that counterman, then Tucker slams you in jail for disorderly, then what?"

Harve relaxed. "Then I don't have to talk to you no more, Blondie."

"Yeah, well, nice try." But she got on the back seat and let Harve drive. No point rubbing it in.

Harve was revving on the shoulder of Bypass 73 when Tucker wooped his siren a couple of times and leaned out the window. "Hey! Ransom!"

"Hold it a second, Harve," Suellen said. "Yeah?"

"Got a message for you from Hillemeier."

"Wonderful. What?"

Tucker waved a bye-bye hand. "It's a fax, which I din't memorize it. Stop by, Vera Jo'll give it to you."

"Who's Hillemeier?" Harve asked.

"Jerk I used to work for. Drive on."

When they were back at the Swamp Road house, Suellen

led Harve onto the screen porch, sat him on the glider, and handed him a beer. She figured the ghosts might leave them alone if she had company.

"Jeez, a glider," Harve said. "My Aunt Jesse had one of these. Kids weren't allowed on it because we always got it going too far, and banged it back against the wall."

Suellen shivered a little. "Let's keep it under control, then. Who knew about Hap and the lights?"

Harve shrugged. "Shoot, everybody. He didn't make a secret of it."

"And 'Delta Dawn?'"

"That was one of the themes you could choose. Arizona Sunset, Midwest Morning, Autumn Tones, Delta Dawn. I don't know, couple others. Easter Sunrise, Moses and Aaron. With Delta Dawn, you got the idea you were down south somewheres, with, like, herons, steamboats, pickaninnies, that crap. Lot of crackers picked it."

"Why did you lie to me about it?"

"Could we come back to that later?"

"Never mind. Why was it supposedly the worst? Worst for what?"

Harve sipped his beer and sighed. "Old folks can be a little nuts, sometimes. Had an old boy there one time swore there was volts and amps leaking out of his toaster oven, pinching him at night. Volts at one end, amps at the other."

"Noted. Worst for what?"

"Yeah, OK. You know about the so-called "lucent

techniques?"

Suellen thought she could give Harve some rope. "Tell me."

"Well, it was a pretty nice idea. The interior surfaces on all the living quarters were lined with billions of these tiny LED's no bigger than a ant's dick. Like your walls and your ceiling are just huge flat-screen TV's. Theoretically, you could do some kind of special immersion movie experience, like in that Ray Bradbury story about Africa. In practice, up till not that long ago, the software and bandwidth you'd need was just prohibitive for any kind of high resolution and fast action. The most you could do was kind of hint at things; slow outlines like clouds, shadows, like that. Ambience."

"Yeah? But now?"

Harve shifted in the glider, making it wobble off-center and giving Suellen a chill. "Speed and resolution is still pretty expensive. But somebody realized that you could also modulate the brightness of a certain fraction of the pixels. Do it to the whole wall, you'd get a flicker that would drive you nuts. But if the percentage of modulated pixels gets low enough – "

"Somewhere between two and five percent," Suellen nodded, recovered now from the chill.

"You know about this already? Why'm I – "

"Because you said you would. I did a little reading up on it. I'm asking you about what Inglenook did with it."

"Yeah, well ..." Harve scratched his chin and shrugged. "Seemed like a nice idea to me. You observe the patient while you scan for their alpha rhythm, lock it in when they start to react."

"React? Like what, pass out?"

"Nothing like that. It's pretty clear-cut, though. They'll be smiling at nothing. Some people start to sing, you can't hardly shut 'em up."

"Like the old boy down the hall from Faye Bynum."

Harve grinned. "Not sure he counts, but like him, yeah. Keep the modulation down low enough they don't notice it, it still seems to have an effect on people's moods. That's a big deal in a nursing home; client morale starts out poor the day they move in, and goes down from there. Lot of places, they bust their asses trying to cheer the inmates up with crafts, Elderhostels, exercise, what-all. But after a certain point in their lives, the ones that need it the most can't do any of that stuff. All it does is make them realize how far downhill they've come. At Inglenook, you get cheered up and you stay cheered up, long as you have eyes."

"I see. How lovely. We charge you the earth, 'cause lining every room with LED's has got to be a big up-front cost. We bug your room, not to mention there's got to be hidden cameras, or how are you going to monitor response to the alpha rhythms? Anyhow, we serve powdered eggs, we cancel the Elderhostel, we cut corners here and there, we dominate and insult and bully and spy on you and you don't get huffy about it." Suellen glowered, and sang, " 'Cause you're permanently cheerful, thanks to the wallpaper."

"Well, I kind of thought … "

"And if Faye Bynum wants her lights down low, you don't encourage that, I guess. It would mean Faye might get fretful, or say something inappropriate, or God forbid, live her own life and die her own death as she chose. And if some guy actually makes some kind of crusade out of it, goes around stirring up the residents about being involuntarily tranquilized by a bunch of techie Big Brothers, maybe we better – "

"Whoa," Harve said. "Easy. I can see where you're going with this, and let me tell you, Blondie, it wasn't like that."

"Yeah? Like what?"

"There was no effort to shut him up, anything like that. He was a problem for Welles, sure, though I wouldn't know that much about it. She gets paid to handle problems. She's nobody's Big Brother."

"Needless to say. She's Albright's big sister."

"Yeah, and?"

Suellen shrugged. She could feel Harve getting sulky, slipping out of whatever temporary hold she might have achieved by fighting him to a draw. She changed the subject.

"Makes me think of a woman in Gabbro County that never used any kind of artificial light. Not electric, not even candles. She thought they were a big mistake. Got up at dawn, worked all day, and went to bed at sundown. She figured God put the sun there for a reason, and folks that turned their backs on it were asking for trouble. Little did she know. Anyway, that's how she got her name."

"We talking about Annie Godfire here?"

"You know about her?"

"Heard about her, mostly, from clients. She built some kind of a loony thing out of scrap iron?"

"Spirit catcher. It's a hell of a thing."

Harve un-sulked, got eager and boyish. "You've seen it? My soul, I've heard about that thing all my life, and I figured it was a myth. Could you show it to me some time?"

Why, yes indeed, Suellen thought. I can do better than that. "How about right now?"

"Now? What time is it?"

Suellen shrugged. "Night time. That's when it's best." She nodded at a glow beyond the honeysuckle. "It's pretty near full moon. You haven't lived until you've climbed the spirit catcher by moonlight. It's just about a religious experience."

"Already had all those I can take for one 48-hour period, Blondie. You screwed my brains out the other night, and beat 'em back in this afternoon, I'm ready for holy orders, or some sack time, whatever comes first."

"Yeah?" Suellen lifted a corner of her mouth a tenth of an inch, a trick she learned from her tough-cop stepfather. "Can't say I blame you, Harve. Never mind, then."

That's all it took. Ten minutes later, Suellen shut off the Triumph and leaned it against the faded and battered red hand that marked Annie Godfire's drive.

"Annie never much liked motors and such, either. We'll walk in from here."

"She's dead, I heard." Harve was grumpy again, knowing he'd been whipsawed.

"Yup. She died five years ago, the evening she finished the spirit catcher. Story is, she welded the last piece into place, put down her torch, and laid herself out on the very top of it, to join the spirits that were there to welcome her. You willing to bet she's not still here?"

"Nope ... Well. The old boy that told me about her said she was transported bodily into heaven."

"Literally true, if you count being transported a little at a time by crows and vultures. By the time anybody knew about it, there was nothing left but some chunks of pelvis and a pair of boots. The boots were still there, last time I looked."

"Jeez, yuck. Man, only in the South."

"Uh huh. Miz Godfire's granny built the first spirit catcher, but she built it out of pine logs, which is how the Indians used to. Bunch of Klan burned it down in 1920 or so, so Annie's ma and later Annie built this one to be fireproof. She got the materials from folks by reading their palms, helping them out with some basic facts of life by telling them spirits were talking to her."

"Yeah? Like what?"

"Oh, like how Purvis really oughtn't be messing with his sister like that, or Miz Oxendine would do well to show the mister a sweet face now and then. Basic Dear Abby stuff, except she had this talent for figuring out what was really bothering you, behind whatever fool thing you asked her. She didn't take any pay but scrap iron – fire escapes, bikes, engine blocks, barber chairs, train couplers, some rail stock, big heavy stuff it would about bust your ass to lift, she got them up there with a block and tackle and welded 'em in place by herself, after her mother died. County offered her some surplus I-beams left from building a school, and she turned it down flat. She didn't want anything that hadn't made its own way through life, and got soaked in spirit in the process."

"Barber chairs?" They were in deep woods now, invisible to each other, the track a vaguely lighter shade of black at their feet. Harve's voice joggled a little as he tripped over a root.

"Think about it. A barber chair a hundred years old, that's five thousand, two hundred Saturday mornings. Little kids getting their first haircuts, growing up, getting laid, going off to war, getting old, they sit in that chair twice a month through the whole thing. And how many of them had some little piece of spirit to add in? And that barber chair, that might be one piece out of a million things that make up the Spirit Catcher. Bed frames – how many births and deaths, screws and sickness and night fears are we talking about there? Tractor seats, where a woman sat and plowed the corn, realizing there was no way they were going to make a crop and pay the bank this year, just plowing on. Train parts that went all over the country, from Laredo to New York to … I don't know, Laramie, Wyoming, over and over for years, hauling hobos and cabbage and rail dicks through the night. Whatever was used hard, and outlived its usefulness without breaking down, that's what

Annie Godfire wanted. There it is." They stood in moon shadow at the edge of a clearing, before the spirit catcher.

"Shit," Harve whispered. "Holy shit."

It rose fifteen or twenty stories above the meadow, higher than a powerline tower, bigger at the base than a ball diamond. A delicate lacework of junk, tapered to a narrow waist a hundred feet up, and flared above that like a cooling tower. Moonlight ricocheted dully from the million pieces of scrap iron, picking out bicycles, baby carriages, anchors, cutter bars, and a universe of indistinct and unguessable things. Huddled beneath it was the sagging shape of a derelict Airstream trailer.

Harve walked toward it, head bending farther back, the farther he stumbled through the meadow. "No way," he said. "No way one woman built that." He spoke in a whisper, and so did Suellen.

"Believe it. Wait'll you see what it's like up top."

"Bones and boots?"

"Some folks came from the Lumbee towns and buried what the crows didn't take. The boots could still be there, but that's not it. C'mon."

"Wait a second. You're going to climb that thing in the dark?"

Suellen didn't bother with psychology this time. "You too, pal. You'll thank me. It's not dark, anyways, there's plenty of moon."

"OK then. You first."

"Duh. Just put your feet where I do, and don't look down."

"Duh."

Halfway up, Harve said, "I get it. You follow these little paint marks."

"Shh. Good for you, Harve."

"Yeah." He looked around himself at arches, filigrees, and networks of the worn metal detritus of billions of hours of life, motionless in humid moonlight. He thought he heard silent voices from gas cans and gearshifts and garden gates, all of them shining with dew as the iron cooled with the night. He thought of something, and the hair rose on the back of his neck. "This thing's been here how long?"

"It took Annie and her mom their whole lives to build it. The part we're on now, I guess went up thirty years ago. First part, almost eighty. Top, maybe five."

"Uh huh. Thought you said that. How come nothing's rusted?"

"Hm." Suellen's voice was shivery. "Makes you think, doesn't it?"

Annie Godfire had topped the Spirit Catcher with a pyramid of steel ladders, at the peak of which she had bolted and braced a rectangular platform of steel road plates. A warped and weathered pair of work boots, absent laces but reverently aligned, stood on it at one end. Tractor seats backed against the head and foot. Suellen pointed Harve to one, and sank onto the other to puff and look out over miles of moonlit and gently hilly woods.

"How's this?"

"Amazing. Worth the climb. Scary as hell, though."

A little night wind came up, making the spirit catcher croon and mutter. A dozen feet away, Suellen heard Harve's breath shorten with alarm.

"If you talk quietly, and listen, you'll find you can hear everything I say," Suellen murmured. "See?"

Harve's voice sounded in her ear, modulated by the pounding of his heart. "Like one of those whispering galleries. How the hell does that work? There's nothing to echo off of."

"I think it uses the whole structure, somehow," Suellen said. "Just another one of Annie's little surprises. She was at least as smart as Leonardo da Vinci."

"And strong as an elephant, apparently. Are we sure she was a regular human being?"

"Not at all."

"Mm." Harve was silent for a moment. "Listen, that was a pretty good riff you run, about the haircuts and the rail dicks and all. I enjoyed listening to it, letting it sort of wash over me. That's probably more talk than I got out of you in twelve hours the other night."

"Oh. Was I supposed to be talking? I thought we were pretty much doing what you had in mind."

"Not the whole twelve hours. I ... Suellen, listen, did you feel like that was something you'd want to, I don't know ... you know … try again some time?"

Suellen's turn for silence. The excitement of it, the blazing release, the sense of completion and peace the next afternoon, along with the eerie feeling that she'd been somehow alloyed with Harve, displaced from being one hundred percent herself, the Suellen Ransom she'd always and only relied on. But the imperative that she not lose focus on Hap, and on what Harve knew about Hap. She sighed, and raised a shoulder.

"I liked it, OK. I'm not sure we got a possible thing here. I don't even know your HIV status."

"Negative."

"Yeah? So at least I don't have to go get a blood test. Listen, did you have a funny feeling after that, that we'd … " She stopped, and didn't start again.

"We'd what?"

"Oh. Nothing. Maybe we'd be smart to quit while we're ahead, Harve."

Suellen felt Harve's ambiguous relaxation through the spirit-catching web that held them both. "Jeez. Here I thought you wiggled your butt in my nose all this way up, to get me in the mood."

"I brought you up here to show you something I bet you'd never guessed about. Also, the only place we could do it would be this platform, which is where the birds dismantled Annie. You want to move those boots?"

Harve shuddered, making the Spirit Catcher creak. "I don't think so, no."

"Me neither. For starts, it's awful hard to fake when you're on this thing."

"Who was faking? Not me."

Suellen turned to grin at him. "Of course you were. I didn't care, because even faking you're pretty hot, as I'm sure you've been told. No, I mean that's why I talked so much on the way here. This thing kind of does that to you, like truth serum. Don't you feel it? It's hard to lie when you're around Annie's spirit catcher." Her grin faded. "So, Harve, I just want to be sure we get through the bullshit, kind of to ground zero. I won't lie to you, I had a terrific time the other night, almost a mystical experience, and I do want to talk to you about it, some time. But I really need you to level with me about Hap Maryland now, and I need to believe that I can trust what you say. Can you do that? Have you told me everything I need to know about Inglenook, Harve? About Hap Maryland?"

Harve pushed out his lips and swung his feet, like a kid brought into the Principal's office. But all he said was, "Need to know.... Axe me no questions, and I'll tell you no lies."

Suellen sighed and turned a hand. This was the part she'd not wanted to get into, bringing him up here. "Harve, please. I said it was hard to lie up here, but it's not impossible. Let me give you some more incentive."

She cocked her head at the ground, another planet all that way down. "Those paint marks don't work the same, going down. You think back, you'll remember there were about ten places where other lines of marks joined ours. When you try to retrace, you'll find you can't remember which set to follow. You've got ten consecutive fifty-fifty chances to make the right choice. That's a little less than one chance in a thousand. The false trails peter out, or lead to drop-offs and you can't get back to the right one alone, because you'll commit yourself to downward steps that are impossible to retrace without help. Annie did that to keep kids from climbing on this thing when she wasn't around; she knew all she had to do was tell one kid, and every kid in the county would know it within a week.

"Now it's true, when you get a little lower down, you could probably go ahead and drop, and only break your leg or something, like John Wilkes Booth. But to get that low, you'd have to guess right anyhow seven times. That's one chance in 128. What I'm pretty much saying, Harve, you're stuck up here until I decide to help you down."

Harve smiled at Suellen, not seeming much worried. "Saint Annie showed you the way, I suppose."

"She showed Hap Maryland, and he showed me. Come on, we got unfinished business about Hap, so talk, OK? And we can go home. Maybe you can talk me into letting you sleep over, though I doubt it."

Harve sighed, and cocked his elbow over the tractor seat. "You liked Hap, I guess. You're sure as hell giving a lot of time to figuring out what happened to him. Well, Suellen, believe me, and this is the truth. You don't want to know."

Suellen shook her head, mad now. "Harve? You want to stay up here a week? How hungry d'you think I'll let you get?

Well, double that a couple times, that's how hungry. Also, I heard we got a front coming in – yeah, hey, look at the clouds around the moon, I bet that's the first of it now. It's gonna get a lot darker, and then it's gonna rain, Harve. Lightning, you want to be up on this steel tower in a thunderstorm? So either keep quiet and stay here, or start talking. What'll it be?"

"You think I was bluffing just now? Well, I think you are, Blondie. This really is something you don't want to know."

"Gosh, Harve. Don't you think – "

"Shh!" It came like a hand across her mouth. She heard Harve's voice brushing her ear, barely audible. "Look down."

A narrow streak of light dusted the weeds below them, almost invisible in the moonlight and gone as soon as Suellen saw it. She heard the complaint of aluminum hinges long un-oiled, and the grating of a hasp. As she watched, a small figure, foreshortened into a dark head and a swirl of pale fabric, emerged onto the sagging porch of the trailer at the base of the spirit catcher and sat on the ground to pull on a pair of sneakers.

"Damn," Suellen whispered, and started to clamber down the ironwork.

"Hey," Harve said. The dark figure below them sprang to its feet, peering up into moon-dazzle, and ran toward the road, stopping once to hop and yank on a loose sneaker.

"Morgan!"

No answer but the fading breath of sneakers in sand and weeds. Suellen lowered herself along the line of paint-marked footholds, telling Harve to sit still and be quiet, yelling after Morgan Baley, climbing down as fast as she could while her beaten-up joints yelled in rebellion. When she'd gone maybe fifty feet, scrabbling from one dew-slick handhold to the next in the dubious moonlight, her foot slipped on a pump handle, and she lurched head-first into an anchor from the Lake Erie tramp *City of Ashtabula*. Stunned, waving her arms for balance, she fell onto a section of fire-escape that hinged downward under her and dumped her into empty space.

She may have fallen fifteen or 20 feet – far enough to break bones if she had landed solidly. But the space she fell through was the narrowing that defined the waist of the spirit catcher. She landed obliquely against a playground slide, bounced from it to a bedspring, and from that to find herself – for that instant woozily exhilarated at this Spiderman stuff – heading for a pole polished to a shine by the sliding bodies of sixty years of Fayetteville firemen. She tried to grab it, but slammed against it crossways, knocking her wind out and bruising her forehead on the knee that came around the other way to meet it. Stunned enough to miss the opportunity to grab something solid, she let out a breathless caw of alarm and fell another five feet through a grinning archway of welded chain onto a sewer grating that extended into the interior space of the spirit catcher, still eighty feet above the roof of the Airstream. She had enough consciousness left to know that this was her last chance, and she wrapped her arms around the grating with what tenacity she could muster.

13.

Francesco Maryland lay back on the stained and stuffy mattress and listened as rain began to drum on the ceiling. It was a peaceful sound, and it matched his mood. Sister had been in, brought him food and prayed with him, and that always made him kind of sleepy and excited, at the same time. A delicious feeling, really. Life had gotten very hard for a while there, and Sister made things easier. Made things so easy, really, that Cesco couldn't always remember why life had always seemed so hard to him. Sometimes he had dreams about the hard time, when if it wasn't other kids and fights and teasing, it was girls, or it was school, and before any of that it was his parents.

Cesco missed his parents, now that they weren't around. Sister said they would go back and see Mom and Dad as soon as Jesus made him better. He hoped that would happen pretty soon. He missed Mom, particularly, and sometimes he cried about her, remembering her tender dark face, and her comfortable lap. Then things got hard to figure out, and his head felt like it was stuffed with shit instead of brains. The only thing that helped was working on the picture. Cesco wasn't sure it was any good, but Sister cried when she saw it, and said it was the most beautiful thing there ever had been on God's earth.

Cesco had lost somewhere his automatic doubt of all superlatives; that seemed to belong to another life. Even so, he wondered if it was possible that out of all the lovely things on God's earth, certainly including Sister herself, one fairly messy picture could possibly be the most beautiful. It was terribly frustrating working on it, and he could only do it for a little while at a time, and only during daylight. Drawing what he saw and remembered was easy enough, certainly, but that was only the outside. Trying to get all of it, that was so hard, and unless he could get the whole picture, it wouldn't be right, wouldn't be worthy of Jesus, and then maybe Jesus would shrug and turn away, and never finish his healing. Cesco cried a little now, hugging the smelly pillow until he fell asleep again.

*

The rain caught Morgan a half-mile from home. She allowed herself to hope that its noise would cover what she made returning her bike to the garage and negotiating the screen door. But when, soaked and puffing, she opened that door, the nightglow of appliances revealed Bethany at the kitchen table with a cup of coffee, waiting for her.

"Morgan, honey, what on Earth?"

Morgan had not wasted the time she'd had to think on the way home. She had a story ready, a replacement for the I-couldn't-sleep-so-I-took-a-walk that she'd honed to perfection over the nights during which she had in fact returned to her bed unchallenged. Still, it was a damnable lie, she knew. When she raised her face to Bethany, she learned again what it is to plan the deception of those who love you. The knowledge brought a freshet of tears to mix with the rain and sweat on her face. Even so, she steeled herself.

"I thought I had an idea where Cesco might be, Momma."

"Really? And it was such a good idea you had to run off in the middle of the night to see?"

Morgan shook her head, not looking at Bethany, and said, "No. It was so dumb I didn't want to bother anybody with it."

"I see. But still too good to wait for morning."

"Yes, ma'am."

"And what was this excellent idea?"

Morgan considered. It had sounded like, and surely was, Aunt Suellen calling after her from the spirit trap. Her story would have to square with dead-certain revelations from that corner. "The spirit catcher. You know, where – "

"I know. And was he there?"

"No'm."

"I didn't hear you, Morgan."

Morgan raised her head and looked Bethany square on. Her face solemn, her eyes a little shuttered, she said clearly, "No, ma'am. He was not there."

Bethany's look as she rose from the table to rinse her coffee cup nearly broke Morgan's heart. Why couldn't Jesus have managed this better so she wouldn't have to lie to her own mother? What's the point of being God's son, if you get things into the same kind of stupid mess anyone else would?

"Morgan," Bethany said at last. "I guess I have trouble believing everything you're telling me."

"You think I'm lying? You think I'm a liar? Mother!" Morgan put her head on the table and dissolved into unfaked tears.

Bethany put a hand on Morgan's head. "A liar is someone who lies all the time, for the sake of lying. To fool people and take advantage. I don't think you're that kind of person. But I don't think you're telling me the truth right now. Or maybe not the whole truth. I'm not a detective and I don't want to be."

No, Morgan thought, but Aunt Suellen is, and Aunt Suellen could pull into the driveway any minute. If she was going to save this situation, she'd have to do it right now. She looked at her mother with streaming eyes.

"You don't always tell me the whole truth."

Bethany smiled a little. "I think Daddy and I have brought you up not to be this kind of impertinent and disrespectful. But we don't, and that's a fact. Sometimes we wait to see if it's something you're old enough to hear. Usually, it doesn't amount to anything one way or the other, in the long run. Did you have something particular in mind, or are you just sort of looking for something to say? If it's that, then I think we can get back to the real subject. Morgan, what were you doing out in the rain in the middle of the night?"

Morgan stood and walked to the sink. Her legs felt like moonlight. She seemed to be gliding over the kitchen floor without using them. She pulled a paper towel off the roll over the sink and blew her nose.

"If I answer that truthfully, will you answer one question from me, truthfully?" It seemed the best deal she was likely to get.

Bethany turned her from the sink, brisk and severe. "I should slap you and send you to your room for this kind of rudeness, Morgan. Many a mother would, and wake up to a more mannerly child in the morning." She sat again at the table. "It would depend on the question, I suppose. It had better be a good one."

"Yes, ma'am." Morgan glanced at the kitchen window, checking for headlights, seeing none. "Then who is my real father? It isn't Daddy, is it?"

Bethany sighed. "Daddy was there when you were born. He's been your father from the first breath you drew."

Morgan didn't answer, and didn't have to. Bethany smiled, and kissed her. "And I was about to tell you a lie by not telling the whole truth, wasn't I? All right, Morgan, I guess this is the moment for it. No, Daddy isn't your biological father."

Morgan's airy legs collapsed her to the kitchen floor. "I knew it," she squeaked. "I knew it." She was laughing and crying together, drowning in sorrow and relief. "Do you know who was?"

Bethany laughed too, merry as a carnival barker. "Well, what do you think? You think that's the sort of thing could happen when I wasn't paying attention? Or maybe I was having sex with so many fellas I lost track, is that it, Morgan? Is that what you think of your mother?"

Morgan shook her head, speechless, no longer in control of her voice.

"Well, daughter, let me tell you." Bethany ran a hand through her hair, exhaled, and knelt to put an arm around Morgan's shaking shoulders. She lifted Morgan and steered her toward the kitchen door.

"Let's walk. This could lead to some yelling, and I don't want to wake folks up."

"It's still raining."

"What do we care? You're already wet, and I don't mind. Maybe it will wash us up a little, you think? We won't melt, that's for sure."

They walked through the garage and into a steaming downpour. Before they'd gone ten steps, Bethany was as wet as Morgan, and Morgan was wet through. What they said, they spluttered through a film of warm rain, arms clutched each to their own bosoms, heads down and dripping.

"Daddy and I never told you about your ..." Bethany sighed. "Your genetic father – I will not call him your real father, Daddy is your real father – because he's no longer living, and for ... reasons that I'll get to in a minute."

Morgan didn't answer until they were at the road, then

turned to Bethany. "Are you my real mother?"

"Oh, yes, honey. Yes, indeed. I knew all about you from the morning you were conceived to the day you were born, and every day after that right up to – well, recently. Now I'm not so sure. But I can't ask you to be honest with me if I'm not honest with you, can I?"

"No."

"No. So, if I am honest with you about your father, will you promise me one thing?"

"What?"

"That you'll still honor Daddy, who married me in the delivery room, out of the kindness and love of his heart, and loved you from that moment as if he'd been the one to put the seeds of you in me."

Morgan nodded. "Daddy's sweet, but you might as well know that I haven't believed he was my real ... my genetic father for more than a year. Maybe this will help me be more ..." Morgan lifted a hand to wipe rain and hair from her eyes. "You know. Accepting."

"Maybe. All right, then. The man who actually did ... well, provide the necessary..." Bethany sighed. "Well. The man who impregnated me was a very brilliant, original man. A poet, a minister of the Gospel, and a great teacher."

Morgan smiled. "I knew it! And did people drop whatever they were doing and follow him?"

"Yes, they did." Bethany sounded surprised; whether at the question or at its answer, Morgan couldn't tell. "I was one who did. When I was twenty years old, I thought he was one of the saints of all creation. He told me I might make a good disciple. He wrote a flattering inscription in a copy of his book that I took to him to sign."

Morgan hugged herself with delight. Her breath began to hiss in her ears, and she raised her eyes. Rain fell through the air like silver light, like the tears of the blessed Virgin. *Did your heart not burn within you*, she wanted to say. And was on the point of saying, when Bethany spoke again, her voice flat and emphatic, as if she were reading a sentence of death.

"He kidnapped me and raped me, not once but again and again over the course of a day and night that I can never forget. He very nearly killed me."

Morgan froze but Bethany walked on, eyes on her feet, mind in the past. "When I realized afterwards that I was pregnant, I nearly killed myself. But I sat down every day and talked to the baby that was growing in me, and I purged every trace of that man from my heart and from you. I never allowed his name to be spoken in my presence. I completely removed him from me, so he couldn't contaminate you. He was a wicked, cruel, sick old man whose name even now makes me want to vomit."

Morgan stood in the road, a small statue of consternation. "That can't be true. That's a lie," she screamed after her mother, and her foot stamped a sheet of muddy water from the road. She clutched her head, rivulets of hair streaming through her fingers like blood. "Oh, Momma, how can you tell such a wicked, awful lie? God will – " She broke off, not sure which was worse, the fact of the lie, or its content, or the thought of the punishment that her mother must suffer for telling it.

Bethany flared, turned, and saw Morgan squatting in the road with her hands pressed against her head, rain drumming around her and plastering her nightie against the ridge of her spine. She sighed, and her hands dropped to her side.

"Come here," she said, and she walked back toward Morgan, opening her dripping bathrobe. "Come here to Momma. We could talk all night, so I'm just going to show you something. Come on. Put your hand there. No, it's all right. Feel that? And there? And – no, don't worry, give me your hand. Right here? Morgan, your biological father gave me all those scars, all in one night. Put your hands on them and believe it."

*

When Suellen woke in streaming darkness, she thought she was still hugging the sewer grate. But whatever she was on was breathing, fast and shallow, sounding a little desperate. It appeared that she was hanging down Harve's back like Superman's cape. Her arms were around his neck, clamped there by a sweating hand. Beyond the back of his neck, she saw his exhausted face plastered against a filigreed rectangle of steel bearing the dim legend, "Koken." The footrest of a barber chair, she thought, and concluded that they were still somewhere on the spirit catcher. From that it followed, she supposed, that she had not yet fallen into the front yard of the Airstream. She hitched herself up to take the pressure off his windpipe.

"Man," Harve said. "That's an improvement. You doing OK?"

"I guess so." Suellen felt banged-up, nauseated, and weak. "What's going on?"

She felt Harve jiggle with amusement. "What's going on? We're a million feet up on the damn spirit catcher, and I just ran out of places to go, trying to get us down. Keep this up, I could run out of breath."

Suellen spotted a solid-looking dumpster lid, and got herself shakily onto it to look around. Everything hurt, but the spirit catcher was pinging and sighing with warm rain. She smelled wet forest and the fresh ozone of thunder, and raised her face into the rain to get oriented and clear her head. The narrow waist of the spirit catcher loomed three stories over them.

"My God, Harve, you climbed down here and fucking rescued me? Like in the movies? And you were trying to find your way down this thing in the dark, carrying the swooning girl around your neck?"

"Well ..." Harve shrugged. "I guess, yeah. Time I got down to you, the rain was making things a little slick, and you were about ready to slide off that grating. Kind of a close call, really."

"Well, for – " Suellen looked for breath, felt the new bruises of her fall burning against the background of the established bruises from the fight; and raw streaks across her belly that might, in fact, have come from sliding over the edge of a sewer grating. She opened her mouth, looked down at the Airstream, and closed it again.

"So," Harve said. "Is there a way to get a person's butt off this thing, once you lose the sacred trail?"

Suellen nodded weakly. "Uh huh. You work your way sideways and up until you run across a paint trail."

"How do you know if it's the right one?"

"You don't. You follow it up until it joins another trail, and then either that one is the right one, or the one you were already on is. If you ever knew the right trail, you recognize where you are at that point."

"I could have figured that out."

Suellen smiled and ruffled his hair, a little refreshed by a quick pop of affection. "Sure could, if you'd known the trail to start with. Listen, never mind. Thanks for saving my butt."

"Butt Watchers would've come down on me bad if I let that one get dinged up."

"Yeah, well... I owe you a big one, Harve. Let's go see what's in the Airstream. Bet I know, though."

The Airstream didn't much live up to its name. It was airless and dark, with an outhouse stench that made Suellen's eyes water. Harve took one breath, and backed out the door. Suellen covered her nose with her shirt and groped until she heard a squeak of fear, and felt breath on her arm.

"Cesco?"

"What?"

"Good Christ. You want to come home?"

"No," Francesco said. "Sister'll kill me."

"Sister?"

"Yeah. She might cry."

"Well," Suellen said. "She sent us."

"No, she didn't."

"How else did we know how to find you?"

"I don't know. Sister's taking care of me just fine. I have to be here until Jesus cures me."

From the door, Harve cleared his throat. "Hi, kid," he said, in a Biblical tone. "What seems to be the problem?"

14.

Harve leaned against the wall of the screen porch and passed a cigarette to Suellen. He was back in the torn and maculate clothes he'd arrived in; Hap's soggy coverall was hanging over the ruined chaise like a crash dummy. Suellen was wrapped in a coarse-weave hooded bathrobe she found in Bethany's closet. She was pale and scrubbed, like a dateless roommate, and her jaw hurt.

"What do you suppose that guy wants with you?"

"What guy?"

Harve shrugged and tossed his head more or less in the direction of the Pik Kwik. "The one you used to work for. Hill? Hillman?"

"Hillemeier. Got me." Suellen was not delighted to find herself in bed, or on a sleeping bag, with Harve. He'd just been so nice and resourceful back there at the spirit catcher. And, after all, he had saved her life. He hadn't even seemed to be figuring to cash in on it. Still, here they were, somewhere between two and four in the morning, slumped on softness listening to a bunch of crickets, crazed by the humidity, arguing about nothing. He was spending the night, evidently, without trying to cash any sexual credits. Seemed like some kind of scam to Suellen.

"He a cop?"

"Yep."

Suellen decided that was a little brusque, even for somebody sending messages about grateful non-availability. "Fat jerk," she added, to soften it a little.

Harve nodded lazily, acknowledging the gesture. "How'd you get into cop work?"

"Nice girl like me, you mean?"

Harve snorted. "No, ma'am. No, I mean a righteous, self-directed, independent, mature, buff, blonde, autonomous and handsome woman like you, working for a bullshit hierarchy like the cops."

"Maybe I like hierarchy. Maybe I like busting losers, which is a fact. Busted one the other day, he gave me some lawyer shit about I had no right to bust him in North Carolina, so I dragged him back to the state line and flattened the stupid bastard across it and told him the top half of him was free to go, but I was hauling his ass to the pokey in Tennessee." Which was a slight tweak to the facts, but Suellen didn't want to muddy the narrative by getting Trooper Janklow into it.

Harve sighed, and leaned against the porch rail. His cigarette glowed briefly before he dunked it in an Urquell empty. "My stars, you are some kind of bull dyke, aren't you just?"

Suellen let that sit for a while, turning an unlit cigarette end to end in her fingers. When Harve looked at her, she said, "I never liked that language."

"My stars?"

"No, 'Some kind of.' You sound like a crapped-out quarterback doing color commentary on Fox."

Harve stood and stretched. "Mm. Turned a little cloudy, hasn't it, for this time of year. I'll be going."

"Sorry, Harve. I really appreciate your getting me home safe and all, not to mention you were great with that stupid kid. You're still holding out on me."

"True, I am. A person took that fact, and put it in context of the totality of our relationship up to now, they might conceive I must have an awful strong reason to hold out. Otherwise, and I mean this as a flat fact, not trying to turn your head or anything, I would be as delighted to accommodate your wishes in this matter as in any other."

Suellen blinked. "Didn't know we had a 'relationship.' You want to give me a little hint about your strong reason?"

"No. Well, OK, sure. You're a cop, see. If I told you what I know about Hap Maryland's death – though for God's sake it was none of my doing – you might feel duty bound to … oh, start a chain of events, like, that would change my life for the worse. Very worse. And not just mine."

Suellen laid herself back on the sleeping bag and closed her eyes. "Uh huh. Well, that puts a whole new light on it. I wonder you never explained it that way before. I think you were on your way out the door just now."

"Yes. Yes, I was."

"OK. 'Bye."

" 'Bye."

But when Harve got to the front of the house where he'd parked his car, seemed like days ago, he heard footsteps in the gravel behind him. He turned, and she stood in the rough-woven bathrobe, feet apart, arms crossed, and with her head a little to one side in a slant of moonlight, close enough for him to smell her exhaustion.

"I like ladies, you understand."

"Yes," Harve said. "I do understand that."

"Good. But, Harve, damn it all, I … well, you're not that bad yourself. And of course I appreciate being alive, instead of road kill at the bottom of that spirit catcher. Maybe we can figure something out. Meanwhile, thanks for everything." She lunged at him, sending him into a defensive crouch, but just kissed his neck while administering a Dutch rub, punched his arm hard enough to make his palm tingle, and stumbled back to the house, shaking her hand.

When she stood in the kitchen, she could not stave off some very unwelcome thoughts: first, that she had more or less declared herself to Harve, Christ, *You're not so bad yourself. Maybe we can figure something out*, like a mewling virgin. Harve's going felt like he was wrenching something away with him, something that had ached within her, hurt in the leaving, and left behind pain in its absence. It was a small ache, in the context of this bruising day and night, but certainly there.

And then, she was scared to sleep alone on the screen porch or in Hap's bed, and was still unwilling to use the bed she'd shared with Bethany while Bethany swelled with what would prove to be Morgan the problematic daughter. Pain and tiredness overwhelmed her. She sat on the kitchen floor to try to think of an alternative, collapsed, and slept there. Some time in the night, she stumbled to Bethany's bed, brushed her backpack and accumulated laundry onto the floor, and slipped into it without waking. The body is wiser than the will.

*

Bethany and Plummer Baley's house enclosed only one sleeper during most of that time. Francesco, tired of the questions, the tears, the anguished voices, patient explanations and hot denials, curled up with his head on his mother's lap and slept while the parliament raged overhead and into the night.

"The troublesome fact remains," Taylor said, sounding like he and everyone here were a bunch of scholars explicating a knotty Etruscan text, "that Morgan basically kidnapped Cesco and held him prisoner. All the time," he couldn't help adding, "saying she had no idea where he was. That was a lie compounding a felony no less, and it caused us a great deal of pain."

"We don't deny that in the least," Plummer said. "Morgan has done something terribly serious, and it will go hard with her for a long time before – well, before we can think of other things. You can believe that her repentance will be not only complete, but of the sort that so scours a soul that it never forgets and never repeats the offense or anything like it. Nevertheless, I am only saying that Francesco does not appear to have been injured by the experience. For that matter, he was gone a total of two days, and if anything, he seems a little the better for it. At least his language has cleaned up some."

That was probably not a diplomatic thing to have added, and Plummer was sorry as soon as he did. Still, there it was. Cesco between the time of his swimming accident and his disappearance was a scandal and a trial to everyone; the Cesco that Suellen had returned at one o'clock in the morning was – well, maybe a little goofy and sleepy, but amiable. What little talking he did was free of obscenities. It was a remarkable transformation to have taken place in two days. Taylor couldn't help suspecting that it was temporary and possibly drug-induced, but he liked Bethany and Plummer too much to come out with that, yet.

Giulia sighed, and stroked Cesco's head. "An impasse," she said. "Your daughter kidnapped our son, and who knows when she would have brought him back, how long she would have left us sick with worry. Still, we are all family, and no one wants to send anyone to jail. Just now, it is still too fresh for me to say, Oh, never mind."

Plummer nodded, looking so depressed that Taylor took some pity on him.

"Was there any ..." Taylor cringed at the thought. "You know. Any evidence of, of – "

"Of intercourse," Plummer finished for him. "Both

children say not, though she may have implied something of the sort to get him to follow her out there. It near kills me to think that. In any case, Bethany is looking into it, and more than just verbally. I very devoutly hope that she finds Morgan intact. If not, then we are into very deep water."

Water so deep that it closed over the words, leaving the kitchen silent except for the faint regular creak of Giulia's rocker and the peaceful breath of Cesco's sleep. The silence held until Bethany and Morgan entered in matching bathrobes and toweled heads; grim, exhausted portraits of Grandma Lee as child and matron.

No one spoke, until Bethany gently cleared her throat, causing Morgan to raise a hand, signaling that she needed no signal.

"Mr. and Mrs. Maryland," she said firmly. "I apologize from the very bottom of my heart for the pain I caused you by taking Cesco away. I only did it because ..." She stopped at the slight restless stirring of her mother behind her. "I had no right to do that, and it was terribly wrong to hurt and deceive you and cause you such anxiety. I am more sorry than I can say. I know my mother and father are disappointed in me, but I mostly regret worrying you. I would do anything if ... To make it up to you."

Something in the stubborn, formal voice made Taylor smile. "Thank you, Morgan. Speaking just for myself here, I accept your apology. You were about to say something about a reason," he said. "And your mother stopped you, which she was probably right to do. Still, Giulia and I would welcome any explanation of it." Taylor shrugged. "Well, almost any. Preferably, truthful."

Morgan lowered her head at the reproach, and turned to her mother. Bethany nodded to her.

"Cesco's swimming accident was more serious than we told you," Morgan said. "And it's my fault that it was. I was hoping that if I could get Cesco somewhere … I don't know. If I could get him to a place where I could pray over him, that maybe Jesus would be able to heal him, when I couldn't."

Giulia's eyes snapped open and stared at Morgan. "What? How serious?"

Morgan sighed, and her face started to clench. "He hit his head and almost drowned. I pulled him out and gave him CPR, but I don't think it was good enough. It <u>wasn't</u> good enough. It just wasn't …"

She collapsed at Giulia's knees, grinding her eyes into Giulia's nightgown. "I'm so sorry," she sobbed. "It wasn't good enough. I took him swimming in a dangerous place, and he got hurt, and it was my fault. I <u>had</u> to try to make him better, didn't I?"

*

The deferential tapping at the back door coincided with the ricochet of late morning sun from the mirror on the Triumph, through the door, down the hall, and into Suellen's eye. She concluded that the house was on fire, and one of the firemen banging against locked doors was Harve, dressed as Hap Maryland, telling her he'd come to carry her down on his back. She sat up in shock and panic.

"Oh … Christ, just a second."

Whoever was tapping stopped, and the sunlight flickered with what was, Suellen supposed, a cheery wave. She waved back, staggered to her feet and gathered the robe around herself, muttering, Fuck you, Merry Sunshine. Every muscle and bone yelled about yesterday's abuse, and she was pretty sure she had at least two black eyes, though it felt like more.

Opening the back door admitted more light than Suellen could deal with. She glimpsed a pair of khakis, closed her eyes, and spoke from behind a shielding hand. "Harve? Could you just come back in a couple weeks?"

"Um, it's Taylor," Taylor said.

"Oh. Yeah? Taylor? C'mon in. What do I owe this pleasure?"

"Well, for one thing, a little more articulate thanks than you got last night. Thank you for bringing in Cesco."

Suellen shrugged. "Glad to do it. I got lucky." She pulled the robe around her neck and walked into the kitchen. "I expect I'll be making some coffee pretty soon. Want some?"

"Actually, I wasn't sure if you had facilities out here, so I brought some. With or without a splash of bourbon?"

"For … Wow. You're your father's son, you know that? Hold on, lemme get some clothes on."

When they were sitting on the back step with steaming thermos-tops of coffee, Taylor said, "Dad really liked you, you know. He talked about you a lot after you joined the Marines."

"He was a great guy. I had a real father who died when I was a kid, but wasn't worth a crap, and a stepfather that I loved, who died too young. Hap was like bedrock, more like a big brother than anything. I wish to hell I could get someplace figuring out what happened to him. By the way, thanks for not asking what the other guy looks like. He looks worse."

"You look OK." Taylor sighed, and scuffed a shoe in the dust. "I met your mother once, did you know that?"

"No shit? When was that?"

"I was a kid. She had on a black leotard kind of thing, and I could barely look at her without, um, she was so ..." Taylor shrugged. "You know. Spectacular."

Suellen nodded, not smiling. "That's Mom. Was."

"Oh? Uh huh. I'm sorry. Listen, you think you could show me where you found Cesco?"

"Scene of the crime?"

Taylor shook his head. "Little Miss Morgan ... I don't know if 'admitted' is the word. Informed us rather late in the day, that Cesco almost drowned at Riverbend. She saved his life with CPR, but that's the end of the good news. Something happened to him. We're praying it's not brain damage. Giulia and I took him to the hospital this morning, and they helicoptered him up to Duke for a neurological exam. There was only room for one of us to go along, so Giulia's up there with him. Meanwhile, we just have to wait. I was going nuts, so I thought maybe if I saw where he was, I could ... help explain things."

Suellen shrugged, and drank coffee. "He was in Annie Godfire's old trailer, under the spirit trap. You grew up here, didn't you?"

"Yeah, that's what Morgan said. I thought I remembered where it was, but I couldn't find it. I thought it was off the Bozlee road."

"Huh uh, other side of town. So how is Cesco acting? He seemed pretty normal when we found him. Maybe a little dazed, but it was the middle of the night."

"He's – " Taylor threw his arms out. "He's placid and cheerful, which you might think was an improvement. But he's not himself, and he's not talking. I don't mean about where he was, like that. I mean he's not saying anything at all. As if he's forgotten how. It's got us worried sick."

"Man, no wonder. Look, it'll probably wear off. Maybe he's embarrassed about kiting off with Morgan like that. But if it'll make you feel better, sure, I'll show you the place. You driving?"

"Yes. If that's OK?"

"Sure is. Splash me some bourbon."

The spirit catcher looked a lot more ordinary in daylight, Suellen thought. As if it might be a little sleep-deprived too. She twisted the hasp on the trailer door, and opened it to release a ripe stench and the drone of a thousand flies.

"Take a breath before you go in. It was a little close in there."

"Yeah, I thought I …Yeesh, good grief. I thought Cesco had a smell to him, even after he came all that way through the rain on a motorcycle. My God, that's criminal. What the hell was that damn girl thinking?"

"Yeah. Look, you poke around all you like. I think I'll stay out here and hold the door open."

"All right." Suellen felt the Airstream lurching on tired springs as Taylor went from window to window, yanking at sashes. "I'll tell you something, if I'd been held prisoner in a septic tank, I'd say anything to get out. We get back there, I'm going to talk seriously to Plummer about that girl."

Suellen laughed shortly. "Knowing Plummer, I'd say he's already got Morgan wishing he'd burn her at the stake and get it over with. You don't mess with that guy."

Taylor grunted, and was silent long enough for Suellen to sit stiffly on the grass in the sunshine and swirl the last of her enhanced coffee, letting the steam of coffee and bourbon mix with the pennyroyal smell of the meadow. Three good smells to battle the stink of the trailer. Taylor's voice emerged over the babble of flies.

"Holy Christ, will you look at this."

Suellen looked reluctantly at the dark doorway of the Airstream. "What?"

"Well … I can't describe it."

"Yeah?" Suellen stood and looked into the gloom, and saw nothing. "I gotta come in there?"

"You get used to it."

Suellen took a breath and walked into the Airstream. Taylor's back blocked her view at first; then she saw the mural, a monochrome in black on cracked grey panelboard that formed one of the walls of the trailer's entrance. It looked at first like something cheesily erotic, and Suellen was about to say something scornful about vandals. A naked girl crouched over a male figure, kissing so profoundly that their heads were halves of a single object, their faces obliterated by the fusion.

The woman's form was tense, crackling with the desperation of the kiss, while the man lay limp; possibly with desire, but possibly dead. If so, Suellen supposed, the woman would be his death, or some such nastiness. Still, there was something sure and sensuous in the figures, and an economy of line that created, from a minimum of means, rounded, vital, and believable human bodies.

"Boy," Suellen said. "Not bad for graffiti." She waved a hand over it, displacing a cloud of flies. "God, it stinks in here."

"I've seen worse in the Uffizi, and it stinks there too," Taylor said. "OK, turn around."

Suellen turned. On the facing wall was the same couple, the male figure still sprawled unmoving, the woman now kneeling erect by his side. Her arms were outstretched in anguish, her face drawn with sorrow. Again, the figures were rendered with such sureness and economy that they seemed to float within a space completely other than the cracked and fly-specked wall. And their heads, now fully revealed, were of an immediacy that transcended the crude medium – some mix of crayon and fingerpainting, or maybe a sticky brownish charcoal, Suellen thought. Not only were the faces expressive, but – without any of this being clearly represented, only implied by the sparse precision of the features and a few feathery lines of charcoal – one seemed to see behind them into the skulls, the brains and blood and membranes of the human mechanism.

"My God," Suellen said. "My God above. It's – what's that thing? Leonardo, Michelangelo, one of those guys?"

"The Pietà," Taylor said. "Mary grieving over the dead Jesus. Nobody can get in to see it any more, it's so mobbed you can't get even a glimpse. I saw it one time, a guy took me in after hours. It's fantastic, a beautiful thing. If it was a drawing instead of a statue, it might look like this."

"Then what's with the kiss? A porno pietà? Did Annie Godfire draw this kind of stuff?"

"I don't think so," Taylor said. "Look at the faces again. Don't let yourself look through them, the way I guess you're supposed to. Just look at the surface."

Suellen looked, and felt as she had when Harve landed on her. "No way," she whispered. "No possible way."

"If it was a Pietà," Taylor said, "Mary would be giving Jesus CPR, and it wouldn't be working. But it's Morgan and Cesco, after his swimming accident." He pointed to small initials at the bottom of the first drawing, "FM."

Suellen stood between the walls, turning from one to the other, between Morgan's frantic hovering, her despair, Cesco's inertness; and yet the pulsing of life within them both. And the swarm of flies walking over them, probing and dabbling. "It's unbelievable," she said at last. "What are you going to do?"

"Do?"

"Your kid's suddenly a genius. Or autistic. Or both. Whatever, this stuff ought to be in a museum somewhere."

Taylor laughed through a mask of fear. "Oh, right." He wiped his eyes, and his shaking fingers sketched a museum label. 'F. Maryland, Pietà. Charcoal and excrement on Formica.' They'll love that in Raleigh."

15.

After Taylor dropped Suellen and took off for town, thumbing a cell phone, Suellen was at loose ends. She folded the wreckage of the chaise and put it next to the shed with other bulky trash. She wandered around the house gathering laundry – standing with the Jiffy-lube coveralls in her hand, considering, shrugging, coming back to herself with no notion of what she'd been thinking about for a full three minutes.

Suellen realized she was low on blood sugar, groceries, and cash. The solutions to all three were in town, and she didn't much fancy going there. Still, she couldn't sit out here on the Swamp Road like a troglodyte. She pulled the crushable dress out and put it on over the Umbro shorts and a bra she dug out of the back of Bethany's closet shelf. The bra was too big, which did nothing for Suellen's mood; she cinched it in and fastened it on the last hook, and managed to achieve a slight rounding in the vee of the crushable dress that anybody that wanted to could damn well have a look at, and she hoped he did, so she could flatten the sucker, whoever.

Snarling into downtown Gabbro at one in the afternoon, she went to the Gabbro Prudent ATM, got a fistful of twenties big enough that she could imagine a slight sucking sound somewhere in Tennessee, broke one of them at the Terminal for a chili dog, fries and a Blenheim's, and walked down the street to the Suds-Ease, her mouth ablaze and the crushable dress swirling in the drowsy sunshine. When the laundry was started – not enough for separate white and colored loads, so integrated aslosh in cold water – she retrieved the Triumph and blatted north to the County Building on 73 Bypass.

The Office of County Security was quiet and almost abandoned, but there was a motherly-looking presence bending over droopy aspidistra with a watering can.

Suellen cleared her throat. "Vera Jo?"

The motherly lady pursed her lips, finished her watering, and put the can on the floor. When she'd wiped her hands, and a couple of drops that had got on the windowsill, she straightened and lifted an eyebrow at Suellen. "Vera Jo's sick."

"Sorry to hear it. Tucker told me y'all had a fax for me from Commander Hillemeier, Tennessee Highway Patrol."

"Captain Pardee said that? And you would be?"

"Corporal Suellen Ransom," Suellen said. Not to get into a pissing contest with the help.

"Let me look," the woman who was not Vera Jo allowed. Like it would be a strain to remember just one from the deluge of faxes this little place got in a day.

"No," she said after a painstaking shuffle through six or eight papers on a work table, and two that had fallen on the floor. "Nothing here for a Corporal Anybody. Couple patrolmen, a deputy, and a sergeant. Then, of course, quite a number for himself." This with a toss of her grandmotherly head toward a closed door marked Sheriff Tucker Pardee. Sorry,

Miss."

"Did you," Suellen said, picturing the grey head shaved, with a wet sponge on it, "look at the names, or just the ranks? Thing is, I resigned from the force last week, so he might have addressed it just by my name."

"Oh, dear," the woman murmured to the aspidistra. "I'll have to look through them again."

"I'd be glad to do that for you, if you're busy. Won't take a second, I'd recognize my own name in a flash."

"Nice of you, I'm sure, but no. Just a moment, please." She picked up the handful of paper again, dropped one, sighed, picked it up. "Would it be <u>Sergeant</u> Suellen?"

"Not last I knew. Does it say Ransom?" Just slip your legs into these clamps, please, ma'am.

"Ransom?"

"My last name, Ma'am," Suellen said, marveling a little at herself. It must be something in the water here. "Suellen Ransom."

"Yes, that's what it says."

"Well, that's me." Suellen cocked her head at the woman. "Is Vera Jo this ... this careful?" Again, she marveled. She'd meant to say, this fucking dumb.

"I'm sure I don't know. I certainly hope so. The Director of Homeland Security has instructed all of we in the First Responder Community to be just as careful as if the lives of everyone in Gabbro depended on just exactly this kind of apparently innocent transaction."

"Quite right, too. Look. Evidently somebody back in Knoxville made a mistake addressing the fax. I bet anything I'm the only Suellen Ransom in Gabbro and all its contiguous counties. Here's a picture ID, issued by the State of Tennessee."

The woman took Suellen's ID. "It says Corporal."

Suellen fastened a 2000-volt beanie down on the wet sponge, pulled the switch, and smiled serenely. "Funny. That's what I asked about. I think the 'Sergeant' business is just a dumb mistake by some part-time … Some new hire. Suellen Ransom, that's me." She plucked the fax from reluctant pink fingers and slammed out into humid sunshine.

Sergeant Suellen Ransom
c/o Tucker Pardee, Sheriff
Gabbro NC 29987

Suellen Ransom:

You are hereby reinstated, advanced in rank to Sergeant, and requested to report to THP District 11 Headquarters, Knoxville, as soon as practicable, to undertake duties assigned to you as instructing mentor, Protected Class I-F of the Tennessee Highway Patrol. This offer of reinstatement and advancement expires at noon on the fifth business day from this date. Your acknowledgement thereof, and your declared intention to undertake the assigned duties is due in this office at that time.

(Signed) Harold B. Hillemeier, Commandant, District Eleven

(Suellen, for God sake, please get your act back here. Assemblywoman Smiley and her lardbutts give me a batch of half-trained trooperettes that couldn't stop a perp in a bumper car, and don't have the first idea of discipline, investigation, self-defense, or any damn thing else but looking good in the uniform. All the regular troopers are scared to get tough on them. I need you bad to whip some moxie into the best two or three, and you can wash out the rest. Please notice, I said Please)

"You gonna go?" Tucker eased himself out of County Ten, balancing a paper cup of Terminal coffee and a doughnut, smiling sunnily at Suellen's new cleavage.

Suellen let herself wonder for a half-second why he couldn't keep his eyes off the top three-sixteenths of a breast, but wouldn't look at the whole thing on a bet. "You always read other folks' mail?"

"SOP, Honey. It said, 'Care of' me. Got my name on it, I'd have Homeland down my chimney quicker'n antshit if I passed on information that endangered a national asset. Turned out otherwise this time, a course, but how was I to know till I read it?"

"I see. Well, I'll have to let him know in the next two days if I'm going to. What does Mary Worth in there think about it?"

"Mary … aw, you mean Flora. Don't mind her. She's the

wife's cousin, not much I can do about her. She fills in when Vera Jo's got the monthlies, or otherwise unable to perform her duties. Flora's got a permanent case of the monthlies, so it don't hinder her none. Anyways, she don't hold an opinion on your opportunity, there, one way or the other."

"Really. You're sure you encouraged her to speak her mind on it? I'd have sworn she was doing her damnedest to keep me from doing anything at all. I haven't made up my mind yet. You've had longer to think about it, so what do you think?"

Tucker grinned. "Course, we've always missed you pretty bad around here, you and your queer pals and your hookers and your camera. Somebody told me you'd done some good, tough time in the Marines. I'd hate to be some pretty little thing, got put on the Tennessee Patrol outa politics, drew you for a DI. You'll have the poor things beggin for mercy before lunch."

He pushed his hat back and scratched a thinning crop of grey. "Still, not kidding around on this, thanks for finding the Maryland kid. You done me a mighty good turn on that. I hate like fury to get FBI poking where they got no goddamn business."

He shrugged amiably. "Summing it up, one thing an' another, you look just plain stunning in that dress, they's no other word for it. Partic'ly the way the periwinkle tones coordinate with them shiners. Have a pleasant afternoon, sweetheart."

*

The mixed load – a little less contrasting in color, but clean – went into a dryer along with a handful of quarters, and Suellen was at loose ends again. Standing in the Suds-Ease doorway, she looked across drowsy College Avenue to the office of the Gabbro <u>Intelligencer-Bee</u>, that had been the focus of 55 years of Faye Bynum's life.

And in fact, there was a poster in the window that said as much. "Faye Bynum: A Half Century and Then Some." The sunshine on College Avenue seemed suddenly harsh and lifeless; Suellen scuffed across the street to see what else the poster had to say.

<u>A Half Century and Then Some</u> was the title of the books stacked in the window, slender and looking home-printed, with a primary green cover and lettering that looked like what you used to get on the boxes of toys imported from Japan. "The wisdom and insight of Gabbro's hometown chronicler, selected columns from the Gabbro <u>Intelligencer</u>, 1948 – 2003." the poster explained.

The topmost copy was sunstruck to a dubious pale turquoise. But the picture of Faye – taken during the '60's, at the latest – was crisp enough. She looked handsome, Suellen saw, with a pang. At the bottom of the jacket was an endorsement: "Faye Bynum is North Carolina's irrepressible and irreplaceable answer to Abe Martin" – Jack Fogg, The Charlotte <u>Observer</u>"

Suellen was surprised, and a bit scornful, that there was no mention of Faye's recent passing in the window. She went through the door into a plummy-smelling gloom. From somewhere in the depths, she heard the chatter and clank of an offset press, and a phone warbling. Suellen spotted the apparent receptionist behind a good-sized flat-screen monitor when he picked up the phone.

"Intelligencer-Bee," he said, continuing to type. "No, ma'am, we close on classifieds 36 hours before press time." The kid rolled his eyes at the ceiling, thereby spotting Suellen, and got brisk. "No, ma'am. We'd be more'n glad to print your notice in the Monday edition, but – Yes, I understand your sale is this weekend. I'm sorry, but there is just no way in heck we can print an ad for it in the Friday paper. That edition went to bed – Yes, ma'am. Give us 48 hours next time. Yes, Ma'am?"

It took Suellen a bit to realize he was talking to her. His gaze danced a little triangle from one breast to the other to her eyes, and around again, while he groped for the phone cradle. Suellen leaned over the counter to settle him down.

"Can I buy a copy of Faye Bynum's book from you?" she purred.

"Certainly. Yes, ma'am. Sure can." He rose and backed away from the counter, wrenching his eyes to the shelf of green books against the far wall.

"Good. I was a little surprised you didn't have anything in your window about her passing on last week."

The kid stopped on his way to the bookshelf. "Huh?"

"I said, I was a little surprised – "

"Yeah," the kid said. "I heard you. Celeste? Hey!

Celeste?"

"What, fer Chrissake?" A woman leaned out of a door in the back wall, spotted Suellen, and giggled. She looked like carrying about 280 pounds under the Santa sweatshirt and track pants. "'Scuse my French, Miss. What?"

The reception kid looked apologetic. "When'd you say Miz Faye called about her retirement ?"

"What about it? She don't get no cost of living till July, I told her that six months ago."

"What I ast was, when was it she called?"

"Yes'dy afternoon, three minutes to five like she always does, the old biddy. Somebody got issues with her? They can get in line."

Suellen leaned on the counter, for lack of a dignified alternative. "What?"

"What, what, ma'am?" the kid asked.

"Somebody called and said they were Faye Bynum? Didn't she … I thought I heard …"

"She'd passed on? Don't think so, ma'am. We're fixin to run her column tomorrow, which she sent it in two days ago, right on the dot."

Suellen gave herself 30 seconds to formulate a response to this latest perfidy from Harve, telling her Faye Bynum was dead - what was it, "done passed very suddenly, over lunchtime?" - before leaning into a headlong stomp that made people jump out of her path ten yards away. She made furious stops at the Suds-Ease, Brenda's Happy Notions, the County

Library's internet room, the Shade Shack and McLain Hardware (where a grizzled clerk risked the last four years of his life by asking how the other guy looked) before she straddled the Triumph and blammed herself out to Swamp Road. Once there, she stripped off the dress and threw it on the closet floor, and settled down with the Jiffy-lube coveralls, a pair of sewing scissors, needle and thread.

While she worked, she allowed herself to consider which would piss her off more, that Harve had lied to her about Faye's death, or that Inglenook was somehow trying to scam a corpse's retirement check out of the Intelligencer. Harve hadn't known she was coming to visit Faye that afternoon, couldn't have known Suellen in the first place, when he set to work packing up Faye's room. Why would he lie? And she'd seen the County ambulance loafing back toward Gabbro, in no more hurry than a hearse. Which proved nothing, of course, but Suellen believed in her bones that Faye was dead. Otherwise seemed impossible, however she might wish it. The body is wiser than the will.

Much easier to believe that Judith Welles would authorize a small lucrative fraud – or more likely, a whole string of them, an SOP of one postmortem payment from every newly deceased client before the public announcement of death made it official – than that Harve would lie to a stranger for no reason. She sighed, ground her teeth, and began snipping threads. Whoever was scamming on this was going to bleed for it.

In less than an hour, the Jiffy-lube logo on the coverall pocket had morphed to Julie. She briefly considered Jeff, certainly a lot less cutting and patching, but faking a pants number was more than she wanted to try, on top of the mountain of deception she would already be climbing when she got to Inglenook. She put the coveralls on, clipped her new rubber-covered five-cell flashlight on one of its belt loops, clipped a stack of zoning variance appeal forms she'd downloaded from Gabbro.gov on her new aluminum-frame clipboard, put on the deep blue sunglasses from Shade Shack, and the hard hat from McLain's, and checked the result in the mirror. Not too bad, once she changed the flats for biker boots and kicked the hard hat up and down the driveway to knock some of the shine off. Alternate kicks were for Nurse Welles and Harve.

*

"Francesco, if you don't feel like talking to us, that's perfectly all right," the therapist said. He turned to Giulia. "We see this kind of thing from time to time. Usually, it's temporary, a way of saying 'Nobody's listening to me.' Sometimes it helps to offer an alternative way to communicate. Do you think he'd do better writing down what he's feeling?"

Giulia opened her mouth, closed it again, and looked at Cesco. Negative head shake, followed by a shrug and a nod.

The therapist smiled. Get them talking one way or another, and you were halfway home. Before they realize it, they forget whatever kid vow is keeping them mute. "Miss

Bowen, could you bring Francesco a pad of paper please? And a pen or pencil?"

Miss Bowen did, with the firm good cheer of one who guards the office against the bizarre, the inappropriate, the constant undertow of threat from the sick who pass through it every day.

Giulia looked at Francesco, and her eyes were bright with tears. "Cesco, be a darling," she said in Italian. "Talk to Mama with the pencil."

Cesco sighed and said nothing, but his hands got busy while Giulia groped in her pockets and fanny pack for a tissue and blew her nose, and the therapist jotted things on his own notepad. And when, in thirty seconds, they turned to Cesco again, he was holding up the notepad and smiling.

On it, in fifteen or twenty lines – no hesitations, scribbles, or erasures – was Giulia. The eyes seemed to be bright with tears, though Giulia could not have said exactly how she knew that. There was no single line or mark of which you could say, See, here's how he made the tears. But the mouth was smiling, and the tears were tears of happiness. Behind the radiant, parted lips were a few shining teeth, behind them the hint of a tongue. In the lines that made up the whole, you could see that the teeth were rooted in the bones of a skull. And the skull, heavy and tender, was precisely Giulia's, from its shape to its angled repose on the neck, to the least slant of cheek and eye; and it echoed with the delight of being alive.

Giulia took one look at it and burst into tears.

16.

Suellen left the Triumph at the Inglenook gate and walked in whistling, paging through the blank zoning forms on the clipboard. She bypassed the main door and headed around the facade, looking for infrastructure. She found it in a loading dock at the back, a plain pipe railing instead of glossy extruded-aluminum handrails, and a scuffed bell button next to a brown steel door. She pushed at the door, and it swung open on a humming utility room. A bank of inscrutable machinery was providing the hum and, Suellen supposed, institutional amenities to the clientele. There was a cluttered desk with a fairly recent-looking jelly doughnut and an empty paper coffee cup. Suellen looked around for the sweet tooth and heard a toilet flush. A skinny, balding guy emerged from a door that bore a ripped-off gas station sign reading *Regular*. The monogram over his pocket said Rick. "He'p you, ?"

"Reckon so, I guess," Suellen said, trying to look virginal and wary like Carolyn Albright. "We got a complaint from the FCC, some kind of radio interference with flights out of F'etteville. They done triangulated it to this side of Gabbro or possibly toward Bozlee. But we gotta check all the nonresidential facilities, see if it's coming from some kind of PA or monitoring system. You got such a thing here?"

"Maybe. Who's 'we'?"

"Oh. Yes sir. I'm from Tennessee Highline Patrol, we're contracted with FCC for this kind of thing."

"See some ID?"

"Yes, sir. Excuse me just a secont." Suellen turned her back and pulled the coverall zipper down far enough to fish out her THP identity card, which she'd altered with Flair pens to what she figured was the most she could get away with, and clipped to a neck chain. She turned back and waved the thing over the swells and lacy bra-edges that the zipper uncovered, and tucked it back in, prissily re-zipping not quite all the way.

Rick seemed to consider something, his eyes a little out of focus, and he relaxed. "Uh huh," he said, "What do ya need?"

"Basically, access," Suellen said. "Though a Ladies' wouldn't hurt. You got a restroom I could use just a secont?"

"Down the hall, sign says No-Lead."

In the No-Lead, Suellen checked for peepholes and oddly placed mirrors, and saw none. When she thought she'd been in there long enough to get the guy good and interested, she lowered the zipper another couple of inches, flushed the toilet, and emerged, trying to look a little more relaxed. The guy was hanging up his phone and pulling out a set of diagrams.

"C'mere," he shrugged. "I'll show you what we got."

"I surely appreciate it. You'd be surprised, the push-back I get from folks some places. What we wont to do is, rule your facility out, not cause a lot of trouble. But there's a lot of high-frequency crosstalk out there any more. Other day a fella bringing in a Airbus from Singapore called up LAX tower, got a baby monitor instead. Kid was crying, the pilot like to wrack the thing 'fore they got it straightened out."

"Yeah. OK, you got your main building here, and the Maintenance facility, which is where we are. Got your Contagious suites here, and a couple storage facilities. Main and Contagious, they got room monitors. Maintenance staff generally use beepers and intercoms to stay in touch."

"Uh huh." Suellen leaned over the diagram, hunching a little to let the front of the jumpsuit sag. The guy gave it a glance, not much more than that. "The intercoms an' beepers FCC-approved?"

"Sure."

"Good. Is there a kind of central place where the monitors are, uh, monitored?"

"That'd be here in Main basement. Room 012. Want me to call him, tell him you're on the way?"

Suellen considered. She didn't much like this guy, and didn't want to be on his radar much longer. "Aw right, that'd be very nice of you, Mister ..."

"Tallon."

"OK, Mr. Tallon. I'm Julie Morgan. I appreciate your help."

"Yeah. Come to think, I got an errand in Main. I'll walk you over."

This was just what Suellen didn't want, a lot of attention and seamless handing-off from one staffer to the next. First thing, she'd be in Judith Welles' office, and the jig would be up.

And she hadn't even really decided what jig it was in the first place. When they stood outside the little office, Suellen put a finger to her mouth.

"Orient me a little, here. Over there's the main buildin', and – I guess that'd be your Contagious facility?" She cocked her head at a low brick building, more pipe railings and painted concrete instead of the brass and limestone of the Main facade.

"That's right. Hope you didn't want to get in there. Got folks with any number a complaints, West Nile down to pneumonia. You'd need a Level Three clean suit to go in."

"Well, I hope I won't, for sure," Suellen said, wide-eyed. "Let me talk to your fella that runs the monitors. Good chance we can rule out your facility right from there."

"Come on."

Tallon led her up a dirt track to the back of the Main building, and in a ground-level entrance, again of the steel practicality that clients would rarely see, but was good enough for staff. He stopped at a door marked "AUTHORIZED ONLY" and knocked.

A voice said, "Wha - " and Suellen heard a drawer open and shut. "Just a second, coming," the voice added, and a pudgy kid with a shaved head opened the door. He zoomed right in on the negligently zipped coverall, and Suellen felt this might be someone she could work with.

"Yuh?"

"Julie here's checking radio emissions for the FCC. She needs to talk to you about the monitors and such," Tallon said.

"Gimme a call when you're done, OK?"

"OK," the kid said. Suellen clutched her clipboard to her chest and sidled into the kid's lair, walking with what she hoped would read as a vulnerable and virginal bounce. She didn't much like the way Tallon said "Julie," with little quotes in the wiggle of his eyebrows. She was glad to see him walk off toward the front of the building.

"Look," she said to the kid. "I cain't tell you how many nursing homes, hospitals, an' what all I done site visits on this, and they all checked out clean. Thing is, we got a fella call in the other day, claimed he was in approach to F'etteville and his contact with the tower broke off, got some kind of modulated interference as he passed over Inglenook. Said it sounded like an old lady, which I expect you got quite a lot, here. He couldn't hear the tower, and pretty near slammed into a Southwest out of Atlanta on the runway. We run some tests, and it looks like it's coming either from here or from your Contagious facility over there."

The kid puckered his lips. "This old lady mention a name?"

Suellen smiled and tried to look cool while she peeked into the clipboard, tucking it against the coverall to give the kid fast frames of skin behind the flipping zoning forms. "Here it is, yeah. This was pretty distorted, mind. You got anybody name of Byer? Or Byner?"

"Nope. Wait, sure, there ya go." The kid's eyes narrowed shrewdly. "How about this? Jimmy Dyer, in 116."

"He sound like an old lady?"

"Naw, that's right."

Suellen inhaled, exhaled, eyes closed, and got a wet sponge ready for the shaved head. What I get, trying to be cute. "Do you got a resident list I might could look at? Maybe something would jump out at me."

The kid scowled and raised his chin, managing to look like Mussolini with zits. "Sorry, miss. That's confidential information. I'm not supposed to – "

"Goodness, of course. You can bet your sweet life it will not go beyond just the two of us. Thing is, we'd both be in trouble if it was to be a plane crash. We got Homeland all <u>over</u> our behinders on this." Suellen raised her eyes from the clipboard and gave the kid the wide-eyed look her mother taught her. But even Trudi Ransom had never tried it wearing coveralls and a hard hat. The kid's breath caught, and he stepped back, reached behind him, and pulled a printed list of names from a magnetic clip on a file cabinet.

"Numbers without a prefix is Main, 'C' is Contagious," he said, hardly moving his lips.

"Bless you, dear," Suellen chirped, and she all but chucked the kid under the chin.

The list was ordered by room number, not by name, so she had to read through the whole main building before she got to C-102 Bynum, Faye.

Suellen fought for a level, sprightly voice over tension and a growing streak of anger. "This list up to date?" But before she finished asking, she saw the date at the top.

"New list every day, sometimes twice a day," the kid said. "Old folks like this, you got a lot of turnover."

"Mm-hm. Well, this Bynum, now. Says 'Faye,' so she's a lady, I take it."

"Not that much of a lady, but she's female, more or less."

"Mm-hm." Suellen forced herself to keep reading through the list, praying against any other Byers or Byners. When she finished, and there were none, she made herself smile at the young Benito and give him the list back.

"You better hang on to this. I wouldn't want you to get into no trouble on my account. Thanks ever so much, hear? Looks like I'd need to have a look at this Miz – what was it? – Bynum. Her room."

"You're just gonna look? You didn't bring no equipment?"

"Out'n the truck. If I need it, I'll get it. Usually, you kin tell just by looking. So that's the Contagious facility over there?"

"Yup. But you can't go in there, not dressed like that." He considered. "Less you wanted to stay there the rest of your life." He turned to his console and picked up a phone. "I'll call Security, get you a throw-away clean suit. You'll have to take off them clothes you got on now, or – "

The kid broke off because Suellen, driven by frustration, fury, and the relishy undertone when the kid said 'take off them clothes,' lost patience with subterfuge, and popped him behind the ear with her five-cell flashlight.

"In your dreams, zit-face," she breathed, while the flashlight lens skittered across the floor. The kid turned halfway around. He waved the phone and seemed to grope for words of protest, but his eyes were already slits of white. He collapsed across his keyboard. Suellen frowned, hung up the phone, and opened drawers in his desk until she found what he stashed when Tallon knocked: Caged Kittens in Kabul. Suellen flipped open the graphic novel to a half-pager of a cheerleader wearing a pleated skirt and a wrist pom-pom, tied to a chair with some kind of ayatollah gloating in the background. She sniffed. Little heavy up top for my taste.

She pulled the kid off of his keyboard so it would stop saying, "^R^R^R^R^R," dumped him on the floor with the cheerleader across his lap, and fingered a little of the oozing scrape from his skull onto the corner of his desk, making him mutter and protest, but he didn't wake up. Why, my land, he was jes' fine when Ah left him.

Operating now without even shreds of the plan she'd brought into this, Suellen zipped the coverall and walked into the sunshine, shuffling papers on her clipboard, heading for the low brick outline of the Contagious suite. C-102 had to be on the first floor near one end, right? Just four possibilities, assuming a center hall.

And, hey, no problem, except that the door to the center hall was locked tight at both ends, with biohazard warning signs; and that the first floor was elevated enough that the windows began five feet over Suellen's head. The only way she could get a look in them was to nab a wheelbarrow that was leaning against the maintenance building, trundle it under each window in turn, leap from it to grab the windowsill, and chin herself against it. The tedium was hardly lightened when the first window showed her a room full of cleaning supplies, and the second an old gent with a Hustler in his lap and his hand under the covers. The third window, though, was open. It had a browned-off tea rose on the sill and Faye Bynum behind that, paging through a copy of the Gabbro *Intelligencer-Bee*. Faye looked up from the paper, sniffed, and tossed it on the floor. "Well, for the land's sake. Where you been, Blondie?"

"Same to you, lady. Why'd they sneak you off here and tell me you were dead?"

"They thought I was. Fooled them suckers, though."

"What?"

"I took a real bad angina, liked to kill me. I come around in the ambulance, with a EMT pumping on my chest. They tooken me in to Memorial, but then they had a five-car out'n the bypass, and Doc Howard tells me he needed the ICU beds. Said if that'n didn't kill me the next one would, or nothing. So I got a 50-50 chance, the way I see it."

"Wait a second," Suellen grunted. "I'm getting a cramp in my fingers." She pushed herself off from the wall to clear the wheelbarrow, dropped to the ground, and stood the thing against the wall. Climbing onto a brace between the handles gave her a perch that allowed a precarious and tiptoe line of sight into Faye's room.

"Why'd they put you in here?" she puffed. "Angina isn't contagious."

"Thank your stars, Hon, or you'd be looking over your shoulder like me. Time the EMT's got me back out here, they'd already stuck an old boy in my room that's got more money than me. This is temporary. <u>They</u> say. What they mean is, they don't look for me to live long enough to bother with anything else."

Suellen all but bit the windowsill with fury. When she found Harve, she would kick the lying bastard inside-out. Meanwhile – "OK, Faye. Meanwhile, please. I'm not going to try for subtlety and reading clues in a journal – much as I admired it, by the way, and I really want to sit down with you one of these days. But right now... well, can I get a straight answer from you? What happened to Hap Maryland? Is he dead? Or in Boston? Or did they hide him away somewhere? Or what?"

Faye rolled her eyes. "Oh, Honey. Believe me, this is not something you want to know."

Suellen threw up her hands. "Not something I want to know? I just asked you. Who are you, for Christ's sake? Goddamn Harve in disguise?"

Faye shrugged, and drew away from Suellen. "I'm sorry, I'm sure. Maybe I should have said, this is really not something I want you to know. Not something I got a right to tell anybody. Even you." As Faye turned her head away, Suellen felt a tug on the sleeve of the coverall, and a garden rake grated against the brick wall. Rigid with anger, she knocked the thing away, but the wheelbarrow tipped and dumped her on the gravel below Faye's window, at the feet of Mr. Rick Tallon and a security guard. Tallon didn't offer her a hand up.

"Miss, this is a secure area to all but authorized personnel. Can you explain why you feel you have authorization to disturb our patients and endanger your health and that of everyone you contact?"

Suellen got to her feet, trying for dignity without dropping the virginal pose. "I done went over that with your boy in the monitoring office," she said. "I need to see the setup in here, without getting in the building. I was follering one of the monitor wires."

"Yeah? What wire was that, Missy?"

Suellen tossed her head at the much-painted window frame. "My mistake, I reckon. Looked t'me like a wire, turned out to be weather-strippin'."

"Yeah. How'd you like to show Officer Krupa here that ID you waved at me a while ago? I gotta say, I never got much of a look at it."

That was the idea, Suellen thought. But she turned her back and undid the zipper, wondering how bad they could make this for her. When she turned around, with as much zipper undone as she thought Miss Julie Morgan might have allowed if she was dead drunk, Harve was there next to Officer Krupa, grinning at her.

"Hey ... Julie," he said. "My stars, what brings you to Inglenook? You still with that Tennessee outfit?

"Tennessee Highline Patrol," Suellen said, nostrils flaring. "Contracting with FCC. Seems like your bug – your monitors is interfering with aviation some." She narrowed her eyes at Harve. Get me out of this, Harve, so I can kick your balls to Boston.

Harve looked thoughtful. "Seems like I seen something in the paper about that," he said. He grinned at Tallon. "You don't wanta cross this little lady, Ricky. We was in high school, she tossed some jackass was bothering her? Four <u>feet</u> into a pile of tomata stakes, like to kill the guy. She's prob'ly toughened up some since then. Listen, Krupa, it was you I come looking for. Old McLain's serenading the south wing with Cry Me a River again, can't nobody shut him up. You think you could come along and show him reason? I got a family looking the place over for Grandpa, and the lady's fixing to take apoplexy, kids giggling, it's got the residents all in a knot."

Krupa looked at Tallon, who shrugged. "You vouching for this little – this person?" he asked Harve, tipping his head at Suellen.

"Shine," Harve twinkled. "She got more vouch already than Santa got elves. Vouchiest lady I ever knew. I'm just sayin, I been knowing her from third grade, never knew her to tell a fib but one time, which was about who sent me a valentime. She's been with Tennessee Highway Partners for years, helped us out of a scrape over'n Kinston one time. Julie's a straight shooter. She says you got a problem, you likely got one."

*

"Much as I appreciate your assistance back there," Suellen said when Harve had walked her to the Inglenook gate, "don't think it bought you a damn thing. I cannot fucking stand being lied to, Mr. E. Briggs Harvey." She threw a leg over the Triumph and, remembering, zipped the coverall back into place.

"Harve," Harve said. "Just call me Harve, most everybody does. About Miz Bynum?"

"For a start, yes. What else did you want to bring up? There must be – "

"Who told the first lie, can you tell me that?"

"You."

"Wrong."

Suellen started the Triumph and revved it. "You told me Faye Bynum was dead. 'Miz Bynum done passed suttenly,' I believe was your choice of words. Unless that was a goddamn ghost – "

Harve put a hand over Suellen's on the throttle. "At the time I told you that, I and all the staff at Inglenook thought she did. Not my fault she was alive. We can skip over the handsome display of erogenous parts you put on before I ever opened my mouth, though that wasn't exactly straight shooting, Miss Julie – course, it wasn't exactly a lie, neither, come to think of it. Then the next thing anybody said was something about Miz Faye being the best darn teacher you'd ever had, and I don't know what all hogwash. Then it was 'Ah'm waitin heah for a friend, you wont to bah me a beer?' And 'Call me Suellen,' and sucker punches, and 'C'mon up the spirit catcher by moonlight, chicken.' Yeah, and 'Maybe we can figure out something,' sure. Right now, I'm kinda racking my brain to think of anything you told me, I can be sure is real."

Suellen found her hand lingering on the ignition key, and with a sigh, she shut off the Triumph. "Well," she said. "You got some points there, one way of looking at it."

She looked at Harve, and immediately looked away, before she lost her steam. "You still never told me the truth about Faye, after you must have found out. You pretended you didn't know who Hap Maryland was. You … oh, you told me so many lies, I can't remember them all. You jerked me around like a fish, you loaded me with beer and dope and took me to bed, and all the time, you were just so full of bullshit and spin and jive and play-along, I can't think of a bad enough name for it. You make Bill Clinton look like George Washington." She snorted a little, unable to keep her mouth from curling. "Tennessee Highway Partners, for God's sake."

Harve snorted back. "That, of course, was the God's truth, wannit? Gimme credit for getting the tune an' the first couple chords. And if the bed thing was distasteful to you, you covered up admirably, Blondie. I already told you, somebody jives me right off the bat, I'm gonna jive them back till I find out what they're after. And then maybe for a while, just to make sure. Even when it happens I'd rather be jived by you than sung to straight by Ella Fitzgerald."

Suellen tossed her head and reached for the ignition. Harve held up a hand. "However, I can see you feel deeply about something here. Maybe you figure there's some true thing behind it worth lying for. I would be willing to tell you one thing straight about all this, if you'll do the same for me."

"Yeah? What would that straight thing be?"

"My full official, administrative name at this time and for a good while to come."

"Wow. And what would you want in exchange for that priceless information?"

Harve put his hands in his back pockets and shrugged. "I don't know. Maybe just a break. Maybe some little insight into why you're going after Hap Maryland and Inglenook like a rat terrier."

Suellen took a breath, almost run dry on anger, but reluctant to let it go. "All right, shoot. What <u>do</u> they call you in administrative circles, Harve? No, wait, let me see if I can guess. Uh, … Captain Harvey? Agent Harvey? Don Giovanni? Staff Liar Briggs?"

"137596 Harvey, Edward Briggs. Five ninety-six, for short."

Suellen gaped at him. "Fi … You're a con?"

"A loser, I think you like to put it. That's right. I'm out on parole. I fuck up once, get out of line, make the least little wave to piss off Nurse Welles, I'm back in Raeford for another five to fifteen."

Suellen sighed. "In other words …"

"In other words, I'm about as far from being a free agent in this as it's possible to get."

17.

Francesco and Morgan were sleeping; their elders sat in the back yard, sipping cool drinks and discouraging mosquitoes.

Suppose," Plummer Baley said diffidently; "Suppose Cesco is not allowing himself to talk because he doesn't trust his tongue not to betray him? Maybe this is some form of penance for his cursing and bad language. I try not to sound like this, most of the time, but the ways of the Almighty truly are beyond human understanding."

Taylor clenched his jaw and said nothing for four seconds, then could hold it no longer. "Bullshit," he snorted. "What gives you the almighty gall to invoke the hand of God in striking a young boy dumb? You'd sound different if it were your kid. Talk about dumb!"

The last was muttered, but not inaudibly. Plummer sighed and nodded, but Bethany said, "Calm down, Taylor, you sound like you're thirteen, still. You're upset by Cesco's not talking, and of course who wouldn't be? But you're overlooking some other changes. He's amiable and gentle, and his artistic talent is amazing, and truly God-given. The biggest thing is how happy he seems."

Ginnie North, back from the beach and looking tired and sandy, flipped a hand. "The source of Francesco's artistic talent is hardly a matter of theology. He's my grandchild. These things skip a generation, Taylor, so of course you never amounted to much in the arts. But your son didn't fall far from the family tree."

"So," Taylor said. "If you had to choose between art and speech, Mom – not that you ever did – which would you pick for yourself?"

Giulia sighed, and put a gentling hand on Taylor's arm. "Of course, we are alarmed but also intrigged."

"Intrigued," Taylor said grumpily. "I suppose. If you can be 'intrigued' by your son turning into an idiot-savant."

"Oh, for God's sake, Taylor." Bethany stamped her foot. "He's nothing of the sort, and you know it. He's gone through a life-threatening experience, and then a – sure, pretty much a kidnapping, sure, I admit it. Though that piece of silliness doesn't seem to have done either of them any real harm. Anyone his age would be affected by it. You're probably lucky he found some way to cope with it."

"First drawing I see," Giulia said, "I break into tears. But I don't think they are the tears of joy that he draw. Tears of puzzlement, maybe, mix of fear and joy. And anger. Are we to have a boy who seems happy and draws like an angel, but cannot talk? Who would want that?"

"For themselves, or for their child?" Ginnie asked. "There are two other choices here, and both of those came out the good way. Dead or alive – and he's alive, thanks to Morgan. And happy or unhappy. I'm not sure that what we see is all there is, but Cesco was unhappy, and making everyone else unhappy. Bethany's right, he seems very happy. Maybe to him, drawing feels like talking now. Look at Giulia, trying to show how she felt by talking about it, when Cesco got it better and more gracefully in less time by drawing it. The boy gave his mother some very good advice. Cry, but cry for joy. He's operating on another plane just now, where the truth of things isn't to be found in words. Maybe he'll come back to earth, but if he never does, so what?"

Taylor blinked at her. "Goodness, Mom," he said. "I don't agree with one word of that, but it's an awfully mellow thing to hear from you, I must say."

Ginnie smiled lazily and patted snoozing Silvio's knee. "I admit, he will have difficulties getting through life without words. Did anyone ask Francesco why he's not talking?"

"Sure," Taylor said. "He shrugs his shoulders and smiles. And draws something, like as not."

*

Somebody was whispering and scratching at the screen behind the honeysuckle. "Aunt Suellen?"

Suellen groaned and pulled the sleeping bag over her head, giving Harve an elbow in the face. He grunted and buried it in a pillow. One thing had led to another with Suellen and Harve again, though this time there was hardly any role-playing. There were a few half-smiles, shrugs, small touches, an early check-out from work by Harve, and the almost wordless acknowledgement on both sides that, after the fireworks and the house-to-house combat of their last encounters, never simply and mutually taking each other to bed was unthinkable. And if not never – well, why not now? The result, for Suellen's money, had been gentle, happy, and irritatingly gorgeous.

In fact, after Harve's revelation of his jailbird status, Suellen was mostly silent, realizing that if she said anything about it at all, it would have to be, What were you in for? And she just wasn't ready to learn that. Beyond stalking and murdering lesbians – and he'd had plenty of opportunity for that by now – there was nothing Harve could have done that would change how she felt about him. She just needed to figure out what the hell that was.

Christ, you fool, she thought, as she drifted toward sleep again. You don't boff men. There are consequences to boffing men, particularly the same one over and over. You could get used to it. Like they say happens in arranged marriages. If that wouldn't be the absolute crappiest cocked-up ball of balls … Boston …

"Aunt Suellen?"

"Wha. Yeah. . . What?"

"Please, I gotta talk to you."

"Who? Morgan?"

"Yes. Can I come in?"

"Just a second. Come to the kitchen door, OK?"

"Thank you." Morgan sounded pretty ragged, Suellen

thought. She leaned over and whispered, "Stay here, OK?" to unresponsive Harve, and slipped out of the sleeping bag. Hopping from one foot to the other, bumping into a wall, she got into a pair of shorts and a tee shirt on her way to the kitchen door.

Morgan looked ragged too. She was dressed in patched shorts and a pajama top, cross-buttoned and floppy over pale and vulnerable collarbones. She'd cut her hair, or maybe her mother had, to something fit for Joan of Arc.

"Aunt Suellen," she said. "Thank you for ... " She stopped and wiped her nose with the pajama sleeve. "Thank you for seeing m - muh ... meee, Oh, God, I am the most vicious, miserable brat ..."

That seemed to be all she could manage for a while.

"There, now, honey," Suellen whispered, and patted Morgan's hand. There was a watch on Morgan's wrist, but the kitchen was too dark to read it. "There. You're not vicious, or a brat, whatever else. You do seem kind of miserable. What is it?"

Morgan withdrew the hand, made a limp fist, and began to bang herself on the head. "I'm bad, that's what. I'm stupid. I need to just kill myself right now, and I would, but I know it would kill Mom."

"There, see? That's not a very vicious thing to say, right there. Bratty, either. Come on, let's take a walk."

Morgan looked up at Suellen. "Why do people always say that?"

"I didn't know they did. Seemed like a good thing just

now. Get out in the air, work out some sorrow, whatever." Get away from Harve. Suellen yawned achingly, torn between mentoring this little sister in need, and kicking her little butt the hell out and snuggling back with aromatic Harve to sleep and dream. Morgan turned and stumbled toward the door, and the back of her neck was so skinny that Suellen could do nothing but follow.

"Tell me," said Suellen under the stars, "why you feel so down about yourself."

"I am a little fool. I am so foolish and full of myself that it is a mortal sin."

"Funny. You sound anything but, unless you count being kind of focused on what a jerk you are. Think you are."

Morgan was silent while she walked toward Swamp Road. At the road, backlit by the first traces of dawn over Lake St. Luke, she turned and faced Suellen. "Oh, I'm a jerk, all right. Here's how big of a jerk: I was convinced for almost a year – almost a thirteenth of my entire life, mind you – that I was the child of Bethany Morgan Baley and Jesus Christ."

"Mm hm. Really. I guess this ties in with our conversation about stepfathers and real fathers and so forth. How'd you pick ol' Jesus?"

Morgan laughed, a single bleak syllable, and started to walk toward a glimmer of light a mile down the road. "Hey, some kids have their hearts set on, like, Harvard, politics, being President some day. I've always had a kind of religious streak, so 'Why not the best' there, too?"

"So what changed your mind?"

"Well. Start with Cesco's swimming accident. I saved his life with CPR, I guess you heard. Well, ha! Of course I did. Nothing's too tough for the daughter of Jesus Christ, is it? I gave God the thanks and credit, but God, how I hugged myself over that. The Saviour's kid, God's little handmaiden, works her first miracle, ohh! I'm like on <u>fire</u> with shame. At the blasphemy and the ... the vanity and pride. There's proof enough right there, if I'd had eyes to see it, what a jerk and a sinner I am.

"And then it turned out that Cesco, guess what, he wasn't completely OK. My first great miracle was rather <u>flawed</u>, actually. And while I was trying not to face that, while I was lying my head off to everybody I love, including you, Aunt Suellen, and praying to Jesus over Cesco like a kid pestering her daddy for a new pony, I talked to Mom, hoping to get her to ... I don't know. To prove I was right, by saying, Yes, my little one, your father came to me in a vision from the Angel Gabriel and like that. Instead, she ..."

Suellen sighed, and put an arm around the narrow shoulders beside her. "She told you about Derwood."

"Who?"

Suellen bopped her own head. "Shit. She didn't tell you his name?"

"Huh uh. She just told me what he'd done. She showed me the scars."

Suellen was silent for a dozen paces. "Well, forget what I said, then. He was everything your mother told you, and then some. He was a hateful, sadistic bastard and a fraud that should have been born in prison and stayed there."

Morgan crumpled to the sandy road. "So of course, that's why I'm the kind of wretched, rotten, stupid, vain ... Oh, God, I'm my father's daughter. That's what hurts so much."

Suellen bent over Morgan and pulled her up. "No, you're not. Did she also tell you that she completely read him out of her body and yours, during her pregnancy?"

"Something about that. I was so upset that I didn't pay much attention to it."

"Mm. Well, if you want somebody to feel good about in your family tree, you can start with your mother. Everybody, including me and your Grandpa, was yelling at her to have an abortion, but ..."

"She should have."

Suellen tightened her hold on Morgan. "No, huh uh. First of all, let me say, I had one once, and they're no fun. But you do it, and it's over with, for better of worse. Bethany wasn't going to go that way. You want a case of mind over matter, of complete mental and spiritual triumph, ask your mother to talk to you about that. She sat down for hours every day, and she – I don't know, she somehow visualized you, from a little ball of cells up to a full-grown baby, day by day, cell by cell and organ by organ, and she pictured herself going into every cell in every fold and bone of your body, and cleaning out all traces of Der – of the father. Of the guy that raped her, I mean. You think about that, Morgan. Every day for nine months, week in and week out, doing this … this spiritual thing so that when you came, you'd be completely clean and ready to start your life with Bethany as your mother and no one; and I mean no one at all, as your father. I never could have done it. Hell, I couldn't even stand to watch it. Not one woman in a billion could have done it. And don't ask me how it worked, but it worked. Derwood was gone. Maybe that's why you look only like your grandmother, if you want some explanation of that.

"And anyways, then, to top it off, one of the all-time great guys of this or a thousand other counties takes an interest in her, and understands what she's doing, admires her so much that he proposes, and marries her two seconds before you were born. There was never a kid born to better parents than you were. Speaking of Plummer here, not the other guy."

Morgan shrugged. "Well. So then why I am such a vain, stupid jerkpot?"

"I don't happen to think you are. You got an idea in your head – "

"A stupid, blasphemous idea. The kind of idea this, this Derwood, is that his name? The kind <u>he</u> would pass down."

Suellen waved a hand. "Whatever. The kind of idea people sometimes get, and once they get it, it's about impossible to get rid of it. If somebody told you to forget it, it would be like telling you not to think of a cow. You're stuck with it until something comes along that convinces you it's wrong. The really sad cases are the people that never get over their 'sinful ideas' … so called."

Morgan was silent long enough for Suellen to drift into half-conscious thoughts of Harve's admirable butt stuffed all by itself into the sleeping bag. What was she doing out here with this kid? The kid needs me, she thought, sleepily. The mind is wiser than the body.

Something wrong with that. The thought lasted until a tentative pallor spread over the sky and the packed sand of Swamp Road gave way to a stretch of gravel. Suellen's bare feet woke the rest of her to complain.

"Ow. I guess I need to turn around here, Morgan. I didn't think about shoes."

"I'm sorry I got you out of bed, Aunt Suellen. I didn't used to be so ..." She sighed. "Such a problem child."

They started back toward the Swamp Road house in growing light, the east's pallor now decorated with two or three orange wisps of high cirrus. Suellen patted Morgan's shoulder, and felt the pointy bones looking for meat. "Must be about time for breakfast. What say we hop on my bike and see if the Terminal's got their doughnuts ready yet?"

"I need to get home before Mom wakes up. I'm grounded." Morgan sagged against Suellen's hip, and Suellen felt warm tears spreading through the thin cotton of her shirt.

"Buck up, honey," she said. "Things will start looking better."

"It's not that. I did my best for Cesco, and it's not God's fault that it was a fool's best. I just all of a sudden missed Grandpa real bad. Sometimes he'd take me to the Terminal when they were baking doughnuts."

"Oh. I miss him too," Suellen said. "He was like a big brother to me."

"See," Morgan sniffled. "That's another thing I completely screwed up. That's when everything I did started to go wrong. That's why I pretty much turned into a recluse. If I didn't try to do anything with people, at least I wouldn't kill them."

"Oh, come on, Morgan, wait a second. You didn't kill your Grandpa."

Morgan was silent for seven or eight paces, and then put her arm around Suellen's waist. Suellen began to wake up and breathe softly. "Did you?"

"No," Morgan said, "but I didn't save him, either."

"Save him from what?"

"From – " Morgan broke off.

After another thirty unproductive seconds, Suellen prompted her. "From…?"

"I promised Jesus I wouldn't tell."

"Excuse me?"

Morgan shrugged, and said nothing.

Suellen begged herself for patience and a soft voice. "Morgan, honey, this could be real important. I loved your Grandpa, and so did a lot of other people. If you know something about where he is, or what happened to him, you can't hold … It's not fair to everyone else not to tell them."

Morgan turned a tearful face to Suellen, shaking her

head, looking as miserable as Suellen could imagine any kid looking. But she said nothing until they were back at the house.

"The Terminal," she hiccupped, "won't give you service if you're barefoot."

Suellen sighed. Easy does it, Babe, she told herself. How many people get a chance to cross-examine a material witness against a gag order from the Incarnate Word?

When they entered the kitchen, Harve was at the table with a cup of coffee. He wore Bethany's coarse-weave bathrobe with its hood over the back of his head. Suellen was chagrined to find that the figure in the half-light of dawn, and Harve's smile against the mahogany skin and flaxen robe, stirred a lust as sharp as fear. But Morgan stared at Harve, clutching Suellen's tee shirt with a corded fist, breathing hard and shaking her head, the Joan-of-Arc haircut blurring across her face .

"I ..." she managed. "I wasn't ..."

Her eyes fluttered and rolled back, and she collapsed at Suellen's feet.

When Suellen looked up at Harve, he was hunched over the table with his head in his hands.

"Damn it, Harve," she gritted. "I told you to stay put. Now look."

Harve sighed, and shook his head. "How'd I know you'd bring that particular kid in here? I can't stay in bed all day, I got early shift today."

"You know her?"

"We've met."

"Uh huh." Suellen's eyes narrowed. "This have anything to do with your serial number, Mr. Five ninety-six? Is that why you're in Raeford, for God's sake?"

"Of course not. Is that what you think of me, I'm some fucking sex offender? Shit, Suellen, thanks. I'm so goddamn glad I leveled with you on that, I could just split."

Harve stood and stomped out to the porch, leaving Suellen with her arm under Morgan's shoulders. By the time she'd carried Morgan into Bethany's bedroom and dropped her with brisk tenderness on the bed, she heard the kitchen door slam. She got to the front window in time for a quick sight of Harve stuffing himself into trousers, and he was in his car and gone before she got the front door open.

Suellen slumped against the door jamb, clutching her head, and walked back to the bedroom. Morgan's eyes were open.

"Did you see him?"

"Of course I did, Morgan." Suellen frowned and cocked her head at the pale face on the mattress. "Who?"

Morgan stared at her. "Well, Jesus."

*

Suellen got Morgan back to her house in time to meet Bethany exiting the garage with curlers in her hair and fire in her eye. Suellen felt Morgan's panicked fingers clutch her hips, and the hopeless thump of Morgan's head against her back.

"Let me do the talking," she muttered over her shoulder, and got a strangled monosyllable back.

"Lee Morgan Baley," Bethany called as they dismounted from the Triumph. "I recall a very specific order from your father and me, that you were not to leave this house without our permission. Get yourself in here, young lady."

"Um," Suellen said. "Would you be willing to listen to an extenuating circumstance?"

"I would not, thanks. Morgan is grounded under strict and specific orders. Didn't she tell you that?"

"She did tell me that, Beffie. But – "

"Then don't 'Beffie' me, Suellen. I don't know what you think you're doing, helping and defending this disrespectful behavior, but kindly stop, right now. Morgan is my daughter and a very considerable anxiety to me and Plummer. You could help me beyond measure by just for Pete's sake butting out."

It certainly was a temptation. The snarl of the Triumph would be the best answer to that righteous matronliness, and would get Suellen the hell and gone out of this mess besides. Damn Bethany! Damn Harve! Damn Morgan!

When she'd finished that, and then gone back to stick Faye Bynum into the litany, Suellen smiled gently and dismounted from the Triumph. At least Bethany had said "for Pete's sake" and not "in God's name" or some such. Suellen's whole willingness to stay with this hung from that frail thread of good nature.

"Bethany," she said. "Mrs. Baley. May I speak to you privately for just a moment? It will not have anything to do with this business. At least this immediate business."

"I suppose. Morgan, take yourself into the kitchen and make yourself known to your father."

"Yes, ma'am." Morgan slipped past Bethany and into the garage, looking like a collision with a mayfly would knock her sideways. Bethany watched her go, and turned to find Suellen beckoning from the shade of a pecan tree.

"C'mere, Beffie," Suellen said. "I need to ask you a couple questions."

"All right. Don't think you can – "

"Shut up, OK? Just shut up. You know I'm staying at your old house. I'm sleeping on the screen porch. Remember the screen porch?"

"Of course."

"Of course. Do you remember sitting out there with me?"

"Yes. I don't see what that has to do with anything."

"Yeah, nothing probably. Thing is, Beffie, I'm sleeping there because I can't bring myself to sleep in any of the bedrooms. Not Lee and Hap's, for sure. Not the ones you and Taylor had when you were kids, and not even the one Hap added on, back when we were – " Suellen waved a hand. "When we were committed to each other."

Bethany smiled, a little sadly. "That was a long time ago."

"Wasn't it, though. Still, in a way, it seems like no time at all, since he put that wing on the back of his house so you and I could live together in a relationship that he never approved of."

"I see. Is that the point here? Who am I to act the righteous parent when my own father indulged me in a lesbian relationship?"

Good for you, Einstein. "Wear it if it fits. I'm just trying to get you to see how much it means to me to try to understand what happened a year ago. Hap took me in like I was his own daughter, or daughter-in-law, I guess, because I told him I loved you, and that was good enough. What happened to him? Where is he? Why won't anyone who knows anything about it tell me what they know? Okay, I'm just a friend, I'm not a blood relation. Nobody is, but Taylor. But it's like no one else wants to know."

"That's not true at all, Suellen. Of course we want to know. We <u>been</u> wanting to know for a year. Just, wanting didn't make it happen, and doing our best to find him didn't, and we're kind of resigned to not knowing at this point. We need to figure out how to go on from not knowing."

"And Morgan, who was there when he disappeared, after all … Morgan won't give you any help?"

"I don't think she has any help to give. What she said is, they got separated when Hap went behind some bushes to pee. Sounds like he got disoriented, and didn't find his way back to where he'd left Morgan. By the time Morgan went to look for him, he was out of sight. And, I guess, earshot. It's confusing to follow sounds in a swamp."

Suellen shrugged. "Well, it's starting to look to me like Morgan might know more about it than she told you. That, and this business about Derwood, they're killing her, Bethany. She came out to Hap's in the middle of the night to talk to me, because she thinks she's an evil, blasphemous, I forget what all else, brat."

"Brat is getting close. The rest of it, of course - "

"Shut up. She had the idea that – well, she had some crazy ideas. When you told her about Derwood, it knocked them out of her with a bang. And then, she does seem to have some knowledge about Hap's death – if that's what it was – and on top of the other thing, it's killing her."

"And she came to talk to you about it, because …?"

Suellen sighed and shrugged. "Well. She might still be a little sore - hurting, I mean, not mad - from your conversation about Derwood. Or maybe it isn't the sort of thing she feels she can talk to her parents about. For whatever reason."

Bethany sighed, and leaned against the tree. "I'm not going to play the martyred mother here. If she'll talk to anybody at all, wonderful. What did she say?"

"All right. Here's what sense I can make of it. She was with Hap. She didn't say anything about getting separated. But she said she 'didn't save him' from something that was apparently scary, or big, or important enough that she promised Jesus she wouldn't discuss it with anyone."

"Promised Jesus?"

"Yep."

Bethany ground her teeth. "Honest to God, if I hear one more word about Jesus from that girl, or from anybody, including the Reverend Plummer Baley, I swear I'm going to throw up. For Christ's sake, why can't – "

"Man," Suellen said, "You make a vow, it's forever, isn't it?"

Bethany frowned. "Are we going to keep coming back to that? Can't we – "

"No, no. 'One more word about Jesus, I'm going to throw up, for Christ's sake.' "

"What? Oh." Bethany scowled and sniffed, and then couldn't stop a little snort of amusement. "Blehhh," she said, leaning over Suellen's lap. "Barf, bleph, burff." A little pop of emotion made her dig a knuckle into Suellen's ribs, and she hit a spot that Harve's fist had visited. Suellen doubled over.

"Ow! Ow, oof. I give. Ow, stop."

Bethany raised an eyebrow. "My stars, aren't you the delicate thing! I heard you were this big tough marine, and one little teeny – "

Suellen grabbed Bethany's arm, and they rolled in the grass, gritting their teeth, conflicted between laughter and the buried fury of their old selves. Bethany ripped handfuls of grass and threw them in Suellen's face, and ground her knuckles into other places on Suellen's bruised body, looking for more hot spots while Suellen yelped and established dominating holds. For about forty seconds, they forgot about Morgan and Jesus entirely.

"Listen," Suellen panted, when she had Bethany more or less immobilized. "Take my advice, quit now. The last guy I wrestled with had an orgasm and we wound up ... What?"

Bethany, pink-faced, was hushing her. Suellen looked up to find Plummer, Taylor, Giulia, Ginnie, and Silvio in a line at the edge of the driveway, watching solemnly except for Silvio. Silvio smiled a crooked smile, and looked interested. Behind him, Suellen could just see Morgan and Cesco at the living room window.

"Thanks," Suellen panted, "for turning out on such short notice. Now could we all get together and see if we can make sense of this business?"

"There's no sense to be made," Ginnie said. "Hap was a confused old man, and he wandered away into the swamp. That's where he was headed his whole life. Why can't you leave it alone?"

Suellen scowled. "Couple things. First place, he wasn't a confused old man his whole life. He was a friend and a benefactor to me and to Bethany, and one of the bravest, sweetest guys I ever knew. Second place, even confused old men have a right to respect and a decent burial. Third place, I'm a cop, and it always bothers cops when some close relative starts telling us to back off a death. Not that – "

"Not that I'm a close relative. Marrying Hap was one of the dumbest mistakes in the history of dumb mistakes." Ginnie snorted. "I admit, his marrying me is right up there. And, he's

Taylor's father and Francesco's grandfather, for better or worse. All right."

Morgan said something then, too low for anyone to hear. Suellen turned to her.

"What, Morgan?"

Morgan stood and drew a breath. "I said, he was my grandfather too. Maybe he wasn't mom's real father, but I guess I've learned something about the difference. He was the one who raised mom, so he's my grandfather too. That's all."

There was a general, a little reluctant, murmur of assent and admiration. Suellen raised an eyebrow. "And it doesn't bother you that he disappeared, and no one ever found his … found him?"

Morgan's face crumpled. "Of course it bothers me, what do you think? I told you everything I could about it. What do you want?"

"Well," Suellen said. She looked around the room. Plummer and Bethany looking scared silent, Taylor impatient, Silvio urbanely bored. Cesco cross-legged in a corner with a pad of newsprint; smiling, sketching, while Giulia bleakly watched. "I guess I want you to break your promise and tell us what you didn't save him from."

Morgan looked at her feet, head shaking. The wings of her bowl of black hair fell forward over her eyes. "Death," she whispered. "That's all. Just death."

18.

Six hours later, Suellen slumped at a back table of the Trigonal Rose, cheek on her fist, making rings with her beer bottle on the sticky table. She was tired, having spent three hours in a cheesy chain-market gym, making up for a week of lying around drinking and sitting on the Triumph getting her insides shaken around. She was in a bad mood, arising from an offhandedly hostile greeting on Cameron Avenue from Honey, the sulky waitress at Xanadu, who stared at her a little rudely, and said, "You know he's queer as a three-buck whore, don't you," to which Suellen had stupidly answered, Who, and Honey said, "Harvey, that's who. The guy was buying you drinks an' blow the other night, at my table. 'Fugue on Bop Themes,' my ass. Eddie pork you later that night? That'd put you number about 82 on his list for the month. Congrats."

And even though, in the course of what Suellen now thought of - with a smirk - as "the endless night of love," Harve had already told her the tragic story of Honey - a hopeless meth-head, who lived a life of detox, repeated breakdowns, and short-lived jobs - it still sucked to be poked in a spot she'd already made sore by self-castigation. Harve - making it funny, of course - told her of one date he'd mistakenly asked Honey on when they were both sophomores at Pernell Swett High School in Robeson County, that ended in a minor wreck when she yanked on his arm as they drove past the Maxton town hall, a pretty bad beating-up and a night in jail at the Robeson County courthouse in Lumberton for dating a white girl who had not yet at that point been written off by her folks.

Suellen was smarting from the sidewalk encounter, not satisfied in retrospect with her improvised riposte to Honey, and not reassured by Harve's claim that he'd been harassed and pursued by Honey ever since. What did she expect, she started jackassing around "dating," for Christ's sake? She was sick of her own lazy sensual slackness, sick of Harve, sick of ghosts and Jesus and Gabbro and Faye Bynum and the impenetrable swamp of evasion and religion and slack-head half-truths that was her adopted family.

She didn't know whether to put it down to too long a layoff, advancing age, or just bitching bad karma, that the workout had been no fun, that her body had responded indolently and without spark; pouting, reluctant on weights, easily exhausted on the treadmill. The place had been nearly deserted until noon, when a bunch of office workers had taken it over, all of them shrink-wrapped in cutie-pie Spandex outfits, boys and girls both, laughing at nothing and shortcutting their workouts.

Suellen had kept working, succeeding with surprising ease in ignoring their little hard butts and their unlined, mindless faces. When she was more sick of sweat than she was of body guilt, she showered and got the hell out of there.

She had to laugh now at the portrait Francesco had drawn of the family a-wrangle over Hap. The couples – Taylor and Giulia, Plummer and Bethany, Ginnie and Silvio – were shown as Medieval royalty, joined at the waist like face cards fluttering through dark air while Morgan and Suellen gaped at them from below. Morgan was rendered Medievally too, a princess of unearthly beauty, the perfection of whose velveted body was betrayed by the curve of a finger, the tip of a sneakered foot beneath the folds of her gown. Suellen appeared at the edge of a wood, a uniformed Robin Hood of ambivalent gender with ill-matched hands, one twice the size of the other, which it cradled at her belly. Suellen looked at the thing, and at her own reasonably symmetrical hands, sipped her beer and wondered why he'd done that – Cesco clearly had no trouble drawing accurately – and why it seemed right.

She was scowling at it when a couple of women at the next table flared up and then stopped talking at the same time, evidently heading for a quarrel they were both reluctant to push. They both had sticky-looking drinks, but they didn't seem otherwise much in harmony. One – the older, with a surgically stretched face – wore a black wide-brimmed straw hat, a black cocktail dress, and a massive ring. The other, who was still no kid, maybe Suellen's age or more, was in a fits-all Yankees cap with a pony tail flaring from the rear window, bright blue sunglasses, and a sundress that looked like it came from K-Mart.

Stretch-face broke the silence at last. "Honey," she said,

"I guess I don't quite know why we're meeting. If you won't help yourself, then there's nothing I can do to help you."

Suellen sighed and rattled the drawing, and thought about leaving. But hell, she'd just got here, she had no place better to be, and the Guinness she'd about finished on top of the workout was working like Flexeril, slacking her muscles and her enterprise.

"It don't seem like a lot to ask, Momma," Yankees cap sighed. "You and Carl are going to whatchamacallit, so why cain't I – "

"Doesn't," Momma said absently. "We are going to Weston-super-Mare. Is that so impossible to remember? The house is sublet, and the new people are moving in exactly two days from now."

"Well, two days, that gives me a chance to look for another place."

"The answer is no, Weezy. The place is a madhouse with packing and putting things away to make room for the tenants. No, you go back to your own apartment that Carl and I rented for you, and take a policeman with you, if you have to. Tell that lowlife to get out and stay out, and get legal help with it. Here, honey."

Stretch-face pulled out a wallet and shoved a little raft of bills toward Weezy. "Now, let's not quarrel, Weezy. I really, absolutely must run. No, I don't care for another drink, please. I'll call – no, you call me. Call me from your own place, and tell me that punk is history. I'll look forward to hearing it."

She rose and scrammed, not quite trotting toward the door, issuing into the sunglare of Franklin Street, where the flood of undergraduates swept her away like blackish driftwood. Weezy – Christ, Suellen thought, what do people imagine will happen when they give their daughters that kind of name? – sat, not pouting or sniffling, thank God, but sitting upright, pale and bleak.

Suellen went back to the drawing, grinning a little at the deadeye portraits of Taylor, Silvio (a tangle of darkness with iceberg teeth behind smiling lips) and Plummer (Spiderman in a clerical collar). She was turning it over, pausing to puzzle again over her lopsided self, when she became aware of blue regard from the next table. The woman Weezy was looking at her, not smiling, but not deflecting her apparent gaze behind the cobalt lenses of the sunglasses. Suellen gave her a short, buzz-off smile, and raised the drawing to convey a boundary.

The two hands at her waist were different in other ways than size. The big hand – Aha, Suellen thought. Let's see, both hands, big and little are on myself. On "one." I get it. It's a clock, five after one. Naw, baloney. Suellen snuffed with impatience. Bloody artists. Why don't they just come out and say what they mean?

The bigger hand, anyhow, was rendered anatomically; you could see the tendons and the muscles, every one of them in exact working relationship. A hand made to do things. The small one that it cradled was half-drawn, barely formed. A Rorschach that could have been anything from a glove to a tiny bunch of bananas, to a puppy dog or a chick embryo – *Holy shit!* A shock exploded in her belly. Ach, Jesus, no way. Francesco was no doctor, and he didn't have X-ray vision.

But, she fretted, he did see things. Did he see Edward Briggs Harvey Junior in her belly? Is that why her body was so damn somnolent? She remembered instances of birth control during her encounters with Harve, but she couldn't swear it had been there every single time. The all-nighter in particular was a haze of bad memory, false memory, and improvisations in which a condom had played a walk-on, walk-off role. And anyhow, no method of birth control is a hundred percent.

Suellen thought back through the calendar to her last period. Well, she was in a THP uniform, she remembered that much. Quitting the Patrol and coming to Gabbro had broken her routine and screwed the days all around, some of them endless and some over before they began. It was some weeks, that's all she could swear. Christ! Boff men, see what happens, Stupid. Number 82 this month, and how many of us are carrying your progeny, Eddie? She would go straight to the CVS and pick up a pregnancy kit.

She slapped the drawing onto the table, and looked up to find Weezy, unmoving, looking at her still.

"Excuse me," Weezy said.

Suellen sighed. "I don't have room, either. Actually, I don't have a place of my own right now."

"Naw, that's all right. Could I just set with you a couple minutes, ast a question?

Suellen looked around the Trigonal Rose. There were still plenty of empty tables.

The woman looked flustered. She was not as old as Suellen's first flash on her. Maybe thirty, Suellen thought, slender and busty, with knobby wrists, mouse-brown hair and a vulnerable, uncertain mouth.

"If'n you was expecting somebody – "

"No," Suellen said. She rolled up the drawing to make room. "Sit down. Why me?"

"We got something in common." The woman smiled a little, her eyes on Suellen's while she took off the sunglasses to reveal a swollen eye in a polychrome socket. "'Less you got yours from stepping on a rake. That's what I used to say."

"Nope. A guy gave 'em to me, both sides."

"See, I knowed you'd understand."

"Uh huh. Well, maybe not entirely." Suellen sighed. The pregnancy kit would work the same now or in a half hour. "Get you a drink?"

The woman looked at the empty glass in her hand. "I guess. I'm drinking grasshoppers. Get you one, too, hear? On me."

Suellen shuddered and fetched a fresh grasshopper and another Guinness, which prompted Weezy to pull a bill out of the raft she'd just got from Stretch-face. When she slid the green thing in front of the woman, she raised an eyebrow. "My name's Suellen." *Call me Suellen.* She found her left hand cradling her belly, and snatched it away. "Understand what?"

"Louise Mayhew," the woman said. "Weezy's what most folks call me. Understand how I'm fed up with fellas beatin up on me. I'd think you would be, too."

Suellen nodded. "Easy enough to understand that. If it makes any difference to you, I picked the fight, and the guy looks worse. I don't do self-defense, though."

"I wasn't looking for that. Look at me, you think I got any chance tryin to Kung Fu a fella that's a foot taller and a hundred pounds heavier'n me?"

"You might surprise yourself. Still, there's guys out there that don't beat up on women."

"Not in my case, they ain't. I never dated one fella from sixth grade to day before yesterday, didn't sooner or later start in to slam me around like I was some ..." Weezy Mayhew waved a hand, and Suellen saw that one of her wrist bones was a little crooked. "Like they was perfectly well entitled to, and what hurts don't count, long as they have a good time. Well, I'm done with it. I brought Momma here – I knowed she'd turn me down, so screw her – We come here because a friend of mine told me they was, you know ... " Weezy leaned forward and whispered. "<u>Lesbian</u> women hung out at this place."

She leaned back and looked at Suellen speculatively. "I thought maybe one of them might know how to be a friend, have a good time, without to beat up on a person. Would you happen to know if that's so?"

Suellen nodded solemnly. "I've heard that too. Some of them. Some are just as tough and mean as any guy you could find. Most of them are peaceable, that I know of. What kind of good time are you looking for?"

"Oh." Weezy shrugged shakily. "You know. Laugh at things. See a movie. Split a drink or two. And, then, you know." She blushed, frowning, and bit her lip. "Ain't there supposed to be some ... You know."

Suellen didn't respond, wanting to see if this waif could get the word through her bruised lips.

"Of, well." Weezy blushed and looked out at traffic on Franklin Street.

Suellen relented. "Sex?"

Louise Mayhew no more than glanced at Suellen, and the un-blackened eye jumped all over the place. "Sex. You still call it that, even ...? Well, that's right, then."

She toughened her jaw then, and clenched a fist on the table. "That's what I meant, yes ma'am. Sex that's just pleasant, and ... and happy. With no babies and no rough stuff and black eyes and all." She lowered her head and laughed shortly, the pony tail a flag of surrender. "Just saying it sounds like craziness. Well ... would you happen to know how that works? For both folks women?"

Suellen touched the fist with a tentative finger, enclosed it, felt it relax. "Sure, Louise. I got a couple errands to run, but let's see if we can't find you a nice, peaceable lesbian friend."

Suellen's search for a presentable and trustworthy lesbian friend for Louise Mayhew was unavailing. The bartender at the Trigonal Rose opined that the Indigo Girls farewell tour, which hit Raleigh that night, had sucked all the first-string singles that direction.

And besides, damn it, as soon as they started looking, giving up on the Trigonal Rose crowd and sorting through the three or four other close-by spots Suellen was sure of, slinging Weezy on the back of the Triumph finally and rumbling through Durham with no luck, Weezy had started being kind of fun. She stuck a bare foot out on either side of the Triumph, kept track of which hit more bugs in the wind-stream, and made up funny theories to explain the result, complete with advanced statistical correlations to which kinds of fast-fooders and Greek houses they were passing. She had wide-eyed, hilarious things to say about "Dook perfessors," about her mother, and about the mindless swarm of students, about men and about women that finally led Suellen to turn on her in puzzlement, straddling the Triumph at the on-ramp to I-40.

"Damn it, Louise, – "

"Weezy. Everybody calls me that."

"Yeah, well, that's where your trouble starts, right there. It doesn't take much balls to take a pop at somebody named 'Weezy.' Christ, it's like a sticky note on your chin, just asking for it. Anyways, how'd you come to be so sharp about some things, and so goddamn dumb about sex?"

Weezy was silent, and alarmed Suellen by looking at her with wet eyes. "<u>You</u> ain't gonna pop me, are you?"

Suellen blushed. "No, shit, of course not. Is that what

happens when people get exasperated around you? No, no, no. I'm just trying to figure out how a smart, funny, good-looking woman turned into a tackling dummy. You can tell when somebody's going to get rough with you, can't you? Well, you need to start seeing that sooner, and staying away from that kind of jerk."

Silence. Tears spilling down Weezy's grooved and freckled cheeks. Then, "You really think I'm good looking?"

*

Morgan and Cesco had been set to mowing and raking the lawn. Bethany and Giulia sat in Adirondack chairs under the pecan tree, Giulia silent and resigned while she watched Cesco's shirtless form, Bethany alternating between sisterly silence and making sure that Morgan and Cesco kept busy, separate, and in sight at all times.

Morgan was silent too, trudging through the chore, her tee-shirt gathering sweat, her face sick and penitential. Cesco pushed the mower cheerfully, whistling, a hot May sun gleaming from his Heath-bar skin. Every few minutes, they converged at some corner of the yard, giving Morgan time to say something to Cesco under cover of the mower's noise.

"Wish I could take my shirt off." And,

"How can you be so cheerful? You're driving everybody crazy." And,

"They aren't paying much attention. When you finish the

lawn, take the mower to the shed. I'll wait for you there."

To this last, Cesco nodded and smiled as always. Morgan shook her head, and hauled her tarp-load of weeds and clippings around the corner of the house. When she came back, dragging the empty tarp listlessly, she glanced at Cesco closing in on the last strip of unmown grass, and went to stand limply at Bethany's side.

"I need to go to the bathroom."

Bethany nodded at her, impervious to irony, and Morgan disappeared again around the house, disciplining herself to slump, not to look at Cesco, dashing then to the shed when she heard the lawnmower's subsiding chug.

It was hot as a Houston August in the shed. Morgan felt she might faint, the more so when she heard the almost soundless creak of the back screen door and realized that Cesco had detoured on his way to putting away the mower.

"Cesco, for Jesus' sake, what are you doing," she gritted, and she sat against the wall of the shed, a small, soaked and red-faced icon of discouragement. She didn't hear Cesco's footsteps approaching, and when the door of the shed creaked open, she looked up expecting her mother. Cesco slid in, toweling himself, rolling his eyes and whistling wordlessly at the heat. He handed Morgan a rolled sheet of drawing paper, which Morgan ignored.

"Francesco, I don't understand. You just quit talking to anybody ever since you came back from the trailer. Does it hurt to talk?"

Cesco smiled and shook his head, and took the paper out of Morgan's hand. As he began to unroll it, Morgan slapped it away, tears and sweat streaming down her face.

"Cesco, listen to me. I love you, we all love you. You are a wonderful artist and you seem like you're happy. But for God's sake – " Morgan broke off. "No, not God, not Jesus or the Holy Ghost, Saint Mary and the One Holy and Undivided Trinity. Just for us. For your mother, for me. Please, if you can, say one word to me."

Cesco put a hand on Morgan's streaming face. "Look," he said. He opened the roll of paper.

*

Having supper with Weezy involved, as a prelude, some house-cleaning. It started with kicking out the supercilious punk who was squatting in her Carrboro apartment, conducting a Mahler CD with a breadstick and sucking a Bud Lite. That part was kind of fun, and restored Suellen's self-confidence, dented some by her bout with Harve and her unsatisfactory workout.

Neither woman had eaten much, and when they'd got rid of Conrad and his running shoes, his guitar and amps and his rooster, and when the last of the dirty socks, the Purina cock chow and Bud Lite, had cascaded to the dumpster, Weezy got out a half-eaten baguette, cut off and discarded the ragged end with fastidious fingertips, and put the rest and a saucer of extra virgin olive oil and a glass of Chianti in front of Suellen while she phoned an order for pad Thai, spring rolls and Five Delights ice cream from the hash-house across the street. Weezy put down the phone and looked at Suellen, shy because things were getting a little domestic.

"Thank you, Suellen. You got some nuts, I gotta say. Conrad moved in here three weeks ago, and started knocking me around a week after that. He just laughed when I talked about getting the cops." She shuddered, and wiped her hands on the front of her dress. "It was fun to watch his face when you mashed his graphite racket over his head, won't it? You like music?"

Suellen tossed a hand and flexed her newly skinned knuckles. "I needed the workout. Sure, I like music. Got any Brubeck or Johnny Desmond?"

"Huh uh. Who're they?"

"Never mind. Who do you like?"

Weezy shrugged, and – like it was something most people grow out of – confessed that she liked almost any kind of quiet music. Unaccompanied violin or cello, acoustical folk, hushed piano. She put on a CD of Eric Satie and told Suellen to make herself at home while she picked up the food.

"It'll be ready this quick?"

Weezy shrugged. "Sure. They keep a vat of noodles going all the time, and the rest of the stuff is short-order. I'll be back in six minutes, tops."

Suellen wandered the sparse apartment, listening to the

meandering piano music while Weezy was gone, feeling strange, touching her breasts to see if they felt … well, like the breasts of a pregnant woman. Looking at the Chianti, with its label warning pregnant women to for God's sake lay off. Wondering why she didn't feel as upset and pissed off as she ought to about that. Concluding that the time to get mad would be after the pregnancy test showed its stripes.

And what was she up to here, in Louise Mayhew's apartment, a rather nice one Momma and Carl had no doubt picked out for little Weezy? Having failed to procure Weezy a satisfactory female date, having cleared the decks of male jerks, was it now up to her to demonstrate the delights of girl-on-girl? And how did she feel about that?

Before she had made up her mind on that, Weezy was back, apologetic. "They was a big line. You like that music?"

Suellen considered. It certainly was quiet. Transparent, naive, a little sad. "It's restful, sure enough. What is it?"

"This'n is called 'Gymnopedies.' I think it means something about 'barefoot.' Makes me think of being a little girl, walking in the grass, not a care in my head. I used to play like I was somebody else. My favorite was a spy in the French resistance, blonde like you, named Mam'selle Suzanne. You wont some more wine?"

"I probably better lay off. Well, an inch. The Thai smells good too, for that matter."

They ate then, concentrating on the food, letting the wispy piano wrap them in music that was like audible silence.

Suellen polished her plate with a scrap of baguette and finished off her second glass of Chianti, leaning back with a sigh. Weezy glanced up at her, seeming to take satisfaction in the clean plate.

"They's another half a spring roll. Also, wait'll you taste the ice cream."

"Oof. I might have to digest for a little, to make room. Do they explain what the five delights are?"

"Not exactly. I ast once, and they looked at me like I was some kind of redneck, which is the God's truth. It's good anyways, and cold, and not sticky. It leaves a nice taste in your mouth."

"So that's four, right there." Suellen held up a hand of fingers and considered what had occurred to her to say next. Aw, Christ, what the hell. "Maybe it's up to us to provide the last one."

Weezy blushed, and smiled. The Satie fell silent, and she jumped to her feet. "You like Judy Collins?"

"Sure. Look, Louise," Suellen said. "I've had a great time already, I needed a friend today, and I'm happy to be your friend from now to next century. No kidding, you're a terrifically nice lady, and a lot of fun, and I like your music. We wouldn't have to do one more thing, for this to be a swell date, far as I'm concerned."

Weezy half-turned from her shelf of CD's. "That's for me too, Suellen. Don't mind me being a little nervous. I never had no date with a woman. So it's been quite a heck of a day already. Tell you what, you already set me loose. If you want to call it a night, why, you got my grateful blessing. Thank you so much for everything, hear?"

Suellen looked at the twist of Weezy's waist, the purple eye and the wisp of sweat-stuck mouse-hair on the smooth forehead. Her belly stirred a little, and her eyes widened.

"Not," she heard herself say, "without at least a taste of the Five Delights, I'm not calling anything a night."

Weezy smiled, pulling in her bruised lips against sudden emotion. She took the carton from the plastic bag, and whispered, "Here, then." She spooned a chunk of ice cream and extended it, a little shakily, toward Suellen. Staring, her own eyes widening now, into Suellen's. Sitting on the coffee table before them, the ice cream had softened; the spoon sagged, and the offered bite slid off and fell toward the rug.

Weezy broke the spell and caught the gleaming chunk in her other hand. She offered it to Suellen, triumphant, whistling a little at the coldness. Suellen cradled the dripping fingers in hers and tasted it, and it was in fact delightful. So was the sweet skin of Weezy's fingers behind it, and at least five-fold delightful, sharing the alien taste from tongue to tongue.

19.

Leaving Louise Mayhew was not easy. It began with Suellen's foot tangled in the sheet in the milky light of five in the morning, and continued with further entanglement that left Suellen marginally satisfied and Weezy tearful.

"I hate it, you're fixing to leave."

Suellen stretched luxuriously, and walked her fingers up Weezy's centerline. "I know. Me too, W - Louise. You're a very sweet lady."

"But you gotta go?"

"But I do gotta go, honey. You know I'll come back, but to be honest, it'll be a while. Think you can take it from here OK?"

"I don't know." Weezy looked uncertain. "I reckon."

"Listen, you did just wonderful, and I had a great time. You're a natural. Look for women with short hair, rimless glasses, and very clean hands. Stay away from leather."

Weezy giggled. "And which a them would be most important, if I had to pick?"

"There's my girl. Probably the hands."

"Yeah, otherwise I could end up with a serial killer."

Now, speeding south over 501 in a slant of sun, Suellen wondered at her reluctance to start something with Weezy, and her all too evident readiness to leave. Time was, she'd have jumped at the chance to hang around, and relished the landing. This time she'd been slow to get interested. It had been a mental effort, even after the nice boost she'd got from the moment Weezy turned back to her from the stereo and told her she had Weezy's "grateful blessing."

Well, things had been blessed enough after that. Suellen smiled into the wind that swept over her, and stuck a bare foot into the slipstream on each side of the Triumph, playing Weezy's game. She reveled in the yielding warm solidity of the air, even in the occasional ping, on one foot or the other, of a doomed gnat. She pulled to the center of the deserted road then and did some serious research on it, experimenting with various attitudes and positions in the windstream, keeping score as bugs hit one foot or the other. She got up to Right Foot 14, Left Foot 12, remembering Weezy's country-girl grin of amusement, day-dreaming of her lanky charm. There is nothing, she thought, sweeter and more cleanly than the slender body of a woman.

Suellen loved her own body still, in this season of ageing, and she loved sharing it with others like it. She loved the slow mounting of excitement, the expansion of erogenous sensitivity until it was no longer a question of "zones" but of regions, landscapes of delight on which the lightest touch could loose rainbows. It just went to show that sometimes you have to just make up your mind to something and do it. Whatever passive resistance your body might offer, The mind is wiser...

Oops.

Suellen blanked her mind, pulled in her feet, and watched the highway rushing toward her. She'd been about to think something contradictory. If the body is wiser than the will, and the will is wiser than the mind, how can the mind ever be wiser than the body? If you admitted even in one circumstance, as last night, that the mind could be wiser than the body, then it boiled down to a silly three-cornered standoff. Like scissors-paper-rock, for God's sake.

But the first two parts had organized her life since she learned them. The body is wiser than the will, how damn true! How right the Kurdish woman had been to teach her that, after the quarter-century she'd spent trying to subordinate her body to her own will. The will is wiser than the mind; what else had let her smack down the barriers of prejudice and contempt she'd found in the Marines and the THP?

Still, she thought. Is something necessarily more true because you learn it from a charismatic woman who is making love to you under conditions of mortal danger? Couldn't nonsense be passed off as wisdom all the easier under those conditions? Suellen the scientific cop had to admit, it probably could.

OK, but wait. Suppose last night's anomaly wasn't anomalous at all, and her wise body was just trying to tell her willful mind that sex with Weezy was going to be a bore and a dumb idea? Well then, compared to what? Sex with Harve? Working her way up from Number 82 for the month?

Suellen snorted, and then – the will is wiser than the mind – she made herself consider. First of all, that 82 from Honey was BS, and if Suellen had not been #1 for the month, so what? Second, had the pleasure she had shared with Weezy, and the similar pleasures she'd shared all her life with women like Weezy, been comparable to the night-long abandonments in Harve's loft or the painful, bloody, and grass-stained rapture of their all-out fight? Or the sleepy contentment of the screen porch? Well, of course Harve was more fun. But come on, Suellen told herself. Harve was ... well, Harve, and Louise Mayhew was still Weezy. And even with some of the hottest women she had known, it was apples and oranges.

And answered herself, like a catechizing nun, that in fact she had always felt a little contemptuous about apples – easy, take-me-now-and-love-me-to-the-core apples – compared to oranges, with their armor and their mess and their pale hidden webs of bitterness; and their sudden release, that hard-earned burst of delight when you bit down and they broke open at last. Oranges, as far as she was concerned, were in every way preferable to apples. Fine, but was Harve apples, or oranges? Men in general seemed more like oranges; the armor, the mess inside. Still, though.

Realizing that she had the choice of abandoning Kurdish wisdom, or admitting the possibility that, for her, the undeniable and esoteric pleasure of lesbian sex was pale potatoes compared to what she had achieved with Harve, Suellen wisely refused to think about it. She was on the Gabbro by-pass, and NorthPass Plaza had a CVS. She turned in.

Ten minutes later, Suellen had the kit of FetusFinder pregnancy strips in her hip pocket and was on her way to Wiener King ladies' to use one, when she felt a tug on her elbow.

"Suellen, Honey, wait up. You got sand in your ears? I been calling you for a block."

"Uh. Hey, Beffie. A block's pretty far away. And I got something on my mind. How's everybody?"

"Well, the last time was from three feet away. And everybody's in a uproar, that's how. I need you."

The Problem in the Pines. "Yeah? What now?"

Bethany ignored the attitude. "Cesco drew a really lovely portrait of Hap and Lee, and it's got Morgan all upset. She's locked herself in her room, crying. I give up on her for a while, and come into town for Ginnie's heart medicine, which she's gotta have a refill today. I believe she'd listen to you."

"I got nothing to say to Ginnie."

"Nuh-uh, me neither, I meant Morgan. Please, Suellen? I'm about to the end of my rope."

Suellen sighed. She'd still be pregnant, or not, in another hour, or whatever this bullshit would take. "What the hell."

Bethany led an unmerry chase back to her place. Suellen, following with less urgency, had time to see Giulia and Plummer under the pecan tree, looking up into its graceful foliage, as she came up the drive. She parked in the back and found Bethany fidgeting at the door.

When they walked into the kitchen, the house was silent. Silvio looked up from a copy of the *Gazetta dello Sport* and made impatient, finger-flipping motions toward the CVS bag in Bethany's hand. Bethany tossed it to him and continued up the stairs, beckoning to Suellen.

"Out front," Silvio growled after them.

Morgan's door stood open, and her room was empty. Bethany stood in the hall looking left and right, her face fearful.

"Why don't we try out front?" Suellen said. "Being a gangster doesn't mean everything he says is a lie."

When they walked up to Giulia and Plummer under the pecan tree, Giulia was calling, "Cesco, come down. She don't want to talk to you, honey. You can see that."

"Mom," Cesco said, with no apparent difficulty. "I need to explain it to her. Privately if possible.

Suellen looked up. Cesco was standing in a crotch, maybe fifteen feet off the ground, peering into the high branches. Thirty or forty feet higher, on a sprout so slender that anyone heavier would have cracked it, sat Lee Morgan Baley.

"There is nothing to explain, Francesco," Morgan called. "I am here to consider whether ending my life right now would be enough to divert you from the folly you have in mind."

Suellen turned to Plummer. "Folly?"

Plummer passed a hand through his hair. "There's an old photo of Hap and Lee on their wedding day, been in the spare room where Cesco's sleeping, for years. Pretty bad faded by now, really, what with the heat up there and all. Cesco took it in his head to do us a hand-drawn copy, which he did, and very handsomely too. Morgan seemed to like it at first, and then she got – I don't know, kind of uneasy, and then this morning she's in her room, crying her eyes out. Time I could turn around, she was out her winda and down the azalea, and now here she is up this tree. Anybody tries a rescue seems like liable to break that branch."

He scuffed his shoe in the grass. "I pray night and day on this, but that child gets beyond human understanding sometimes. Anyway, Taylor's bringing down some mattresses to pile up under her. You could help with that, if you would, while I stay here with Morgan. Fire department's on its way."

"Well, be glad to, Plummer, just a sec. Morgan?"

"Hi, Aunt Suellen. Please don't get yourself involved in this. It will be over with before you can change anything."

"What would I want to change? How could things be better?"

Morgan was silent at that, maybe a little shamefaced. She cocked her head at Cesco, all that way below her. "You could get him down before he hurts himself."

Suellen looked at the tree. It was vase-like, with multiple trunks fanning from the base. The one next to Morgan looked like a lot easier climbing than the one Morgan was on. Suellen shook her head and rolled her shoulders, sore from the workout and not feeling any the stronger for it. She began to climb, in the style of a Pacific islander climbing a palm. When she got to

Cesco's level, she switched to a different trunk and leaned on his.

"What's the deal, Cesco?"

Cesco sighed. "Really, if everybody will go away and let me talk to her, I think …" He stopped, frustrated. "I don't know how to say what I mean."

Suellen raised an eyebrow. "You're doing pretty well, seems to me. What was this no-talking stuff?"

Cesco looked up at Morgan, who was looking tearfully at the horizon, gripping the trunk next to her shaky perch. "At first, I couldn't talk without swearing, so I decided I just wouldn't. As soon as I did that, and even more when Morgan took me out to that trailer, I found I could look at things and really see them. See the whole thing, not just how it looked on the surface. My whole life, I've been such a talky brat, I never took the time to look at anything. Like I was always shut up in this bubble of words, and I couldn't see past them. And then, all of a sudden, it seemed like it was the easiest thing in the world just to draw things, and the more I drew, the easier it seemed not to talk. I started to worry that if I did talk, I would lose this new thing, this new way of seeing. I knew it was upsetting Mom, and people, but I thought I could make them see it."

Suellen shrugged. "Not everybody is tuned in to that."

"No. Grandma Ginnie was. She understood. And I was hoping I could make Morgan understand."

"Is that what caused all this?"

Cesco reached into a pocket and pulled out the rolled

drawing. It was a little torn and crumpled, but Suellen could see that it was a really fine likeness of Hap and Lee: Lee smiling tearfully, Hap looking dazed and disbelieving, a couple of economical and masterly strokes suggesting a wedding cake and streamers around the happy couple. Suellen grinned. "Nice job. Really nice. Why's Hap so dark?"

Cesco smiled and shook his head. "Because," he said. "Because I … it's…" He shrugged, and burst into tears.

Suellen looked at the picture again, smoothing it against the tree. She felt a little shock, and began to laugh with delight. "Because," she said, "Oh, goodness, Cesco, because it's not Hap and Lee, is it?"

"Huh uh," Cesco said. He shook his head and wiped his eyes, smearing tears and dirt across his face "Me and Morgan."

"Well," Suellen said, "what's so terrible about that?"

She was at Morgan's level now, on the next trunk over. It gave her the willies to see the branch under Morgan bending when Morgan shrugged impatiently. The thing was green wood, no thicker than a broomstick. Fifty feet below, the pile of mattresses looked laughable, something you'd see tried, and failing, in a Roadrunner cartoon. It wasn't even clear that they were under where Morgan sat. From the direction of Gabbro, she could hear a siren. She hoped to hell whoever was coming had something better up their sleeves.

"Have you looked carefully at it, Aunt Suellen? Can't you see?"

Suellen considered how to answer that. "Cesco," she said, "is a brilliant artist. Draftsman, really. He sees things that are there to see, and he's found a terrific skill, or gift, or something, for getting them down on paper. He doesn't see things that aren't there."

"I agree. You remember when I showed you that picture of me with my parents and I asked you where Plummer was, in my face? Well, that was the wrong one to look for, wasn't it? Mom took one look at this thing and she went all funny and quiet. And she still thought it was Grandpa and Grandma. What did she see?"

Suellen held up the drawing. Cesco's face was a dark version of Taylor and through Taylor, you could look straight back to his father Hap. The grace-notes of Giulia were there too, plain to see for anyone who knew them both. The kid was really more than a draftsman, if maybe not quite an artist. He saw things. And in the woman's face – yes, Bethany and Lee. But also something that neither Bethany nor Lee ever was. Something speculative, intelligent, and cruelly dangerous, all in the eyes of a young girl grown to be a formidable woman.

"Derwood," Suellen said.

"Yes," Morgan said. "I knew him the instant I saw him. I don't know why I never saw him before. I rushed to a mirror, and he was there. He is in my face and he's in my soul. Mom didn't exorcise him, you can't do that. It was a nice story, and maybe it got Mom through her pregnancy – that she never should have carried to term, you <u>can't</u> deny that now, Aunt

Suellen."

"Yes," Suellen said. "Yes, I can. You carry Der - that guy's DNA, sure you do. Maybe that's where you get your seriousness and your religious bent; he wasn't all bad. But, Morgan, listen. We all carry the genes of bad people. Killers and rapists and liars and damn fools, and – I don't know what all. There's not a person alive that doesn't have failures and idiots and criminals in their family tree. Huh. I bet that's where the notion of Original Sin started, you think? Anyways, nobody has immaculate genes. What matters is what you do with them. Not what somebody else did, who died before you were born."

"What were we talking about? I don't care about his sins. I'm talking about my sins, that I committed because I'm stained with his rotten, murderous ..." The siren was nearer now. Suellen reached across the space between herself and Morgan.

"Is this about Grandpa Hap?"

"Yes." Morgan's free arm wrapped her head.

"Why don't you tell me about it, Morgan? Maybe it won't seem so bad if – "

"Oh! Don't say stupid things, Aunt Suellen! Francesco wants to marry me, no less, and if I don't kill myself right now, he will keep after me, and some year, when we're older, I will not be able to say no to him. Then what will it be? Will I kill him in the night some night? Tie him up and give him scars like mother's? Or drown our babies, how about that? How can you talk about 'not seem bad?' Jesus Christ!"

Morgan banged the branch beneath her, and the recoil of

her body brought a stretching, cracking noise from it. She turned pale, and grabbed the trunk next to her, and then smiled and let it go. "So, how's that? Either I took the Lord's name in vain, or I was really asking Him for help, and He started this branch cracking. I think I hear the answer."

"No, Morgan, please. You didn't kill Grandpa Hap. You didn't harm him in any way."

"Oh, no? Were you there? How do you explain Jesus coming and taking him away because we were kissing?"

"Kissing?" Oh, not this.

"Yes," Morgan hissed. "And not some little Grandpa kiss, either. And Jesus didn't just pop out of the bushes. He ran across the water, like on the Sea of Galilee, because I was ..." She pulled herself closer to the trunk, and the little branch quit creaking. "All right. I am going to confess to you, and then I am going to let go of this tree and jump off this branch, and there's nothing you can do to stop me."

Suellen tried not to look at the fire truck that stood now below them on the road, all flashers and diesel and radio squawks. "All right," she nodded. "Confess."

Morgan glanced at the truck. "Listen good, because there won't be time for questions. I'll need to jump before they can get their dumb ladders set up."

"So, get going."

"All right. You know I used to take Grandpa Hap for walks in the country."

"Yes."

"And you know, toward the end, he used to sometimes think he was walking with Grandma Lee, instead of me. Because I look so much like her, and because – well, he got mixed up sometimes."

"Is that why you changed to 'Morgan'?"

"Um … well, that's part of it. The day Grandpa died, he took me on a canoe trip into Indian Girl Swamp. He said he was going to tell me the story of the Lost Princess, and show me the very place where she was supposed to have disappeared."

"Is that where it happened?"

Morgan shook her head violently. "Stop asking questions, Aunt Suellen, or I'll have to jump before I can finish, and then you'll have my immortal soul on your conscience."

Suellen nodded. She knew the place all right. So did half of Gabbro. Morgan must have deliberately misled everyone about where she and Hap were. "Go on."

"He told me the story while we were canoeing. It was a beautiful afternoon, just spring, and the swamp was soft and golden, little shafts of sunlight diving down into the water. Grandpa was a wonderful story teller. I could really see the princess, and her father coming after her. And the magical cape that protected her, but not her lover. How she took it off and put it on him, but too late, he was already shot by the father. How she took the arrow out of her lover and plunged it into her own heart, and died there with him, and they walked off to Heaven together. It was just a terrific story, and I was so happy and grateful to Grandpa that he told it to me. And just at the end of the story, the canoe slid onto the bank of this island where it all happened. I got out first, and I turned around to give Grandpa a hand up out of the canoe."

Morgan looked analytically at the business down on the road, the ladder beginning to unlimber, orders being given, Gabbro firemen peering up into the leaves.

"I'll have to hurry now. I guess I must have looked really happy, smiling at Grandpa and holding his hand. And he looked happy too. But then he got one of his funny spells, and I could tell that he thought I was Grandma Lee. He looked so happy that he'd pleased her. And just for a second – and here's where Derwood showed himself – I wished that I was Grandma Lee. That I could be the person for Grandpa, that he really wanted to be with. So I did a terrible, terrible thing."

Morgan's voice became flat in a way that her mother would have recognized. "He leaned down to kiss me, and instead of ducking, which I usually did, I pretended to be her. I made my voice deep and soft, and I told him I had always loved him and always would. And I kissed him back."

Suellen leaned her head against the trunk she was on, aching for Hap, and for this guilty little girl. "Well, sweetheart, maybe that wasn't very smart, but it was a kind, generous impulse. It probably made him very happy. It wasn't some terrible sin."

"Jesus didn't think so."

"Oh, yes. Running across the water." Jesus was a sailor in a boatload of bonehead disciples. No, he was a convict named

596 Harvey.

"Yelling at Grandpa to let me go, yelling and furious. He ran right onto the island and grabbed me away from Grandpa. Grandpa whispered, 'Jesus,' not like he was mad or like that. Like he was scared. Jesus told me, 'Little girl, I want you to forget all about this. If you tell anyone about it, you'll go to hell.' And I deserved it! I had led Grandpa into a terrible sin, and brought judgment down on him. On us both. I was so scared and ashamed that I think I fainted. When I woke up, he was gone."

"Grandpa, or Jesus?"

"Both of them. I expect Jesus took Grandpa off to judgment, which is where I'm headed, evidently." Morgan looked at the ladder pushing through the leaves toward her, a booted fireman reaching for her arm. "I gotta go now, Aunt Suellen. Thanks for hearing my confession. I love you. 'Bye."

"Stop." Suellen held a hand up at the ladder. "Don't you want to know what Jesus was doing in my kitchen?"

Morgan slid farther out her branch to escape the fireman. It bent badly, leaving Morgan perched on one thigh, gripping the branch with trembling hands. "Sir," she said, "If you so much as touch me, this branch will break. If I see that net moving into place under this tree, I'll jump before they can catch me. Get back, or I'm gone."

She looked up her sagging branch at Suellen. "All right, make it quick. What was he doing in your kitchen? I have to admit, that's bothered me. He was definitely the very same one

I saw on the island."

"I'll tell you, but I'm not proud of it," Suellen said. "It's my turn for confession. Hold my hand?"

Morgan looked cold disbelief. "Do you think I'm a stupid child?"

"Well ... frankly, yes."

Morgan smiled at that. "So why are you crying?"

"Because I happen to love some stupid children. You're one. Cesco's another."

Morgan looked the fireman's hand away like a shortstop looking a runner back to second base. And reached out to Suellen. "Tell me."

Suellen took the offered hand lightly, trying not to scare Morgan into pulling back. "You're not going to like this. I had just spent the night with him. He was my lover. But it wasn't Jesus."

Morgan smiled uncertainly at Suellen, shaking her head. "Aunt Suellen. You're going to Hell for saying that. It <u>was</u> Jesus. I saw him clearly both times."

Suellen shrugged. "Not today, I'm not. Anyway, it's true, on my honor as a trooper, a woman, and your aunt. So; would you rather believe that Jesus would spend the night fornicating with your Aunt Suellen, or that you might be mistaken about who he was?"

Morgan hesitated, puzzled, thinking it over. There was a brief growling sound from the fire truck, and the ladder crashed through the last leaves toward Morgan, the fireman straining toward her, yelling, "Hold on to her, lady." The end of the ladder smacked into Morgan's branch, jostling her downward while Suellen leaned as far as she could, holding Morgan's wrist. The branch snapped and went vertical. Morgan, still looking puzzled, slid down, gathering a handful of leaves, dragging Suellen with her into green and blurring free fall.

20.

"Are you pregnant, Ma'am?"

"What's it to you? Is that how you pick up dates?" Suellen struggled to focus.

The EMT leaned back from the gurney. "No, Ma'am. I gotta ast you that before we offer you no sedatives, painkillers, antibiotics, like that. So, are you?"

"How would I know? If people would leave me alone for five minutes maybe I'd get a chance to find out." Suellen tried to sit up, and found herself immobilized. "What?"

"Ma'am, you was lucky they got that net into place no more'n a secont before you hit it. I believe, at that, we might have a fracture in your distal radius there, where you hit the frame."

Suellen looked at her arm. "Feels OK to me. Why have you got me fastened down like this? What happened to Morgan?"

"The little girl? She walked away – naw, I'm lying, they had to drag her off'n you. I meant th'other un, Ma'am. That'n smart a little?"

Suellen looked at her left wrist. It was taped to a short board, bent about twice as much as Weezy's, and there was a menacing purple bump under the skin on the outside. She tried to turn it to get a better look, and just about passed out again, because that was the best alternative to the orange boulders of pain that rolled up her arm all the way to her ear.

"Ow, Christ!"

"Yes, Ma'am. Are you pregnant? Allergic to any drugs?"

Suellen looked at him woozily. "We better figure I am," she panted. "Better that than the other way." Just, she thought, so she could keep options open.

*

Late in the afternoon, Suellen sat in the bathroom at the Swamp Road house, holding a FetusFinder strip into a slant of afternoon sun. The damn thing showed a double stripe, which meant it was just as wrong as the first one, curling and drying on the counter. These things can give false positives, she knew. It said so right on the box. It also gave the likelihood of that as "less than 0.2%."

Did that mean, Suellen wondered, that getting two false positives would have a chance of 0.2% of 0.2%? She couldn't do the math in her head, but she could in the dust on the windowpane. Four chances in a million that it's wrong. Four chances, that's not too bad. In a million, though. Less than one chance in 250,000. Aw, to hell with it, Suellen thought. I'm pregnant. I got myself pregnant with a liar and a con man who's serving time in a redneck county caboose.

She let her head sink onto her good arm. When the beam of sunlight departed from the bathroom window, she stood, wiping tears, and zipped herself up, shaking her head. The feeble, pregnancy-compatible painkillers the EMT had given her had long since worn off and her wrist – the one the strong right hand had been cradling in Cesco's picture, and that it was cradling now in its new brick-red cast – hurt.

Man, she thought. That Cesco, he sees things. And, hey, way to go, Harve, you fountain of unstoppable sperm. Well, this did not need to stand. Even in North Carolina, pregnancies could be terminated. She wandered toward the screen porch, thinking that she did not need this, the pain and inconvenience and the expense. The abortion Wet Parsonage kindly bought when she arrived under his care, pregnant at thirteen, had hurt, and had troubled her for years. She did not, not, want to go through another.

No, of course not, Honey. Let's do childbirth and raise a baby instead. That'd be the ticket for her career with THP for sure. That Sarge, she's a tough one. Too bad she's knocked up.

Oh, and she came of fine, baby-friendly stock, didn't she? Her mother, leading her into a life of drift and grift, was her only model. Serving Suellen up to the guy she was hustling one night when Momma had the sniffles and didn't feel like putting out, that was her formative training in child care. I can't wait to have a kid of my own I can try that out on. We'll have such fun, just us girls. Suellen carried that onto the screen porch, wondering if the humic ghosts of Hap and Lee might have comfort. Or another shock of horror to induce an abortion.

But the porch was silent, abandoned by humans, dead or

alive. And besides, what ghosts could be worse than what had already happened? Suellen settled onto the sleeping bag with her toothache wrist and her uninvited fetus to look at the ceiling and silently to cry the dusk into night.

The night was hostile country, bringing tormentors who visited and mocked and departed, leaving sweat and tousle and silences that ended in sudden gasps under fathoms of air as wet as the oceans. Grifter mom was there, pinkly blowing her nose, flirting and tucking. And Jesus of course, and Jesus' little handmaiden Morgan and Harve and Rick Tallon and Faye Bynum. And Weezy, laughing fit to bust. Clean hands, she said. She doubled over, clutching her sides, holding a dripping scoop of Five Delights. Clean hands. Look at yourself.

And all of them turning her over, dressing her, undressing her, fighting with each other over rags and scraps of clothing, while off to the side, Hap Maryland's bones smiled and nodded, smiled and nodded.

*

"Birdie, birdie," the loudmouth cardinal yelled. "What cheer?"

Suellen groaned and rolled over onto her cast, which woke her a little more. She was inside the sleeping bag, and she had no memory of getting in it. Or out of her clothes, for that matter; but there they were, folded neatly on the glider. She was wearing a cotton shift she'd last seen in one of Bethany's drawers, and a pair of what felt like cotton panties. She peered at them in the dimness of the sleeping bag and read the faded and blurred legend: "Thursday."

"Birdie, birdie, bir - "

"Shut your beak, jerk," Suellen yelled. She slapped the screen and the cardinal decamped, leaving a falling red feather. Suellen dragged herself to a sitting position. There was something on the glider, under her folded clothes. A manila folder. My dossier. Homeland must have paid a visit in the night.

Suellen pulled her legs out of the sleeping bag and sat against the screen, snuffling, trying to get awake enough to be puzzled, or scared, or upset about the disorienting facts that surrounded her. She wished her hair were long enough to ruffle in frustration. She ruffled it anyway. The glider sat there, holding its little pile of clothing.

Suellen made it to her feet, and was standing at the glider, looking at the label on the folder. (MARYLAND HARPER F) when a soft footfall came from the dining room, and Morgan Baley put a shy and downcast head through the doorway. She had a bruise on her forehead and the beginnings of a black eye.

"Good morning, Aunt Suellen."

Suellen snuffled again, immune to surprise. "Good morning to you, sunshine. Looks like you don't bounce a whole lot better than your Auntie. Well, us old folks, we get kind of brittle. We may have to cut back – "

"I'm so sorry. How many really, really stupid things do you suppose I've done in the last year? And here I am, apologizing for another one."

"Well." Suellen considered. "I think only about one. But you do keep doing it over and over. Are you going to be in trouble for coming here?"

"No. Mom knows. She let me stay here overnight."

"Really? Well, good for her. Is that where this, whatever it is, this folder came from?" Suellen jiggled the folder at a passing fly.

"No," Morgan said. "Mister. ..." She sighed and blushed. "Mr. Harvey left that for you."

"Harve was here?"

"Quite late. He helped me get you into bed."

"Charming. And introduced himself, then." She yawned at Morgan. "Harvey of Nazareth, I think they call him."

Morgan smiled. "Aunt Suellen, you are about the nicest person I have ever known. I am so sorry I made you fall out of the tree. Does your arm hurt?"

Suellen patted Morgan's back. "Only when I cry. So, are you going to marry Cesco after all?"

"Mom and Daddy think we should wait a while. Like about forty years. But if nothing changes in the next ten years, maybe so."

"Things can change in that much time. What does Uncle Taylor say?"

"I think he's pretty much against me, still. That could be a problem, I guess. If we get that far. Grandma Ginnie says anybody who gets married at all needs their head examined. She says Cesco and I should come to Italy and live together in a villa in Rimini. Silvio has three or four he's not using. I expect I should probably get back to studying for the biology exam."

"Clear thinking. Did Harve say what was in this folder?"

"No. He asked me to tell you, be sure you read the whole thing."

"Really. I can't wait."

It was written in ball-point on copy paper.

Suellen –

OK, here is what you wanted. I hope it is worth it after all. I can't stand having you think bad of me. But I'll tell you, Blondie, if you talk to people about this, I am a dead man. Welles will can me, I'll be back to Raeford, and there are guys there who'd just as soon kill me as blow their noses. Anyway, here goes.

(1) You were right, I was given the job of staying close to Hap Maryland after he started to make problems for Nurse Welles. Some of his griping was getting back to the Board of Directors, and they were passing it on to Welles. Welles knew I had Special Forces experience,

No shit, Suellen thought. What outfit?

because it's on my prison dossier. So she figured, I guess, hey, a skill set we can use, and cheap, too. I was just supposed to sort of keep an eye on him, but I got to where I kind of liked the guy, watching him being nice to Morgan, and of course giving Welles a hard time. A couple of times I was able to steer him out of jams – like the day he sat down in a ditch on the Plank Road and kind of passed out. I brought him back to Inglenook through the back way, without anybody seeing him. Since I only showed myself to him when he was out of touch, I never knew if he really saw me or not. He never seemed that surprised when I showed up and pulled him out of something.

(2) What happened to him: I still want you to think twice before you read this.

Think, think, Suellen thought. OK, get on with it.

It was the first nice day last spring. Morgan came for him, and they walked a hell of a ways out through the County, up to the edge of the swamp. There was a canoe there, and next thing I know, they're getting in it. Even after all the rain, the swamp isn't that deep anywhere, so I could pretty much keep them in sight by wading from one hummock to the next. They didn't go that fast, and Hap was talking all the time. Still, I got pretty damn wet and sweaty, mosquitos eating me alive, and it's not long before I'm getting pretty pissed off.

So, why didn't you go home, sleuth-boy?

After a while, they stop at this island, way back in the swamp. Morgan got out of the canoe, and when Hap gets out, he sort of grabs her, and starts kissing her. Shit, what was I supposed to do? I couldn't let that go on, and they're way out in the backwaters, where I can't call a cop. I ran after them, and grabbed Morgan away from him. He goes, "Jesus Christ," and falls down kind of funny, like somebody pulled the plug. Same thing with the little girl, she takes one look at me and passes out. Now what? Here I am, two people lying on the ground. I figure I can't just fade into the bushes, because what if he starts up on her again? While I'm standing there wondering what to do, Hap makes this funny foaming kind of a sound, and kind of bucks once or twice, and subsides. I checked him for pulse and respiration, and guess what, he's dead. I started to try CPR on him, but then I'm thinking, what for? So he can go back to molesting little girls?

So I made up my mind to a hell of a thing. I decided, look, here's a guy that everybody seems to like. I like him myself. He's led a long life, and if this kind of thing gets out, his name will be ruined. Even if I can bring him back, which is doubtful, what kind of a favor am I doing him? He's out of trouble now – and I have to say, he looked about as happy as I've ever seen anybody – so why start it all up again?

So I dragged him off under a thicket and left him there. If you really feel like you've just got to find him, get a good GPS unit and let it take you to W 77°31'22.4", N 34° 48'53.3". He's under a laurel bush. Thicket, more like. When I got back to the little girl, to Morgan, she's coming around, looking at me like I was Godzilla. I told her, her Grandpa'd gone to heaven, and she wasn't to tell anyone at all anything about this. I brought her and the canoe back to where they'd found it, got her headed home on her bicycle, and I took off. It was a bad thing, I know, to leave the old man out there – but neither Inglenook nor I could afford to know anything about it. I figured Morgan would lead people to where she'd been, and they'd bring him in, in a day or two. When it turned out otherwise, I have to say, I wasn't all that upset. Much better for the guy to just disappear, than *to have a lot of questions asked about how he died, and who was there.*

Suellen looked up at Morgan. "Why didn't you tell people about all this?"

Fleetingly, Morgan looked perplexed that Suellen could ask such a dumb question. "Well. When Jesus tells you to forget something that happened, and when your own mortal sin caused it, you forget."

"OK. And when Edward Briggs Harvey tells you, then what?"

"If I'd known ... I'm still not sure. Grandpa and I did something truly shameful, Aunt Suellen."

"Oh, come on. Ill advised, maybe. You were an innocent little girl, and he was in a terminal delirium."

"Well. I didn't know either of those things."

Suellen sighed. "No. No, you didn't, honey. But if I get my hands on Harve, I'm going to pound him into cigarette papers."

Morgan looked at Suellen with tears in her eyes. "Why? He didn't know Grandpa was delirious. He thought he was a dirty old man who was ... was taking advantage of a little girl."

"Well, but ..." Suellen ran a hand through her hair, wishing again it was long enough to tear out. "But how could he just leave Hap to rot out there in the swamp, for God's sake?"

"Harve didn't do that. I did."

"And you did because Jesus told you he'd gone to heaven – How on God's earth did you get Harve mixed up with Jesus? And for that matter, why'd you tell me Harve was gone when you woke up?"

Morgan sighed. "There's no hope for me. I hope to God Cesco meets a nice Italian girl and marries her. I lied about that, Aunt Suellen."

Suellen shook her head. "Why, this time?"

"Well, by the time I told you that, I was beginning to think maybe it wasn't Jesus. I mean, really, why would Jesus be having coffee in your kitchen? If it was just a regular guy who was there with you, I didn't want you to think he'd been part of the deal on covering up Grandpa's sin. Or, well ..." Morgan shrugged. "How he died," she said, miserably.

"OK," Suellen said. "Let's lay this out. Grandpa has a delusion that you're Grandma Lee. You've seen this before, but this time, you don't duck out of it, you go along with it. That makes Grandpa happy, but you know it's – well, it can't lead to any good end. It also fools Harve, who's spying on you, into 'rescuing' you from Grandpa. The shock of his sudden appearance either kills Grandpa or Grandpa was dying anyway. It knocks you out, and when you wake up, Grandpa's disappeared, and Harve is still there. He tells you Grandpa's gone to heaven, which you buy because you think he's Jesus. And you think that because ... help me out here."

"Because he came running across the water. When I saw him the second time, he had the marks of a crown of thorns on his brow. They were still bleeding, Aunt Suellen. He looked exactly like in the Bible. Also, Grandpa called him that, though I admit, he could just have been taking the Lord's name – "

"Right, right, hard as that may be to believe. OK, so by this time, Harve is lying to you about where Grandpa is, and he takes you out to the edge of the swamp and points you toward home. This is probably four or five in the afternoon. So why'd you get home at eight o'clock, muddy and exhausted?"

"I waited until Harve drove off, and I started wondering about all of it. I went back into the swamp to find Grandpa. But I never found him. I never found the place again."

"Gosh, Morgan. You just never do the straightforward, sensible thing, do you?"

Morgan shrugged and hung her head. "No'm."

"I'll say, 'No'm.' OK, then why didn't you tell all this to your folks when you finally did come home?"

Morgan opened her mouth, and shut it.

"Never mind," Suellen said. "Because you didn't want the whole thing to come out. So you make up a story that covers the case, you misdirect the people who went looking for Hap – "

"I did not! I told them the wrong place to look, because I was wrong about it myself. I guess."

"Didn't you tell them it was on Lost Princess Island?"

"Sure, I did. There was nothing there, and when they took me out to help look, it didn't look exactly the same. I guess it's possible Grandpa got mixed up about it."

"Ya, I expect that's right. So then Harve jives me about the whole thing because why?"

"We talked about that. He could see you thought Hap

was a great guy, and he didn't want to have to tell you otherwise. He says he knew you wouldn't let go of it, until the whole truth was out, which he thought would make Grandpa a scandal and make all his folks ashamed." Morgan sighed. "Mainly me, I expect."

3. *I got onto you at first, because old Miz Bynum asked me a couple of days after all this, where Hap had got to. I did my best to jive her like I did you, but that old lady don't jive easy, and getting her into bed wasn't really an option. (Also, I'm not half as good a liar as I try to be.) So she got it all out of me, a little question here and another little question there, what happened to him. I figured if you found out, you'd go right to Nurse Welles with it. I tried to keep tabs on you, but you're a little too sharp, and all I did was make you suspicious. Seemed like maybe just as well when Miz Bynum passed away, but I kind of liked her, so I wasn't all that sorry she came back from the dead, either. It was me that persuaded Welles to stick her in the Contagious ward. I should have blown the whistle on you when you found her, but I didn't know what she might have told you about Hap by that time. (And anyhow, you were cute as the dickens in that coverall outfit with the hard hat and all. Like to give me a hard hat, myself.)*

4. *You have been very kind not to ask what it was that sent me to jail. I'll tell you; I pounded the crap out of a white boy that didn't like nigger fags and didn't mind saying so. I'm not sure if he meant me or somebody else, but I always did have trouble turning my back on a fight. This was in a place where the cops, judge and jury were pretty much of the same opinion as the white boy. White brothers in Raeford*

let it be known, I'll wake up dead the first week I go back there. I'm in for ten to twenty, which will be I've done five in August, and might get out in another two if I keep my nose clean and my ass out of Raeford.

5. Don't be too hard on Morgan. I like her a whole lot, and it's not just because she thinks I'm Jesus Christ.

6. You're very beautiful when you're sleeping, did you know that? I noticed it on our very first date. I have felt weird since then, like I'm part you, and you're part me. What could that mean, do you think?

21.

Suellen watched a pair of twinned whirlpools recede behind the canoe, marking the last place her paddle had broken the dark mirror of Indian Girl Swamp. Duckweed rode giddily through them, dividing and rejoining, breathless. A flicker called somewhere ahead, hardly stirring the silence. The swamp had the sharp sweet smell of wilderness; light struck through the canopy overhead where it could, leaving most of the water dark as dreams. Suellen watched while a gnat hacked manfully through the wilderness of hair on her unbroken wrist, looking for clearance to take off, slithering in the cool condensation of sweat and haze.

The GPS on her lap uttered a small sound, like a dog who begins to recognize that something very desirable lies just ahead. Suellen's belly contracted. She dipped her paddle, and the GPS expressed satisfaction with a doubled sound, a little louder. Suellen took a breath, and held it trembling with her diaphragm. Fifty meters, bearing 342, the GPS said. Forty-five, bearing 341. Suellen corrected, overcorrected, came back. Forty meters. This is nowhere near Lost Princess Island, Suellen saw. Distances in a swamp are deceptive, but this place – now thirty meters away – was a good mile from where everyone had searched for Hap.

Suellen leaned forward, searching the maze of alder and

cypress, shadow and mirror and motion. Twenty meters, fifteen; now ten. A hushed implosion of sound, and a heron rose from a snag at the edge of her vision and skimmed the water, aloof, fading into a flickering maze. Stillness, a blue wing, again nothing. The peace of sunlight and shadow and flat water returned.

The GPS began to pulse yellow, hooted once, and fell silent. Less than five meters. Close as I can get you. Suellen confronted the toppling wall of vines and brambles that edged the island. Beyond them, the land rose enough to support a pine and some laurel, both of them out of place in this aquatic forest. She dug her paddle into the dark water and began to work to the left, looking for a spot to land. The island was no more than fifty yards long, and a sandy clearing sloped to the water at the far end. Suellen beached the canoe there and sloshed ashore to stand on the slope, listening to the dying ripple of water and her own breath.

The sand showed no tracks, drag marks, threads snagged on bushes, discarded signet rings, ticket stubs, or stigmata. Just sand, dappled with rain marks, cris-crossed by windrows of dark sediment left by higher water. Behind Suellen, it sloped so gently into the water that she could follow it half-way to the next island before a dazzle of sunlight hid it.

She walked to the edge of the water and put on a pair of Polaroid glasses. The water was nowhere more than an inch or two deep along a ridge of sand that connected this island to its neighbor. Suellen could easily imagine herself running across that drowned ridge, and if someone were surprised enough at the sight, and dazzled by the sun, and in a state of crisis, they might easily believe she was running across the surface of deep water. Anything was possible, she supposed, except that the fluid sands of Indian Girl Swamp would hold footprints, or even their own topography, for more than a week. She turned back to the island. Her breath was calm in her ears, but it was there. She looked at the canoe, seeing Morgan jumping out, turning back to Hap with a smile of such bottomless dark promise that his last thoughts must have been of falling.

Behind the single pine, a thicket of laurel and alder jostled for rootholds: fierce, unreconciled, impenetrable. At one place, an animal trail dove beneath the tangle; a fox or a possum could negotiate that, Suellen supposed. Or a very determined man who didn't mind getting crown-of-thorn marks on his head Not a woman with no motivation and her arm in a cast. Suellen lay on her belly and looked up the dim tunnel of the fox-trail. Maybe there was something in there – something pale, fragile, and complicated. Something you might be able to get in there by yanking it along by the wrist, when the wrist was still part of the stringy cage of tendon and flesh.

Not a very dignified way to exit the world's stage, but Suellen supposed dignity was the least of Harve's priorities at the time. In any case, there would be no retrieving it short of burning or bush-hogging the whole thicket. And for what? Suellen returned to the sandy beach and sat with her back against the pine, the silence of this place singing in her ears. It was neat, more or less satisfactory. Still, it seemed to her not right.

Or, what was right? Who was guilty, who needed forgiveness? Not Morgan, who had been foolish for the kindest of reasons; not Hap, who had already entered the delirious borderland of his dying. And not Harve, who acted at risk to himself to protect them both from the perils of that dying.

And besides, Hap had lain in that unmarked thicket on this nameless island for more than a year. He was at home here now, one of the regulars. It was peaceful, uninhabited but by small scavengers, and maybe once in a while a fox. Amenities were limited: the quiet of the grave, and its darkness at night. But there was also birdsong, air and sunlight, the sound of rain and wind, the changing barometer, the majesty of herons, the turn and fall of the seasons. Many a rich man lay in a colder, meaner mausoleum.

Suellen rose awkwardly, keeping her broken arm out of it, and turned to face the thicket. She thought about Hap then, and found herself crying, though not exactly from sorrow. "Bye, Hap," she said. "Thank you for everything. You were always a lovely man."

Epilogue: Wiser

Bypass 73 flashed beneath the Triumph and dwindled in the mirror. Behind Suellen was her bungee'd bundle of clothes, the crushable dress now cradling Cesco's family portrait with its looping, tumbling grownups, its perfect princess, and its baffled, asymmetric Robin Hood. Before her, a green sign rose from the back of a small hill:

Exit 115 NC 73 South Gabbro
left exit 5 mi.
Exit 116 I-40 West Asheville Knoxville
6 mi.

Suellen was tired, the low sun in her eyes made her head ache, and she was not sure she could make it all the way to Knoxville in one shot. Well, she would see how she felt when she got into the mountains. It would be cool there, the air would be clean and sweet, and there would be no dark water, nor a leaf of duckweed within a hundred miles. If she was still tired, she would drive into the Pisgah somewhere and sleep. The main thing was, she was free at last of Gabbro and its population of nuts and bolts and lies and secrets and half-truths and relationships, Lord! Suellen threw both arms into the windstream and shouted with the liberation of it.

She still had 19 hours to report in to Hillemeier, get fitted for a sergeant's stripes, and start in on his class of trooperettes. Suellen couldn't wait to see which of them would make real prospects, and get them shaped up. Bang them from a bunch of Weezys – or less, much less – into hard, clean troopers. Succeed in that, go on to the next thing. Bust some loser who will turn out to be on the Most Wanted list in 14 states and the FBI. Celebrate by calling up Weezy.

Weezy, God. Weezy's music started to whisper in the drone of the motor. Maybe she could invite Weezy out to Knoxville for a weekend, show her around, flaunt her under Hillemeier's nose. Let any who might be interested among the trainees get the idea, far as that went.

And to for god's sake get the abortion. Suellen grimaced and shook her head to clear it of the thought. It would be necessary, though. She couldn't imagine doing what Hillemeier needed her to do – being, in the end, what those recruits needed her to be – with her belly sticking out like a horse's rump.

She would have to tell Harve, she supposed she owed him that much. She took her eyes from the road to glance down at the flat bundle of sinews that held the interloper. Sorry, kid.

Hi, Mom. I'm leaning out for love.

Suellen shook her head. I'd be a shitty mother to you, little guy.

For sure. What kind of a mother murders her child?

My own did. Damn near. Got me pregnant and put me on a bus. If I'd died, that would have solved a big problem for her. That's the kind of stock you come from.

What did you tell Morgan about that? "Nobody has immaculate genes."

Kid, shut up. You don't know what you're asking.

I'm asking for my life.

Yeah, well … some life. Rattling around in a trooper barracks while Sergeant SingleMom sets an example to a bunch of girls about discipline and organization and clean living.

Who said Single Mom? What about Harve?

Harve is a convict. You want to be named Susie Ransom-596? That what you want, visiting Daddy through bullet-proof glass?

He's an orderly at an old folks' home. You could live with him, and help him.

Help him change the wet beds?

Help him get over changing wet beds. Harve needs you. I need you and Harve. It's that simple.

Kid, you don't know what you need, and you're nothing but a corner of my mind, so shut up. The will is wiser than the mind.

The small voice fell silent. Suellen drove on. Fugue on Jazz Themes struck up in the smoky back reaches of her brain, displacing Satie and Judy Collins. Harve's muscular slenderness, his amusement, his soft expertise at love. What would be so godawful about sleeping with that every night? Three or four nights a week of mind-bending sex? She ought to tell him what she was going to do. Not let it end in this cowardly way, lamming out of town, send him an e-mail. Hey, why not a postcard? He deserves to have it in person.

Yeah, stupid. That'd be easy, wouldn't it? He'd give me one look, tell me how lovely I am when I'm asleep, and there we'd go again. I'm part you, you're part me, *la la yada yada, one two three.* The next thing, there would be decisions, commitments and promises and compromises. Let that go on, at some point probably I'd have to tell him whether I <u>love</u> him, for Chrissake, and I don't even know if that's so, or what it would feel like if I did. I go on to Knoxville and start some little no-commitment thing with Weezy, or one of the trainees, it's all clean and easy, no babies, no dilemmas, just fun, and on to the next one. Each one making it easier to forget about Harve and the damn continuum, the gay-straight, male-female, Harve-Suellen cock-up. A career in the THP, proving myself. Some day maybe taking Hillemeier's place.

Suddenly, it sounded like a recipe for old age, for ending up in a bugged bed in a smelly room at Inglenook, keeping a secret journal. Gradually aging - and middle age was just over the next hill already - as the dyke THP drill instructor. Could life as a mommy, living with Harve, be as bleak as that?

Yes, of course it will, yes! We'll have quarrels and fights, jealous bullshit, one-upping, nagging about who changed the last diaper. Between Beffie and Afghanistan, I've had all the pain I care to deal with for the rest of my life. He'd hurt me, I'd hurt him, I'd get bored with -

Yeah? Boring, wasn't it, that night I got started. Brubeck, rain, thunder, neighbors banging on the wall, you hollering your brains out, nobody remembering birth control because you were both so hot and bothered you couldn't think about anything but the next -

Shut up. I'll be lucky if he didn't give me HIV then or afterwards.

He's negative.

I thought I told you, shut up. I'm not going to hook up with a fairy.

He isn't all gay, and neither are you, mom. Evidently. What about those potatoes? Looks to me like just enough in both directions, you guys could probably make up sex nobody ever thought of, publish papers -

Stop it. The body is wiser than the will.

Just what I'm telling you.

I am a sergeant in the Tennessee Highway Patrol, and I like it that way. I am not some darky's barefoot pregnant common-law trailer-trash –

You are barefoot, and pregnant. Darky, I guess; that's it, isn't it?

Don't be stupid.

Me stupid? Whose mind is it I'm just a corner of?

Silence again in the Triumph's racket. See, the will is wiser than the mind. No, wait; the mind is wiser than the body. No, but the body …

To hell with it. Suellen saw the exit lane for Gabbro a half-mile ahead, and put the Triumph's wheels squarely on the white line between it and the through lane. No sliding scale of options here, she would have to choose to exit or to keep on toward Knoxville. She would give herself every chance to go either way, if she could just figure out which way to go. Or, hell, obviously this whole thing was way too hard for her to figure out, so if anybody wanted to just bloody tell her what to do, she would listen respectfully.

Something delicate and green-blooded whacked against the windshield, and gave her the answer. She would play Weezy's game. She put a bare foot into the wind stream on either side of the Triumph. She didn't have time to keep a running score, so whichever foot hit the first bug, that was the way she would turn; left for Gabbro and Harve, right for I-40 and Knoxville. If Jesus, or Fate, or the kid inside, had any wisdom to offer, they could push a bug into the path of the ordained foot. That didn't seem beyond the powers of the Son of God, did it? C'mon, Nazareth, you got thirty seconds.

Suellen held her breath, symmetrical and poised, waiting for the smack of chitin that would tip her one way or the other. And there was no signal, no guidance because there were no bugs; she was passing a bunch of used car franchises, bare baking asphalt with no weeds or puddles to encourage bugs, probably reeking with bug spray.

But ahead, the bypass dipped to cross Indian Girl Creek. Reeds, cattails; warm, lazy water. There would be a billion mosquitoes, gnats, Suellen didn't care what. She'd take her chances with a dragonfly, if it would tell her what the hell she was supposed to do. As she crested the rise and started down the slope, she could see a bunch of swallows darting over the road. Great, lots of bugs. Here we go, Jesus; line 'em up.

Looking down, Suellen noticed that one of her feet was sagging a little, offering a smaller target for bugs. She straightened the offending foot, found that she had strayed from the lane divider, and got things lined up again and wiggled her toes in the warm blast of air. OK, bugs. Come on now.

Beyond the viaduct over the creek, she could see the Jersey barriers that defined the exit. The white line she was riding headed straight toward them. Some bug better show up pretty quick, she thought, or the whole question would be moot in a cloud of dust and splatter.

Nothing, still, as the Triumph roared and the exit loomed. Suellen gritted her teeth. Listen, bugs, this is important. Right: Knoxville. Sergeant Ransom and a lineup of Weezies, a career, a clean upward path to Assisted Living. Left: Gabbro. Harve, babies, love, pain, and living assisted by the Harve-Suellen potato-cluster continuum. Please don't make me pick.

She tensed up and lowered her eyes to keep from seeing the barrier coming at her at seventy miles an hour, a tenth of a mile away. Still no bugs on either side. But now the same lazy foot was drooping out of the windstream again, cringing, all but pointing bugs toward the other foot, which was ramrod straight, looking for bugs, giving them a big target.

Well, Jesus, she thought. Look at that. And at the last instant – just about killing herself while the white lines slashed beneath her, the skidding Triumph spraying gravel against the Jersey barrier, her heart in her throat and leaping into the world with her cry of sorrowful thanksgiving when she saw the direction her body chose …

At the last possible instant, that is the way she went.

In case you missed it ....

Assisted Living, the last of the Hap Maryland series of novels, is the sequel to Dancing With Granny. For a brief excerpt from Granny, turn the page.

You can order your copy of Dancing With Granny, and all the other Hap Maryland adventures through Amazon or, at a savings, directly from Tom Blackburn Books, 1504 Irving St. NE, Washington DC 20017. Prices and availability: contact tom@tomblackburnbooks.com

From <u>Dancing With Granny:</u>

Prologue

The summer had been a dream of life on the road. The kid and the very experienced woman were more like sisters than daughter and mother. Both sexy; one leggy and fresh, the other athletic and knowing, dancing from town to town across the broad and believing Midwest, grifting a living as resurrection angels for a traveling evangelist. Coming down the aisle in hooker clothes and getting dunked and saved night after night, from Shullsburg, Wisconsin to Dickeyville, from Toolesville, Iowa down through Missouri, slipping into Knob Noster and Diggins, glimpses of slick bodies in wet angel robes sliding into the narrowed eyes of farmers, and scandalizing their wives.

But now the Old Reverend was gone and the weather was chilly, sliding always north toward November. Instead of sunshine and laughter about the hick name of the next town full of marks, there were cold winds and tears and morning sickness. The last of the easy money went for a one-way ticket on Trailways.

They stood in a place called Lonnie's Convenient and Transmission on Missouri 266, a couple of miles west of Springfield. There was snuff and oil filters, and Little Debbie snacks made of cornstarch and foam. The kid scowled at these, and turned away. She looked to the guy behind the counter like thirteen or fourteen; skinny, pissed-off, the way a kid that age always is; and dressed light for the weather. Straggly pale curls.

"Don't be stubborn," her mother said. "You don't eat, you won't make it past goddamn Indiana, for shit sake. Take something, I'll pay for it." She dropped her voice a little, not much. "You're eating for two now, you little whore."

The counterman – Lonnie himself, or a successor in the business, or dependent – raised an eyebrow and looked west up 266, where it curved behind a limestone bluff. He was sixtyish, lean, badly shaven, and stricken by some disease that made it hard for him to straighten his back or discipline his hands to make change. The oaks outside were the color of dried blood, tossing under the wind. The girl turned her back on the counter to stare at the sun rising into the far deck of cloud.

The counterman saw a flash in the west, reflection from a flat windshield. "On time, pretty much," he said, wanting to cheer folks up. "Third time this month."

The mother smiled. "And today just the seventeenth. Good sign, don't you think? Come on, honey, it's your new life." The girl looked a dismayed appeal that her mother missed, being focused on the bus that was slowing, easing off the pavement onto the dust and gravel. A paper cup tumbled ahead of it, fleeing the west wind. The bus blew off some air pressure, and the door opened.

"Here's your ticket, through to Fayetteville. You get to St. Louis, you change for Charlotte. Charlotte, change for Fayetteville. Think you can keep that straight for three days?"

The girl shrugged and sighed, "Fuck you, Mommy." The appeal and the dismay were gone, covered by sulk.

"That's my girl. You'll thank me when you get some sense. Here's the twenty bucks you should of charged that bastard to knock you up. Your new dad is a cop named Wetmore Parsonage. You can call him Daddy or Wet, but if you laugh about that, he'll slap you silly. He'll be in Fayetteville to meet the bus." Anyways, she thought, soon as I call. She kissed the sullen girl on the forehead and ran to her car.

She left Lonnie's parking lot fast, almost clipping the bus driver headed for the Men's. Her tail lights, bright in the dawn gloaming, shrank westerly to the bypass. The girl looked out at the bus, retched a little, and opened the door. The counterman stumbled after her and stuffed a Moon Pie into her coat.

1.

We could start this like a '20's farce, with a ringing telephone on an empty stage.

A maid enters and picks it up. "Good afternoon, the Maryland residence." And right away, you know where you are.

But Suellen (who was nobody's maid, anyhow) had gone into town for the day. I was a little surprised to hear the phone, really. It had kept pretty quiet since Suellen's project - what she called her Strumpet's Seminar - hit the news.

Not the Gabbro *Intelligencer* or WGAB - "All Country, All the Time" - of course. If our media had one principle, it was that Gabbro, North Carolina was a crime-free zone, right down to prostitution and parking. (And yes, I know, prostitution is both a legal crime in most places, and almost everywhere a nasty form of violent slavery. Just, not so in some little places like Gabbro, North Carolina, where it was something more like a cottage industry that gave a few smart, handsome, and - OK, a little lazy - ladies a living where there was no other ready source, and some lonesome men a sad, forgivable illusion of love and companionship.)

But the Raleigh *News and Observer* had got wind of it, and filled a white space inside their "Life Styles" section with a headline, "Hooker Unrest in the Cotton Patch" and a thumbnail photo of Suellen with Gabbro's two prostitutes, and three from the neighboring town of Bozlee, around our kitchen table. They were planning a job action, and that's what had caught the editor's fancy, limning a country town's mustachioed pillars going without their fun because the prostitutes were on strike for better working conditions. Little they knew. It was passing truckers, not hypocrite city fathers ...

Hell. If I don't get that phone, I'll never finish this.

"Hap Maryland speaking."

Brief silence. A telemarketer, then. I was ready to slam it down when a country kind of voice said she'd been hoping to speak to Miss Ransom.

"Suellen is not available just now. Can I take a message?" Figuring another client for the Strumpet's Seminar, emboldened by the jolly-looking picture in the *N&O*.

"Well, if you could please have her to call Miss Darlene Feely at (417) 555 - 5100. May I ask when you expect her?"

Darlene Feely, sure, I bet. "I'll do that, Darlene. I expect her back around dinnertime. Is this about ... Are you a ... are you interested in the job action?"

"I beg your pardon?"

Survival instinct kicked in. "May I tell her what your call was in connection? With?"

"I am secretary to Mr. Amos Verry, Esquire, of Morris, Gerard, and Verry in Springfield, Missouri. I cannot be more specific than that. If you would kindly see to it that Miss Ransom gets my message? It is important, but not urgent. Thank you."

"I will do that, Ma'am." Just as soon as I get her attention away from hooker uplift.

Suellen Ransom was raised by a hooker for a life as a hooker, and escaped it by the sheerest of luck. I think she felt a moral obligation to reach back and give a hand to girls who hadn't.

Oh, well, there are a few unfair things about that. For one, Trudi Ransom, Suellen's mother, wasn't exactly a prostitute in the full frontal sense. No, she was a woman without other advantages, who used her looks and what tools came to hand to make her way and raise her daughter in a mean and horny world. From time to time, intercourse was one of those tools, and she would use it freely when she could to obtain advantages, cash, or other good and valuable considerations.

For another, Trudi, by Suellen's testimony, did what she could for as long as she could, to keep Suellen from having to do the same. Though when the time came that she could think of no easy and pleasant alternative, she was
ready enough to serve up Suellen steaming on Venus' half-shell, rather than starve. And finally, Suellen escaped the life she was headed for almost entirely by her own intelligence and determination. She was helped a great deal by her foster father, a Fayetteville part-time cop, who inherited her from Trudi abandoned and pregnant. Wet Parsonage gave her a home, applied the flat of his hand to her fanny once or twice when she needed it, and otherwise stayed out of her way.

Suellen, the upshot of this nature and nurture, was a tough twenty-something, and a cum laude chemistry graduate from Gabbro College who was deciding when or whether to take up a fellowship at Chapel Hill to become a doctor of the philosophy of chemistry, such as that might be. And she was a lesbian feminist with a social conscience. It was this last that she'd brought to the service of Gabbro's ladies of the afternoon. Suellen happened to be in the bar of the Holiday Inn and Truck Stop out on the bypass one July late afternoon when Sheriff Tucker Pardee got a little rough, hustling DeLoris Potter out. DeLoris being Gabbro's leading, and senior in terms of service, trollop. Tucker rued the incident, as I know because he told me.

"Shoot, Hap, I hadn't got hardly no sleep the last five-six days, what between night duty and then the baby. DeLoris was kinda slow about movin on from the bar, which I flat had to clean up cause the Chamber was meetin there in ten minutes. I hustled her along, I gotta admit, and
she caught a heel in the doormat, which is one of them kind with little holes in it just the size of a lady's shoe heel. Hell, a hooker's, more so. Anyways, she got hung up and started to fall. She yanked on me, and I lost my balance. I expect it looked a little like police brutality, from a certain angle."

From the angle, he meant, of a quick-eyed photographer that the least you could say of her, she was no Gabbro girl, even if she did live there. Suellen got a good shot of DeLoris sprawled knee and elbow on the welcome mat with her little black skirt hiked up around her rump, and Tucker lurching over her in a way that you figured, at least, a Rodney King incident right here in Gabbro.

Tucker had never been completely reconciled to some of

Suellen's ways, and had made no secret of it with her. So more to irritate Tucker than anything, Suellen had gone on from there, sitting DeLoris down in the bar as her particular guest, buying her a pink lady and interviewing her about how many times this kind of thing happened to working girls like her. DeLoris, at first at a loss what Suellen's angle was, loosened up under sympathetic questioning and a second pink lady and said, yeah, it was kind of tough, when a girl had just come out to the Holiday because it was a good sort of place to meet nice fellas, and once in a while get asked for a date.

"A date?"

"Sure." DeLoris took in Suellen's minimalist chest, leather wristbands and streaked buzz cut, and figured she
might have to spell it out a little.

"I like fellas, see. And they like me. They like a good time, what it is."

"Who doesn't? Do they pay you a fair price?"

Pay? Of course not. What did Suellen take DeLoris for? Truckers have a lonesome and boring job, and a lot of them, they like to look at a friendly face after staring at four, five hundred miles of concrete. DeLoris was more than glad to be that face, when her other option was to clerk the 7-11. She let them pick up the tab for drinks and a meal, maybe, because it made them feel like civilized men, and not some goddamn gypsies. And if they wanted to give her something nice because they had a good time, enjoyed her company, got a break from the road, well, what was wrong with that?

"Not a damn thing," Suellen nodded. "Fact is, though,

you're a hooker, aren't you? Listen, I was one myself, and my mom before me, and proud of it. The thing is, though, it's dangerous work, and tough to keep your dignity and sense of self, all that. I'm not knocking you for it, long as you can do it on your own terms. Do people appreciate you for the service you provide? Does Tucker Pardee?"

DeLoris snorted, maybe a little doubtful about Suellen's claim to hooker credentials, and maybe a little unsure about what "own terms" might mean. "Appreciate? That what that looked like to you?"

Suellen had gone on from there to talk to one or two of DeLoris's colleagues and then a few truckers - I think she lost the leather and put on a skirt for it - long enough to find out, and get it confirmed, that Gabbro County was known from Florida to Cleveland as an oasis. It was one of the few spots left to get laid cheap and clean, with girls that were too innocent to ask themselves what they were getting for the same thing at South of the Border or Myrtle Beach.

Of course, it wasn't like oats or pork bellies, where you get the high, low, and trend on the WGAB farm report every morning. The fact is, when prostitution is an entrepreneurial cottage industry not regulated by mob pimps - which blessedly was the case in Gabbro County - there is no real Market in it at all, the way people mean when they talk about the Invisible Hand and letting the Market prevail. Gabbro's harlots didn't talk to Charlotte's strumpets or Fayetteville's hookers, so it was devil take the hindmost. The truckers knew this, and swore each other to reticence when they talked price with the girls. I do not dare think what wiles Suellen used to open them up.

"Shit, Hap," she said to me the next morning over breakfast. She was wearing boxer shorts and a tank top that presented a vee of sweat front and back, letting me know that she'd done her workout already, some time before I came out at 6:30. "Those girls are getting screwed twice. They need a goddamn agent."

"You?"

"Oh, no," she said. "I can't get bogged down in that kind of stuff. Just, it kills me to see somebody as dumb as DeLoris Potter risking her life and pissing it away fifty bucks a trick, which barely pays her rent. It never occurred to her those guys'd pay anyhow two-three times that, which seems to be the market along I-95. And that's for girls that are so used up and drugged out, it's a miracle a trucker can even get - "

She broke off, and waved her toast at a fly. "Anyways, no. Her age and looks, she could make a good living at it for a while, save some money for whatever comes next. I'm gonna get her and whoever else she wants to bring along together, and give them some advice about hygiene and managing assets, and that's the seminar."

She poured herself some coffee and aimed the pot my way. "You wont your coffee jacked up?"

She glanced at me, and put down the coffee. "Shoot, I'm sorry, Hap." Her voice was gentle.

I sat back and looked at the ceiling, and then smiled at Suellen. "That's OK. You know what, I'm almost, almost over it.

You go ahead and ... "

Damn, damn, damn. Sure I was almost over it. So why was it so hard to talk, all of a sudden? What it was, Suellen sounded so much like my late and horribly missed wife Lee, when she said "You want ..." whatever, anything, in the Gabbro County voice she'd picked up by living here. Lee was forever asking if I wonted my coffee jacked up. I cleared my throat savagely, gritted my jaw, and told Suellen she could go ahead and talk any way she wanted. What I really wonted, was my life jacked up. Or given shape, or brought to a close. Without Lee, it had become a leisurely helter-skelter of coming and going, doing and neglect, with no more purpose or content than one of the fitful dust devils that moseyed up the road outside our house, tarried, and dispersed. Suellen scraped her chair and came to stand behind me, cradling my head and giving me a dutch rub. Her belly was as hard as a post.

"I miss her too, Hap. You're such a good guy, shoot, you don't deserve this kind of grief." The knuckles slowed, to my relief. "Well, that sounds flippant, doesn't it? I meant literal, grief type grief."

"I know. Thanks."

I ran a hand through my thin and rumpled hair. Grief. Another good word done to death by hip talk that made it into something no worse than bother. Until you experience the real thing. Suellen started clattering breakfast stuff into the sink. "You ever thought of hooking up with somebody?"

I patted her butt. "I've enjoyed being hooked up with you, up to now. Otherwise, no thanks. It's my turn on the dishes."

Suellen turned and looked me in the eye. "Hap, I meant actually getting laid. It's been more than a year."

That was one good thing about Suellen Ransom. She always said exactly what she meant.

www.ingramcontent.com/pod-product-compliance
Lightning Source LLC
Chambersburg PA
CBHW062036170626
46813CB00001B/351